"It's been a long time."

Alisha nodded. "Yes." *Five years, two months, three days.*

"How've you been?"

"Fine. You?" She couldn't stop staring at him. He looked wonderful. Gone was the skinny boy in patched clothes, and in his place stood a ruggedly handsome man dressed in a crisp white shirt. She wanted to ask him why he had never sent for her, but she couldn't summon the nerve. She smiled wistfully.

"What are you thinking?" Mitch asked.

"Nothing, really. Just remembering." It was on this very rock that he had taught her how to kiss. . . .

The Novels of Madeline Baker . . .

"Rich, passionate, delicious."—*Romantic Times*

"Magnificent . . . glorious . . . moving."—*Affaire de Coeur*

Also by Madeline Baker

Hawk's Woman

APACHE FLAME

Madeline Baker

A SIGNET BOOK

SIGNET
Published by New American Library, a division of
Penguin Putnam Inc., 375 Hudson Street,
New York, New York 10014, U.S.A.
Penguin Books Ltd, 27 Wrights Lane,
London W8 5TZ, England
Penguin Books Australia Ltd,
Ringwood, Victoria, Australia
Penguin Books Canada Ltd, 10 Alcorn Avenue,
Toronto, Ontario, Canada M4V 3B2
Penguin Books (N.Z.) Ltd, 182–190 Wairau Road,
Auckland 10, New Zealand

Penguin Books Ltd, Registered Offices:
Harmondsworth, Middlesex, England

First published by Signet, an imprint of New American Library,
a division of Penguin Putnam Inc.

First Printing, September 1999
10   9   8   7   6   5   4   3   2   1

 REGISTERED TRADEMARK—MARCA REGISTRADA

Printed in the United States of America

For the real Mitch
Thanks for the inspiration

She was with me
when I was fresh
smiling with one touch of
love

she was with me
as I moved through
the phase
of pain life holds for all

she
was with me
when I stabbed her heart
with words of
release
and good-bye

she moves with the light
as easily
as you breathe
she lives in the darkness
swallowing its pain

she
laughs at you
when you mock life's love
devouring your words
as easily
as the wind pulls
a child's hair
caressing her face
with giggles

she will carry my soul
when time tires of me
and I wither
like our fathers'
fathers. . . .

when you see. . . .
She. . . .
You have to smile
with one simple twinkle
her eyes
hold your soul

She was with me . . .
and I was glad. . . .

—Mitch Dearmond

Chapter 1

Canyon Creek, New Mexico
1869

He was back.

Alisha Faraday heard the news at least a dozen times in as many minutes. It seemed everyone who saw Mitch Garrett ride into town that rainy Friday in late April felt duty bound to stop by the schoolhouse and tell her the news. Her first instinct was to run away just as fast and as far as she could.

Hands shaking, she tried to concentrate on the test papers she had been grading, but it was no use. The words, whether neatly printed by Betsy Hazelwood or haphazardly scrawled by Bobby Moss, made no sense. How could she be expected to think about nouns and verbs and proper sentence structure when *he* was back?

Oh, Lord, what would her father say?

If only she could crawl under her desk and hide—from Mitch, from the prying eyes of the town, from herself.

She folded her hands on top of her desk to still their trembling. Funny, she had never known she was a coward, until now. She glanced around the schoolroom. Nothing had changed. The chalkboard was still covered with the multiplication tables she had written out for the class earlier. The empty desks stood in neat rows, like soldiers at attention. The books were neatly stacked on the shelves; the world globe was in its proper place. Heat rose from the big, old black cast-iron stove in the corner. Her old winter coat and hat hung on a peg near the door, along with her umbrella.

Taking a deep breath, Alisha looked out the west window, staring at the rugged snow-capped mountains that loomed in the distance. She was worrying needlessly. Mitch had ridden out of her life five years ago. She had been little more than a child then, barely seventeen. No doubt he had forgotten all about her by now.

She hadn't forgotten him, though. Not for a day, not for a minute.

And now he was back.

Putting her head down on her folded arms, she closed her eyes, and lifted the lid on the Pandora's box of memories she had kept tightly closed for so long. . . .

Alisha sat in her chair, eyes wide, while the schoolmaster meted out punishment to the boy who had stolen her lunch out of her pail. Mitch Garrett, the town bad boy, stood in front of the class, his head high, one arm outstretched, while Mr. Fontaine struck his palm with a ruler. The usual punishment for breaking one of the school rules was ten whacks, but Mr. Fontaine hadn't stopped at ten.

Mitch stared at the back wall, his face an impassive mask, his eyes dark and angry as Mr. Fontaine meted out an additional ten blows. Mitch hadn't flinched, nor had he cried out. He just stood there, his body rigid, looking old beyond his years as the schoolmaster counted the blows out loud.

Tears stung her eyes and dripped down her cheeks as she imagined his pain and humiliation. She had told Mr. Fontaine she didn't care that Mitch had taken her lunch, but Mr. Fontaine hadn't paid any attention to her.

"The boy is no better than a common thief," the schoolmaster had replied brusquely, "and he must be punished."

Cringing in her seat, she listened as Mr. Fontaine counted out the remaining blows. She thought he looked as though he was enjoying it far too much.

"Eighteen."

Smack!

"Nineteen."

Smack!

"Twenty."

Smack!

"You will stand there and contemplate your sinful behavior until class is dismissed," Mr. Fontaine said curtly.

And Mitch had stood there, his gaze still fixed on the back wall. She had the feeling he wasn't really there at all, that his spirit had somehow slipped out of the classroom, leaving them all behind.

When school was dismissed an hour later, he trailed behind her as she walked home.

Wondering if he meant to do her harm because of what had happened, she whirled around, her heart pounding. "Why are you following me?"

"I want to know why you were crying," he said, his voice and expression sullen.

She looked up at him. He was eleven, and tall for his age. A lock of unruly black hair fell across his forehead. His black cotton trousers were worn and faded. His shirt was tight across the shoulders; the sleeves were too short. She risked a glance at his hand and he shoved it into his pocket, but not before she saw that his palm was still red and swollen.

"Go away," she said. "I'm not supposed to talk to you." Her mother and father had both warned her to have nothing to do with "that boy." Her mother thought it was shocking that a bastard of mixed blood should be allowed to go to school with the children of the town's leading citizens. Alisha didn't know what the word *"bastard"* meant, but she had known it was something bad by the tone of her mother's voice.

"Why did you cry for me?" Mitch demanded.

Alisha shrugged, embarrassed that he had seen her tears.

"Tell me!"

"I felt sorry for you," she mumbled. "That's all."

"Well, don't ever do it again. I don't need no little girls crying for me."

"I'm not a little girl," she retorted, even though it was true. She was short and petite, like her mother, and very sensitive about the fact that people thought she was no more than six when she was actually eight and a half. "Why did you steal my lunch?"

He glared at her as if he hated her. " 'Cause I was hungry, that's why."

"You should have told me you forgot your lunch. I would have shared mine with you."

He looked away, and she saw a flood of red climb up his neck. "I didn't forget it," he muttered, and before she could ask any more questions, he turned and ran away, splashing across the creek to where the town's poor people lived.

He hadn't come to school the next day, and then it was Saturday, and there was no school.

She had wandered through the house, looking for something to do. Mama was ironing her Sunday-go-to-meeting dress; Papa was working on his sermon. Usually, she loved to read, but that day her books and her games and her dolls held no interest, so she had left the house and walked down to the creek. She wasn't supposed to go down by the creek alone, but she told herself it would be okay to go down there just this once. She wouldn't go in the water; she would just sit on the edge of the creek and maybe put her feet in the water.

She walked along the bank until she came to the big flat rock that jutted out over the creek. Sitting down, she took off her shoes and stockings, then, her legs dangling over the edge of the rock, she swished her feet back and forth in the cool water.

"This is my spot."

Her head jerked up and she saw Mitch Garrett standing on the far side of the creek, his hands fisted on his lean hips. "Is not," she retorted. "Besides, it's on *my* side of the creek."

"Doesn't matter," he said imperiously. "Go away."

"Make me."

He glared at her a moment, then waded across the creek. Her heart began to pound wildly as he scrambled up the slippery bank. Every instinct she possessed urged her to run away as fast as she could, but before she could stand up, he was there, towering over her. He wasn't wearing a shirt, just some funny looking thing that tied around his waist. A long flap covered his privates. He was so skinny, she could count his ribs.

"Go away," he said. "This is my place."

"Why are you so mean?"

"Take after my old man, I guess."

She looked up at him, then reached into her pocket and withdrew a shiny red apple. "Want a bite?"

"No," he said, but she could almost see his mouth water.

"I'll give you the whole thing if you let me stay."

He regarded her for a moment, then shrugged. "Okay." He took the apple from her hand and devoured it, core and all, in a few quick bites, making her wish she had brought two.

"Why weren't you at school yesterday?" she asked.

He looked away, his expression guarded. "I was . . . I was sick."

"Oh. Well, I'm glad you're feeling better."

"Yeah." He sat down beside her, his long legs dangling over the edge of the rock.

"What's that thing you're wearing?"

"It's a breechclout."

She frowned. "I've never seen anything like that. Where did you get it?"

"My ma made it."

"Oh?" She would have asked more questions, but something in his voice warned her not to.

"Wanna go swimming?" he asked gruffly.

"I can't. I don't know how."

"You can't swim?" He looked astonished.

She shook her head.

"I could teach you, if you wanna learn."

"Really?" She looked at the water, then shook her head. "I don't think so."

"What's the matter?" he asked, the challenge in his

voice matched by the look in his dark blue eyes. "You scared?"

She was, but she wouldn't have admitted it to him, not for anything.

He stood up and held out his hand. "Come on then."

She didn't want to, but couldn't think of any way to refuse, and then, to her relief, she heard her mother calling.

"I've got to go," she said. Scrambling to her feet, she grabbed her shoes and stockings and ran all the way home.

She started taking extra food and sweets in her lunch pail after that, sneaking them to Mitch when no one was looking. Even as a boy, he had been inordinately proud. He had hated her because she knew he was poor and hungry all the time, had hated accepting her charity, and yet he had been just a boy and all the pride in the world wouldn't fill his empty belly.

She saw Mitch often that long, lazy summer. Her mama was in the family way and so sick that the doctor told Papa she should stay in bed until the baby was born. Papa hired a girl from town to look after her and Mama and do the housekeeping chores, but Chloe didn't care what Alisha did, so long as she didn't cause any trouble. It offered Alisha a kind of freedom she had never had before.

She went to the creek every chance she got, drawn to Mitch without knowing why. She took him apples and fried chicken and when Chloe baked, she took him sugar cookies and bread fresh from the oven.

One sunny afternoon not long after their first meeting at the river, he taught her how to swim. Clad in her

8

underwear, she followed him into the creek where the water ran deep and slow.

"You scared?" he asked, and she shook her head.

She wasn't scared at all, not with Mitch there beside her, and before long, she was swimming. It was exciting, exhilarating, and she swam until she was exhausted and then they climbed out of the creek and flopped down on a patch of sun-warmed grass. She stared up at the cloudless sky, basking in the warmth of the sun.

"What does your daddy do?" she asked when she caught her breath.

"He doesn't do anything," Mitch replied sullenly.

"He must do something," Alisha insisted. She had seen Mitch's father in town from time to time. He was a tall, handsome man with cold blue eyes. She had never seen him smile.

"He's a gambler," Mitch said.

Alisha's eyes widened. "Really?" Her papa often preached against the evils of gambling, declaring that saloons were dens of iniquity.

Mitch looked at her, daring her to say something. She wisely changed the subject. "Tell me another story."

She loved the stories he told her, stories his Apache mother told him about Coyote and Trickster and why the raven was black. "Please?"

He sighed. "Did I tell you the one about how death came into the world?"

Alisha shook her head. "No."

"Well, a long time ago, people lived forever. Nobody got sick, and nobody died. I don't know why. Maybe nobody ever thought about it. But one day, when the earth started getting crowded, they knew they had to make a decision about it. Coyote didn't want death in the world. He thought it would be a bad thing. He said he was going to throw a stick in the river. If it sank, people would begin to die but if it floated, people would go on living forever. So he threw the stick into the water, and it floated.

"Then Raven decided he should have a say. He said he would throw a stone in the water. If the stone floated, there would be no death but if it sank, people would begin to die. So he threw the stone in the water, and it sank to the bottom. And that's how death got started."

Alisha clapped her hands. It was a foolish story, of course. Young as she was, she knew it wasn't true. Papa had told her Adam and Eve had brought death into the world, and Papa wouldn't lie. Mitch's story was just a fairy tale, like the ones Mama told her at bedtime, but she loved Mitch's stories, just as she loved the hours she spent with him.

In the days and weeks that followed, he taught her how to snare a rabbit and cook it on a spit over an open fire. Once, she asked him to teach her how to fish, but he had refused. When she asked why, he explained that *Usen* did not intend for snakes, frogs, or fish to be eaten. Likewise, the Apache did not eat pork or turkey. They shunned bear meat, believing that the spirits of evil people sometimes returned to earth in the bodies of bears. It was no wonder he was always hungry, she thought, when there were so many things he wouldn't eat. And yet, to her horror, he told her he had eaten gophers and squirrels.

He taught her a few words of Apache. *Gah* meant rabbit, *gidi* meant cat, *dloo* was the word for bird, *baya* meant coyote. *Ashoge* was the word for thank you, *ya a teh* meant hello.

It was the best summer of her life, until her mother died and the baby with her. Papa told Alisha the news, then took her by the hand and led her into the dark bedroom so she could kiss Mama goodbye. Alisha stared at the body on the bed, with its pinched, waxy gray face, then turned and ran out of the room.

Sobbing, hardly able to see where she was going for her tears, she cried Mitch's name as she ran down to creek, praying that he would be there. She stumbled once, scraping her knee on a rock, but she hardly noticed the pain. Mama was dead.

She found Mitch sitting cross-legged on the rock, tossing pebbles into the creek. He had taken one look at her tear-stained face and opened his arms. He held her while she cried, held her and rocked her, soothing her with his presence. He didn't tell her she had to be strong, or that Mama and the baby had gone to a better place. He just held her until she had no more tears. And then he had washed the blood from her knee and patted it dry with her handkerchief.

"Will you come to the funeral, Mitchy?" she asked, sniffing.

"Sure, if you want me to."

The funeral was the next day. Alisha stood between Chloe and Mama's best friend, Mrs. McKenny, trying to be brave while Papa talked about what a good woman Mama had been, how she had loved her family and been a good example to others, how she had cared for the sick and taken food to the poor and the infirm.

Alisha glanced over her shoulder from time to time, hoping to catch a glimpse of Mitch. He couldn't stand at the graveside with the other mourners, but she knew he was there, out of sight behind a tree.

Later, after all the mourners had told her how sorry

they were, after everyone had gone home and Papa had shut himself up in his study and Chloe was busy in the kitchen, she crept down to the river and into Mitchy's waiting arms.

Nothing was the same at home after Mama died. Papa didn't laugh anymore. His sermons, once filled with hope and joy and a love for life, grew dark and somber. Chloe stayed on to keep house and cook.

When Mitch turned fifteen, he quit school and went to work full time in one of the saloons. She had been afraid she wouldn't see him anymore after that, but he had sought her out, especially in the summer.

She was thirteen and Mitch sixteen when he kissed her for the first time. They were sitting on the rock near the creek—she had come to think of it as their rock— when he drew her into his arms. His lips were gentle and sweet as they claimed hers. He had closed his eyes, but she had kept hers open. His eyelashes were short and thick.

With an oath, he drew away from her.

"What's wrong?" she asked, disappointed that he had ended it so quickly.

"Damn, you sure don't kiss like a little girl!"

She glared at him, and he laughed out loud.

"I know, I know," he said, still laughing, "you're not a little girl." He looked at her as if seeing her for the first time, making her feel self-conscious of her budding breasts. "You're not a little girl at all."

She stuck her tongue out at him, angry because he had ruined the most magical moment of her whole life.

"Don't stick that tongue out at me unless you mean to use it."

She frowned at him. "What do you mean?"

He didn't answer. Instead, he grabbed her and

pulled her up against him. And then he kissed her again, showing her just what he meant.

She gasped as his tongue slid over her lower lip, licking, sucking gently, then slid into her mouth. Her gasp of surprise soon turned into a muted sound of pleasure. She melted against him, her body pressed intimately against his, her breasts crushed against his chest. Heat flooded through her. Her eyelids fluttered down. Her heart began to pound.

It was, she thought, a kiss she would never forget. . . .

And she never had. Alisha lifted her head from her desk and looked out the window. That kiss was burned into her memory like a brand.

And now he was back.

With a sigh, Alisha graded the last paper, then stood up, stretching the kinks out of her back and shoulders. Extinguishing the lamp on her desk, she put on her coat and hat, pulled on her gloves, picked up her umbrella.

Leaving the schoolhouse, she closed and locked the door, then stood on the stoop for a moment, staring at the rain. She frowned as she faced the prospect of slogging through the mud and then, with a faint grin, she remembered another rainy day, years ago, when she'd stood at the window of her house, watching the lightning streak through the clouds. She hated rainy days, hated them because they kept her from the river. From Mitch. She wondered what he was doing, if he was missing her, too.

She had been turning away from the window when something pinged against the glass. Looking down, she saw Mitch standing outside, looking up. He grinned when he saw her, waved for her to come out.

Laughing, she opened the window and leaned out over the sill. "Mitchy, what are you doing here?" she called in a loud whisper.

"Waiting for you," he called back. "Come on out, Lisha. Let's go for a walk."

"A walk? Are you crazy? It's raining."

He shrugged. "So what. A little water won't hurt you. Besides, you can only get so wet."

She grinned. What was a little rain when Mitchy was there, waiting for her? Happiness bubbled up inside her, as it always did when he was near. "Be right down."

Bundled up in coat, boots, hat, scarf, and gloves, she tiptoed down the stairs and out the back door. He was waiting for her behind the ancient cottonwood tree where they always met. Alisha shook her head. As usual, he was wearing only a shirt and his clout. She had never seen him wear a coat, and wondered now if he even owned one.

"Don't you ever get cold?" she asked.

Mitch shook his head. "Warriors don't get cold," he said with a touch of arrogance.

"I suppose they don't get wet, either," she muttered.

But he only laughed. "Come on," he said, and reaching for her hand, he started to run.

Feeling happy and light-hearted, she followed him. Mitch loved to run. Once, she had told him that proper young ladies did not run, it was unseemly. But he had just laughed at her. "You're not a lady yet, proper or otherwise, Miss Alisha Faraday," he had retorted. "Besides, ladies never have any fun."

She had thought about that a minute, and decided he was right. None of the ladies in town ever seemed to have time to have a good time. They were always complaining about something . . . the price of sugar, the new saloon, the speed with which their children outgrew their clothes, the ever-growing Indian problem. Alisha had promised herself she would never be like them.

They spent the day in the rain, running, exploring, swimming in the deep part of the creek. Later, they took shelter in a cave Mitch had found the year before. He laid a fire and they huddled beside it, he clad only in his clout, she in her chemise and drawers, while their clothing dried.

They sat close together, one of the blankets Mitch kept in the cave draped over their shoulders while they chewed on hunks of beef jerky. He had told her he came here sometimes, to be alone. Though he had never said so, she was sure he came here to get away from his father. She knew Mitch's father beat him. She had, on occasion, caught a glimpse of bruises on his arms and back. She suspected that, on those occasions when she didn't see him for a day or two, it was because he was too badly hurt, or because the bruises were where he couldn't hide them and he was too ashamed to let her see. Knowing how proud he was, she had never mentioned them.

As always, she couldn't keep her eyes off him. He fascinated her, with his long unruly black hair, dark skin, and deep blue eyes. She had always thought Indians had black eyes, but Mitch's were dark blue, like his father's. She knew her father would have been horrified if he knew how much time she spent with Mitch. He would have locked her in her room and thrown away the key if he knew, if he even suspected. But she didn't care. She would have risked anything to be with Mitch. He made her life fun, exciting. . . .

*   *   *

Taking a deep breath, Alisha opened her umbrella and stepped off the stoop into the rain. Her life wasn't fun anymore. It was as cold and dreary as the weather.

And as for exciting . . . schoolteachers weren't allowed any excitement. She was expected to be the epitome of decorum at all times. She had to be careful of what she said, what she did, what she wore. She must never utter a cross word, never do anything that could be construed as unladylike, never wear bright colors, never rouge her cheeks or paint her lips. The fact that she was also the preacher's daughter only made things worse. She must be outgoing and friendly at all times so as not to offend anyone. She must never gossip, or listen to gossip, be careful of the company she kept, avoid even the breath of scandal.

She heard the clock in the church tower chime the hour. Four o'clock. She would have to hurry. Her father expected dinner on the table no later than five.

But she wasn't thinking about what to fix for dinner when she reached home a few minutes later. Instead her mind was filled with memories of the man she had thought she'd never see again, and what she would say to him when, inevitably, they met face-to-face.

Chapter 2

Mitch Garrett rode directly through the main part of town. Canyon Creek had grown considerably in the five years he'd been away. The old mercantile owned by George Cox and his son was gone, and a new, two-story white building with dark green shutters stood in its place. A new sign read HALSTEAD'S MERCANTILE *AARON HALSTEAD, PROPRIETOR.* There was a new boardwalk, a new hotel with a restaurant adjoining. Dixon's Livery was wearing a new coat of paint. He chuckled softly as he saw old Mr. West dozing in a rocker outside the barber shop. Some things never changed.

He was aware of the curious stares that followed him, the whispers, the speculation. He didn't stop, didn't look to the right or the left, just kept riding down Front Street until he reached the narrow dirt road that led to the winding creek that clearly divided the town, with the leading citizens residing on the north side and the riffraff on the south. The creek ran deep here, screened from the town by an overgrown mass of shrubs, weeds, and berry bushes.

He had grown up in this town, held in derision not only because of his Indian blood but because his father had worked in one of the saloons, gambling away his pay as soon as he earned it so that there was never enough money for new clothes, and sometimes not even enough to buy food.

Things had gotten a little better when Mitch turned thirteen. When he hadn't been at school, which he hated, or out hunting in hopes of putting food on the table, Mitch had worked a couple of hours a day at the saloon, emptying spittoons, washing bar glasses, sweeping the raw plank floor, unloading cases of whiskey from the back of the supply wagon that had come through town every month or so. He had learned to play poker when other kids his age were playing catch, downed his first shot of whiskey when the other kids were still drinking milk.

Hat pulled low to shield his face from the drizzling rain, he dismounted and made his way to the flat rock that jutted out over the creek. It looked smaller, he thought, remembering the warm summer days he had spent on that rock, basking in the sun with Alisha.

Alisha. A hard knot formed in his gut when he thought of her married to a worm like Smithfield. He recalled the day he had stolen Alisha's lunch, the smug look on Smithfield's face when he stood in front of the class while old man Fontaine punished him. The tears in Alisha's eyes. He wondered if she still lived in town. She and Smithfield probably had three or four kids by now, he mused, surprised that the thought of her having another man's children could still cause him pain.

Smithfield! Of all the men she might have married, why had she chosen Roger? He recalled the day the two of them had come to blows. It had been a long time coming, fueled by a mutual dislike, by snide remarks on both sides, by threats and taunts and dares.

It had all come to a head one day after school when Smithfield called Mitch's mother red trash in front of Alisha and a half dozen other children. It had been the last straw. He had laid into Smithfield like a fox after a chicken. Surprisingly, Smithfield managed to give about as good as he got until Mitch broke his nose. At the sight of blood flowing down Smithfield's face, one of the boys had run for old man Fontaine, who came out and broke up the fight.

Smithfield had been chastised by old man Fontaine. Mitch had been expelled for a week. He would have quit school then and there, but his mother had insisted he go back.

Mitch peered through the tangled berry vines that screened the rock from the path. He could just barely see the roof of the Faraday house. He had never told Alisha, but he'd snuck into her house one Sunday morning when her family was at church. It had been easy enough, since Reverend Faraday would no more think of locking his front door than he'd think of locking his church.

Mitch's family had still been living in that tar-paper shack at the time and Mitch had been mightily impressed as he wandered through the Faraday house. The furniture had been clean, not stained with spilt liquor. There had been colorful rugs on the floor, lacy white doilies on the tables, photographs on the mantel and on the wall.

He had swiped an apple out of the kitchen, then gone upstairs, curious to see Alisha's room. It had been just as he imagined, all done in pink and white, with a ruffled coverlet on the bed and a rag rug on the floor. A shelf held books. A porcelain doll sat in a small rocking chair in one corner.

Standing on the rock, his hands shoved deep into his pockets, Mitch turned and faced the north. The sprawling ranch house that his father had won in an all-night poker game the year Mitch turned twelve stood at the far end of town atop a lofty rise. The old man had moved them into it, but Mitch's mother had refused to stay there. After a few months, she had packed her meager belongings and gone back to her own people. Mitch had wanted to go with her, but the old man had refused to let him go. He had never figured out why his father wouldn't let him leave. Finally, he'd decided it was just his father's way of proving who was the boss. Mitch had run away several times, but his father had come after him every time. Each beating he had received for running away was more severe than the last, but it wasn't until his father told him that his mother had died of pneumonia that Mitch stopped running.

He blew out a breath. It was his house now, such as it was. It could have been a nice spread, but his father had gambled away the cattle and let the house go to hell.

Across the creek, huddled together beneath the lowering clouds as if they were ashamed to stand alone, stood the 'dobe and tar-paper shacks where the town's poor lived. He wondered if the shack he'd been born in was still standing.

Squatting on his heels, he listened to the raindrops as they hit the water. How many times had he and Alisha come down here so they could be alone? For the first time in years, he let himself remember. . . .

Alisha begging old man Fontaine not to hit him for stealing her lunch. He had always been hungry in those days. There hadn't been a lot of big game near the town, but rabbits had been plentiful. He grunted softly. He hadn't eaten rabbit since. The old man had taken the lion's share of whatever game Mitch brought home, taking it as if it was his due. Mitch had shared what little meat was left with his mother. He pushed the thought of his mother from his mind. It had been here that he had taught Alisha how to swim, how to catch a rabbit and cook it, how to kiss. . . .

Damn. He had kissed a lot of women since then, but he had never forgotten the first time he kissed Alisha Faraday. He had always though of her as no more than a kid until that day.

Picking up a small stone, he tossed it into the creek, watching the ripples fan out across the water.

His life had been like that, spreading out from this place. He had run away, determined never to return, yet here he was, back where he'd begun.

He tossed another rock into the river, then swung into the saddle and rode toward the ranch. The old man was dead, or he never would have come back here. He would settle the old man's affairs, sell the house, and move on. If he was lucky, it wouldn't take more than a couple of days.

He snorted softly as he urged the big bay gelding into a lope. When had he ever been lucky?

Mitch leaned forward in the saddle, his arms folded over the pommel, as he regarded the house that was now his. The place hadn't changed much in the five years he'd been gone. There was still a hole in the roof of the barn. The house still needed a coat of paint.

Swinging out of the saddle, he hitched his horse to the post beside the front porch. Then, taking a deep breath, he climbed the three steps to the porch, opened the big oak door, and entered the foyer.

He stood there a moment, feeling as though the weight of the house was settling on his shoulders. He had never been happy here, never felt as if he belonged. Old memories rose to the surface, echoing down the corridors of his mind. He heard his father shouting at his mother, demanding that she give up her "Injun ways and become respectable." He heard her cries when his father slapped her, heard his own voice, high-pitched and afraid, as he tried to defend his mother from the old man's fists. He had never told Alisha just how bad things were at his house, how abusive the old man was when he was drunk, or when he had lost at cards. To spare Alisha's tender feelings and his own pride, he had made light of the beatings he received, avoiding her company when the bruises were fresh and ugly.

He remembered the day the old man had walked in and caught his mother teaching him to speak Apache. He hadn't been more than five or six at the time, but it was a day he never forgot. With a roar, the old man had grabbed his mother by the hair and slapped her, again and again, yelling all the while, cursing at her for teaching his son Injun ways.

Later, when he was older, he wondered why his father had lived with his mother if he hated the Indians so much. Wondered, but never found the courage to ask.

He forced himself to go into the parlor. It was easy to see why his mother, who had been a woman of light and laughter, had hated this place. The walls were paneled in dark wood. The furniture was heavy, upholstered in a dark brown fabric. Heavy, dark green drapes covered the windows.

The old man had hired a housekeeper to do the cooking and cleaning after Mitch's mother left. Mrs. North had been a sour-faced old crone with iron-gray hair, pinched cheeks, close-set hazel eyes, and no sense of humor. He had never heard her laugh, never seen her smile. She had insisted the drapes be kept closed so that the sunlight didn't fade the carpets and the furniture. She refused to let him have his dog in the house, insisted he wash before dinner and after dinner, that he bathe once a week. She had tried time and again to make him cut his hair, but Mitch had flatly refused and for some reason he had never understood, his father had backed him up.

Striding across the floor, Mitch flung the drapes aside. Standing at the window, he watched the raindrops run down the glass. They reminded him of the last time he had seen Alisha, reminded him of the tears that had slid down her cheeks . . .

"Why are you leaving?" She looked up at him, tears glistening in her eyes. "Where are you going?"

"I don't know. I only know I've got to get out of here. Away from this town. Away from him."

"Away from me," she murmured.

"Lisha."

"Please don't go." Tears spilled from her eyes and ran down her cheeks.

"I've got to. I can't stay here any longer. I'll kill him if I do."

Sobbing, she had locked her arms around his waist and held on as if she would never let him go. He groaned softly as she squeezed his rib cage. He didn't want to leave her. It was the last thing he wanted. But he had to get out of town, away from his old man. He couldn't take any more, knew with a cold, crystal clarity that if the old man hit him one more time, he would kill him.

She looked up at him, her eyes shining with love, and the knowledge that he might never see her again twisted his insides. Alisha. Bending his head, he kissed her. He had meant it to be a kiss of good-bye, but she kissed him back, kissed him with a desperation that seared his soul. Clinging together, they sank down on the grass. She was silken fire in his arms, her skin smooth and warm, her lips sweet, so sweet. He kissed her deeply, his tongue seeking hers, heard her gasp mingle with his.

When he would have pulled away, she wrapped her arms tighter around him. Her hands slid under his shirt, playing over his back, kneading the muscles in his arms, sliding over his chest, down his belly. Somehow, their clothes were gone, the barriers were gone.

"I love you." She whispered the words over and over again, her hands fanning the fire between them.

He groaned her name. "Alisha, we've got to stop." It wasn't right, making love to her when he was leaving. It would only make his going more difficult, more painful.

When he would have moved away, she clasped him to her, her hips lifting, moving in silent invitation. Knowing it was wrong yet powerless to resist, he buried himself within her. . . .

Sanity returned slowly. He gazed down at her, loving her as never before, knowing in his heart that he could never let her go.

"I'll send for you, as soon as I get settled somewhere." He slid his hand into her hair. "Will you come?"

She looked up at him, hope shining in her eyes. "You promise, Mitchy?"

Mitchy. He grinned. She hadn't called him that since she was a little girl. No one else had ever dared call him that. "I promise, but it might take a while."

"I'll wait," she said, smiling through her tears. "However long it takes. Forever, if I have to . . ."

Mitch grunted softly as he turned away from the window. Apparently four months had been longer than forever. But times had been hard back then, jobs scarce. He had finally found a job working on a cattle ranch in Wyoming and once he was settled, he had written to Alisha, telling her to come to him. He had sent her money and a train ticket. She had returned both, along with a brief note which had said, in part, that she had reconsidered his offer and had decided to marry Roger Smithfield instead.

He had left the ranch at summer's end. Being a cowboy had been hard work. Roundups, branding, long hours spent in the saddle. He quickly came to the same conclusion as the other cowhands. Cattle had to be the stupidest creatures the good Lord had ever created, forever getting tangled up in barbed wire or mired in bogs. The job had been bearable when he was doing it so he and Alisha could be together. Without her, it had been just hard work.

For a time, he had drifted from place to place. He had been a young man from a small town who'd been nowhere, seen nothing. An angry young man with a broken heart. He had tried to forget her, tried to drown her memory in booze, in the arms of other women.

Nothing had worked, but, in time, the ache had grown less and he quit running. He had stopped in a little Colorado mining town to spend a few days and ended up wearing a badge. He had stayed there for almost three years before the itch to move on hit. During those three years, the name Mitch Garrett became a name to be reckoned with. The town had been wide open when he pinned on a badge; it had been a quiet, law-abiding community when he left, a place where decent folk could walk the streets without fear. He had been in a Nevada saloon when he got word of his father's death.

And now he was back in Canyon Creek, back where he had started.

But not for long.

Chapter 3

Russell Faraday sat at his desk, his hands clasped in an attitude of supplication. It couldn't be true. After all these years, Mitch Garrett was back.

Russell closed his eyes, an urgent prayer wending its way toward heaven. *For my daughter's sake, don't let him stay.*

Even now, over five years later, he could remember how shocked he had been when Alisha told him she was in love with Con Garrett's half-breed bastard son. Not only that, she'd said, but she was going to marry young Garrett as soon as he found a job.

Russell had stared at her, unable to believe his beautiful, angel daughter had been spending time with young Garrett.

But worse things were yet to come. Two months after declaring she was in love with Garrett, Alisha had come to him in tears to tell him she was carrying Garrett's bastard. Pain had clutched Russell's heart, so sharp and intense he had been certain he was going to die.

It was at that moment that he had fully realized how much he had relied on his wife. Angela had been his strength. When she died, a part of him, the best part, had died with her. He had needed Angela then as never before, needed her strength, her womanly intuition to guide him. For the first time since his wife passed away, he had admitted that he wasn't strong enough, wise enough, to raise their daughter alone. Self-recriminations followed. He should have paid more attention to Alisha, spent more time with her, listened more intently, instead of shutting himself away from her. Obviously, she had been searching for the love and affection he had denied her.

He had spent the rest of that night in his study, on his knees, fervently praying for help, for guidance, for wisdom.

The following day, he had put Chloe and Alisha on a stagecoach. He told his congregation they had gone east, for a visit, which was both the truth and a lie. They had gone east, but only as far east as the next town.

He had been there when the child was born. He remembered how his daughter had cried when he told her the baby had been stillborn. Two days later, he had taken Chloe and Alisha home.

They had never mentioned that awful time in their lives again.

Alisha had become the schoolmistress a year later when Mr. Fontaine retired. She was a respected member of the community. She played the organ in church on Sunday and for the choir on Wednesday night. She was engaged to be married to a decent, hard-working man. Her life was settled. Respectable. Above reproach.

And now Garrett was back.

With a sigh, Russell Faraday sank to his knees, praying that the house of cards he had so carefully built would not come tumbling down around him.

Chapter 4

Alisha took off her gloves and tucked them in the pocket of her coat, then hung her coat and hat on the hall tree inside the door.

"Father? I'm home."

"In here, Alisha."

Alisha followed the sound of her father's voice to the study. He was seated at his desk, working on Sunday's sermon. She felt a rush of tenderness as she looked at him. He had taken her mother's death hard, and it had aged him. His hair, once dark brown, was now gray. His eyes, once a deep emerald green, seemed to have faded. He rarely smiled anymore.

He looked up from his desk as she entered the room. "Good evening, daughter. How was your day?"

"Fine."

She sat down on the arm of the sofa, wondering if he knew Mitch was back in town.

Alisha took a deep breath. Might as well get it out in the open and get it over with. "I guess you've heard the news."

He didn't pretend ignorance. "Yes. Are you all right?"

"Of course." She pasted a smile on her face. "Why wouldn't I be?"

"I know you once thought you were in love with him."

"That was a long time ago."

"Yes," he said quietly. "A long time ago."

"How's your sermon coming along?"

Russell shrugged. "Fine, fine."

Rising, she walked around the desk and gave her father a hug. "I know it'll be wonderful, like always. I'll go fix dinner."

In the kitchen, she stared out the window while she waited for the stew to heat, sighing as her thoughts turned toward Mitch, as they had been doing all day.

Why hadn't he sent for her? When her father insisted she leave town until the baby was born, she had made him promise he would forward any mail she received, but none had been forthcoming. Still, she had waited, hoping, for months and months. Every time her father went to the post office to pick up the mail, she had been certain that she would hear from Mitch, but the days and weeks passed, and there had been no word from him and finally she realized he was never going to send for her, that his love, like his promise, had been a lie. Even now, she could remember how devastated she had been when she finally admitted to herself that she was waiting for a letter that was never going to come. She had felt so lost, so lonely, so bereft. She had cried until she was certain she had no tears left, and then she had cried some more.

She had been determined to put him out of her mind, and she had turned her every thought to the baby she carried. She might not have Mitch, but she would have his child.

But even that comfort had been denied her. She had never seen her son. The baby was born dead, and her father had told her that it was for the best if she didn't see the child, that she should put the whole affair behind her and go on with her life. For months afterward, she had dreamed that she heard her baby crying, that he was wandering in the dark, searching for her.

Gradually, the dreams had stopped and she had sought to take her father's advice, to put that period of her life behind her. She had thought herself quite successful at it until today, when just hearing Mitch's name brought it all back, made her remember how desperately she had loved him, how her heart had ached when he left her, how empty her arms had been when the child she had longed for was taken from her.

Tears burned her eyes and slid down her cheeks and she dashed them away. She would not cry for Mitch Garrett. Not now, not ever again.

She was going to marry Roger Smithfield. They had grown up together, gone to school together. He was a good man, an ambitious man, and she cared deeply for him. Soon he would have his own business. They would have a home of their own, a family of their own. She was going to be the best wife any man ever had. And if Roger didn't make her heart sing the way Mitch had, if Roger didn't make her flesh ache for his touch, well, she could just live without that. Love and lust had brought her nothing but misery and despair.

Sniffing back her tears, she removed a pan of biscuits from the oven, filled two bowls with beef stew, and went to tell her father that dinner was ready.

Chapter 5

Mitch shook hands with his father's lawyer then left the man's office. Closing the door, he stood on the boardwalk for a moment, then shoved the legal documents into his back pocket. The ranch was legally his now, to do with as he pleased. Ironic, he mused as he descended the stairs and crossed the street, that the first piece of property he had ever owned should be a place that held nothing but unhappy memories.

He muttered an oath as he stepped onto the boardwalk. Why had he come back here? Why hadn't he just written to the lawyer and told him to sell the ranch, lock, stock, and barrel, and send him the money?

Shit, he knew why. He had come back to Canyon Creek hoping for a miracle, hoping that *she* would still be here, that he would have a chance to confront her, to ask her why she hadn't waited for him, like she'd promised she would. Damn, after all this time, it shouldn't matter anymore. But it did.

Lost in thought, he didn't see the woman exiting the mercantile until he had slammed into her, nearly knocking her off the boardwalk.

"I'm sorry," Mitch exclaimed, grabbing her arm to

keep her from tumbling down the stairs. "I wasn't looking where I was . . ."

The words died in his throat. For a moment, all he could do was stare. "Lisha." She was every bit as beautiful as he remembered, with her honey-gold hair and sparkling brown eyes.

Alisha stared at the man in front of her, scarcely able to speak past the lump in her throat. "Mitch." She tried to smile, and failed. "I heard you were back in town. I'm . . . I'm sorry about your father."

He nodded. "Thanks."

She looked down at his hand, still holding her arm. It was a large hand, dark, callused. Strong. She remembered the touch of it on her skin, the way the merest touch had made her tingle from head to toe. Mitch's hand, caressing her, his fingertips gliding over her thigh, his skin so dark against her own . . .

He followed her gaze, then jerked his hand away. "Sorry."

Silence stretched between them.

I never had trouble talking to him before, Alisha thought. *Now he seems like a stranger.* "How long will you be in town?"

"I'm not sure. Until I sell the old man's house, I reckon. How's Smithfield?" He glanced at her hand, steeling himself for the sight of another man's ring on her finger, then noticed she was wearing gloves.

"He's doing very well, thank you."

Mitch grunted softly, all too aware that they weren't alone, that people were watching, staring. Remembering.

Silence settled between them again, punctuated by memories of what might have been.

"I have to go," Alisha said. "It was nice seeing you, Mitchell."

Mitchell. She had never called him that in all the years he had known her. "Yeah," he muttered. "Nice."

"Well, good day." Head high, she turned and walked away, hardly able to see where she was going for the tears that flooded her eyes.

Mitch watched her until she was out of sight. Going into the nearest saloon, he ordered a bottle of the best bourbon the house had to offer, then carried it to a table in the back corner of the room and sat down, determined to drown her memory in whiskey, to obliterate every thought, every memory, every regret.

It wouldn't work, of course. But then, it never had.

He was about a fourth of the way through the bottle when he heard the gunshots. His years of being a lawman rose to the fore and sent him running out of the saloon, gun in hand. It took only a moment to size up the situation. Three men were exiting the bank, pushing their way through the handful of townspeople gathered on the boardwalk.

Saul Jordan, owner of the Canyon Creek Cattleman's Bank, was sprawled facedown across the doorway. Blood oozed from his left shoulder.

A woman screamed as one of the robbers shoved her out of the way.

Mitch didn't stop to think, just did what came naturally. He fired a warning shot in the air and hollered, "Throw down your weapons!"

He didn't expect the outlaws to comply, and they didn't. They turned to face him, their guns swinging in his direction. Without hesitation, he fired at the man in front. The outlaw went down, and Mitch fired at the second man. The third bandit threw his gun into the street and raised his hands over his head.

One of the moneybags had burst open when it hit the ground and greenbacks fluttered in the air like paper butterflies.

A man swore as the scent of blood and gun smoke rose on the wind. Somewhere in the distance a child cried for its mother.

When the smoke cleared, two of the bank robbers lay dead in the dirt. The third outlaw hadn't moved. He was staring at Mitch, his expression virulent. "You dirty half-breed! You killed my brother!"

"Shut your mouth," Mitch replied mildly. "Or you'll join him."

The outlaw fell silent, but he continued to stare at Mitch, his expression filled with loathing.

"Damn!" exclaimed a man standing near the newspaper office. "That was some shootin'."

"Like greased lightning!"

"Never seen nothing like it!"

Mitch nodded as men came forward to slap him on the back. Two of the bank tellers rushed out of the bank and began picking greenbacks up from the street and boardwalk.

Someone called for the doctor. Another man ran forward with a piece of rope and tied the surviving outlaw's hands behind his back.

Holstering his Colt, Mitch turned away and almost bumped into old man West, who had left his rocking chair across the way to get a closer look at the dead men.

"Where the hell's your sheriff?" Mitch asked.

Mr. West shrugged. "We're sort of between lawmen at the moment."

"Not anymore!"

Mitch glanced over his shoulder to see who had spoken, and saw two men walking toward him. They both wore dark suits, and they were both smiling broadly.

The taller of the two pumped Mitch's hand vigorously. He had wavy brown hair and guileless gray eyes. Mitch figured he was in his mid-forties.

"Casey Waller," he said. "I'm one of the city fathers. This here is Fred Plumber."

"Pleased to meet you," Mitch said. He nodded at the second man. Fred Plumber had sandy-colored hair and pale blue eyes. He sported a handlebar mustache and thick sideburns, and appeared to be about the same age as Waller.

"Unless I miss my guess, you've worn a badge before," Waller said. "How'd you like to be our new sheriff? Pays ten dollars a month, plus room and board."

Mitch shook his head. "I don't think so, but thanks for the offer."

"Now, now, don't be too hasty. We might be able to offer more. Say, twenty a month?"

"Cowboys make more than that," Mitch said, "and they don't have to worry about getting shot."

"Twenty-five," Waller said, "plus room and board." He smiled expansively. "That's a mighty sweet deal for the right man. . . ." He glanced over at the activity in the street. "And we think you're the right man."

"I was getting more than that in Virginia City. Anyway, it's not the money. And I don't need a place to stay."

Waller held up his hands in a gesture of surrender. "All right," he said, obviously exasperated, "we'll pay you forty dollars a month, and pay for your ammunition, too. You can't turn that down! No need to decide right now," he added quickly. "Why don't you think it over for a day or two? We'll be in touch."

Waller pumped Mitch's hand again, then hustled his silent companion into the street where a tall, lanky man dressed in unrelieved black was lining up the two dead bodies while a man Mitch assumed was a photographer for the *Canyon Creek Gazette* set up his equipment and began to take pictures.

Shaking his head, Mitch turned and went back into the saloon. Newspapers seemed to have a fondness for photographs of dead outlaws. He remembered seeing a photograph of the Howard gang. All six of them had been killed during a bank robbery in Tucson. The undertaker had laid them out side by side in their coffins. The photograph had made the front page. Arizona was a colorful place. Crawling with gunmen and gamblers, rustlers and stagecoach robbers, it had earned the name the Southwest Corner of Hell. Mitch had spent a little time there, and he had been inclined to agree.

Resuming his place at the table, he poured himself another drink. Sheriff, indeed. He planned to get shut of this town just as soon as possible. Still, it would give him something to do until he found a buyer for the old man's house.

He laughed soundlessly, humorlessly. For the first time in his life, he didn't have to work for wages. He could fix up the house, stock the ranch with cattle, and most likely earn a comfortable living selling beef to the cavalry at Fort Apache, but the mere idea left a bad taste in his mouth. Staying at the ranch would be like living off the old man, and that was something he couldn't do.

Mitch Garrett, sheriff of Canyon Creek, New Mexico, he mused. It would be a hell of a joke on the town.

By the time he was halfway through the bottle, he had decided to take the job.

Chapter 6

Alisha took a last look in the full-length mirror that stood in the corner of her bedroom, making sure her bonnet was straight. It was a new bonnet, dark blue lined with a lighter blue silk. It had been imported from France. She turned her head from side to side. It was quite the most becoming bonnet she had ever owned, she thought, and then chided herself for her vanity as she tied the long ribbons into a pert bow beneath her chin. It was rare that she spent her hard-earned cash on such fripperies, but she had seen the bonnet in a mail-order catalog and sent for it before she could talk herself out of it.

The chiming of the courthouse clock reminded her she would be late to preaching if she didn't hurry, and that would never do. Turning away from the mirror, she took a deep breath. Her mind had been in turmoil ever since Mitch rode into town. Last night, she had almost burned her father's dinner. But how was she supposed to be able to think of mundane things like cooking and teaching when *he* was back?

Mitch was the new lawman. He had killed two men and foiled a bank robbery. The news was all over town. People were calling him a hero. She shook her head. What had he been thinking, to risk his life like that? And why had he accepted the offer of the town counsel? He had never liked it here. Even if he hadn't wanted to get away from his father, he would have left just to get away from the censure of the town. What was she going to do? Canyon Creek was a small community. She was bound to run into him often, at socials, the Fourth of July picnic, the harvest dance, on the street, in the mercantile. At least she wouldn't have to worry about running into him in church!

She pressed her hand over her heart. He couldn't stay here, he just couldn't. Maybe she could talk to him, make him see how impossible it was.

Grabbing her reticule, she hurried from her room and flew down the stairs. Outside, she smoothed her skirts, took a deep breath, and pasted a smile on her face. It wasn't seemly for the preacher's daughter to be seen running down the street, especially when she was also the schoolmarm. She must always walk sedately and smile at everyone she met.

She reached the church a few minutes later. Entering the sanctuary from the side door, she took her place at the organ and struck the chords of the opening hymn. She couldn't help smiling as the congregation began to sing "Shall We Gather At the River." Nor could she help wondering what had happened to the carefree girl who had once gone skinny-dipping with the town's bad boy . . .

She stared at him, her eyes wide, unable to believe he was serious. "I can't go swimming now," she said. "I didn't bring anything to wear." She wasn't a little girl anymore; she couldn't swim in her drawers. These days, she swam in an old shirt of her father's and a pair of Mitch's cut-off trousers.

"You don't need anything to wear," he had replied with a roguish grin. "I'm not wearing anything."

"Mitchy!"

"Come on in, Lisha. Don't be chicken."

She crossed her arms over her breasts. "What if someone comes?"

"No one's going to come down here at this time of night. Come on."

"We're here." She tried not to stare at him. The water covered him a few inches above his waist. She tried not to think that he was naked beneath the water, tried not to notice the way the water glistened on his sun-bronzed skin, tried not to stare at his broad shoulders, at the way the setting sun caressed his hair, highlighting the shiny black with bright gold.

"Come on," he coaxed. "I know you can swim. I taught you."

He had taught her so many things. Of course, her father wouldn't have approved of most of them.

Mitch smiled at her, his head cocked to one side, one brow raised. "Come on, Lisha, you know you want to."

"You won't tell anyone?"

He winked at her. "I'll keep your secret, darlin'. Haven't I kept all the others?"

She nodded. She had told him things she had never told another soul, her hopes, her fears, her girlish dreams. "Turn your back."

He splashed her once, then turned around, giving her a clear view of his back. It was a beautiful back, she thought, if a man's back could be called beautiful.

But there was no time to admire it now, not when he was liable to turn around at any minute.

She undressed quickly and slid into the river, shrieking as the cold water closed over her. "Why didn't you tell me it's freezing!" she exclaimed. She bent at the waist and crossed her arms over her breasts again.

"You'll get used to it." He turned to face her, grinning. "Come on, I'll race you to the bend of the river."

She shook her head. "It's too cold."

"Don't be such a baby. Come on, I'll even give you a head start."

"Oh, all right," she agreed, knowing he would just rag on her until she gave him his way.

"Count of twenty," he said.

"Make it thirty. And count slow."

"All right. Thirty. Go!"

She struck out, her strokes long and even, the way he had taught her. She could hear him counting, hear the suppressed laughter in his voice. He was so sure he would win. He always did. But not today! Concentrating, she swam for all she was worth. She could hear him coming up fast behind her, but it didn't matter. She was going to win!

She was grinning triumphantly when he reached her. "Ha!" she shouted triumphantly. "I won!"

"So you did," he agreed. "I guess there really is a first time for everything."

She stuck her tongue out at him, then shrieked as he put his hand on top of her head and pushed her under the water. She came up sputtering and swinging, heard him grunt as her fist connected with his eye.

"Oh, Mitchy, I'm sorry," she said, instantly contrite. "Are you all right?"

"Of course I'm all right," he said. "You can't hurt me."

But even then, his eye had been turning red, swelling shut. . . .

"Let us pray."

Alisha bowed her head and folded her hands, but she didn't hear the words of her father's prayer. She was lost in the past. For days after she hit him, Mitch had sported the most gorgeous shiner. She had felt guilty as she watched it change color, from black to purple to bilious green. *Mitchy, oh Mitchy. I waited and waited. Why didn't you send for me?*

She looked up as her father said "Amen," felt her heart catch in her throat as she glanced out over the congregation, and saw Mitch sitting in the second row, beside Mr. West, who was snoring softly, as usual. She closed her eyes and opened them again, certain she was imagining things. But he was still there. What on earth was Mitch doing here? He had never come to church, not once in all the years she had known him.

She looked away before he could catch her staring, only to find her gaze straying toward him again moments later. He looked older, of course, and even more handsome that she recalled. She thought of the baby she had lost. Had her son lived, would he have looked like Mitch? Her son, their son, would be four now. If he had lived . . .

She felt a wave of heat sweep up her neck and onto her cheeks when Mitch's gaze met hers, and she quickly looked away, wondering if the entire congregation was aware of the tension that flowed between the two of them.

She was glad when it was time to play the organ for

the next hymn, though Mitch's presence made her so nervous she made several mistakes, something she rarely did. She caught her father looking at her strangely and shrugged, certain he would comment on it later.

She could feel Mitch watching her, and she wondered again what had brought him to church. He wasn't of her faith, nor did he believe in any of the various forms of Christianity. She had often asked him to attend church services with her when they were children, and he had always refused, saying that he didn't hold with the white man's religion, that, when he prayed, he prayed to *Usen*. She had asked if he couldn't pray to *Usen* in her church, and he had said, no, that the Great Spirit of the Apache couldn't be found within the four square walls of the white man's church. She wondered if he had changed his mind about that, or if he was there today merely to make her uneasy. She winced as she hit another wrong note.

When the hymn was over, she moved to one of the choir seats behind the pulpit. She tried to concentrate on her father's sermon, but all she could think about was Mitch, laughing at her, smiling at her, kissing her.

She drew her gaze from Mitch and searched the congregation for Roger. He was sitting near the back, wearing his Sunday-go-to-meeting blue suit, his cravat neatly tied, his blond hair slicked back. He would expect an invitation to supper, and then, after he spent an hour or so visiting with her father, they would take a walk through town, looking at the store windows, making small talk. He would bring her home, thank her for a pleasant evening, give her a chaste kiss good night.

She sighed heavily, suddenly depressed at the

thought of spending another evening with Roger and her father. She glanced at Mitch again. He had ridden out of her life and taken all her girlish hopes and dreams, all her laughter and good times, with him.

She hated him for that.

She stood up and moved to the organ as her father began to offer the Benediction.

Mitch glanced around the church as Russell Faraday's sonorous voice pleaded with the Almighty on behalf of his congregation. It was a large, square building, with a peaked roof and whitewashed walls. The benches were made of pine, the altar rail and pulpit of oak. A large cross, also made of oak, hung on the wall behind the pulpit. Sunlight streamed through a round stained-glass window. He studied the window a moment. The scene depicted the Good Shepherd standing near a clear blue stream, surrounded by a flock of sheep. One small white lamb stood on the far side of the water, looking lost and forlorn.

Mitch shook his head as the prayer went on and on. His old man hadn't believed in a supreme being, but then, he hadn't believed in much of anything. His mother had worshipped in the Apache way. She had no Sabbath day, as such, no holy days. She had told him that the People worshipped when moved upon to do so. Sometimes the whole tribe would gather to sing and pray. At other times, only a few would join together. She told him that sometimes they prayed in silence, at other times each one assembled would pray aloud. Sometimes an Old One would pray for all. He had never seen his mother pray, yet he knew her faith in *Usen* had been strong and unwavering.

Mitch let out a sigh. He wasn't sure what foolishness

had brought him here this morning. It was the first time he had ever set foot in this church, or any church, for that matter. He had told himself it was because he was now the sheriff and people expected it of him, but that was a lie. He had never done what people expected of him. He had come here to see Alisha and for no other reason.

It was hard to believe that the woman sitting at the organ, modestly clad in a dark blue dress and silk-lined bonnet, was the same girl he had once known. He couldn't imagine this demure woman sneaking out of her house to meet him late at night, or skinny-dipping in the creek.

He had a sudden, inexplicable urge to go to her house that night, to stand beneath her window and call her name and see if she would meet him in the moonlight.

Faraday said the final amen. Mr. West came awake with a start as the strains of "Blest Be the Tie That Binds" filled the air. The congregation rose to their feet and began to file out of the church.

Outside, Mitch nodded to Waller and Plumber, then skirted several groups of parishioners who were gathered together talking about the weather, the sermon, babies, and all the other mundane things small-town people gossiped about.

Crossing the dusty street, he headed toward the hotel, thinking about getting something to eat. Abruptly, he changed directions and made his way toward the river. The water was running high and fast due to the recent rains. Standing on the bank, he looked at the ramshackle huts on the other side. Nobody should have to live like that, he mused, remembering the tar-paper shack where he'd spent the first twelve years of his life. Cold and drafty in the winter; hotter than hell's furnace in the summer. He remembered drawing water from the river to bathe in, collecting wood for the stove.

He remembered his mother. . . .

"Why do you live with that man?" He had been eight or nine when he asked that question for the first time.

"Because he is your father."

He had frowned at her, wondering how his gentle mother could love such an abusive, angry man. "He's mean to you," he said, staring at the dark, ugly bruise on her arm. "He hits you."

"He doesn't mean it, *ciye*."

He hadn't understood why his mother defended Con Garrett, why she stayed with him.

Now, more than twenty years later, he still didn't understand why his mother had stayed with his old man for so long, or why she had finally left him to go back to her own people. He had never blamed her for leaving, only for not taking him with her.

He never should have come back here. Muttering an oath, he picked up a rock and tossed it into the river. It was all in the past and best forgotten.

Like Alisha . . .

A faint rustling from downriver drew his attention. He glanced over his shoulder, and she was there, poised like a doe ready to take flight.

"Lisha."

"Hello, Mitch."

She had changed out of her dark blue dress into a gray skirt and white shirtwaist. She wasn't wearing a hat and he had a sudden urge to loosen her braid and run his fingers through the thick golden strands.

"It's been a long time," he said quietly.

She nodded. "Yes." *Five years, two months, three days.*

"How've you been?"

"Fine. You?" She couldn't stop staring at him. He looked wonderful. Gone was the tall, skinny boy in patched clothes and in his place stood a ruggedly handsome man dressed in a crisp white shirt, black wool trousers, black boots, and a black hat with a snakeskin band.

"I'm doing all right."

"I guess you're planning to stay awhile," Alisha glanced at the badge pinned to his shirt pocket, "now that you're the new sheriff and all."

He shrugged.

She smoothed a hand over the front of her skirt. "What have you been doing all these years?"

"Not much. How about you? You happy with Smithfield? He treating you all right?"

"Of course. We're getting married in June."

"You're not married yet?" He stared at her. He had heard of long engagements, but five years? Hell, it was none of his business. There was no point in bringing up the past. She was engaged to Smithfield. And even though he had never cared much for the man, he had to admit that Smithfield had turned out to be a decent sort, honest and hardworking. No doubt he would make Alisha a good husband.

She ignored his question. She didn't want to talk about herself, about why she had waited so long to marry. "What about you? Are you married?"

"No."

She wanted to ask him why he had never sent for her, but she couldn't summon the nerve. Besides, it didn't matter now. She had been engaged to Roger for the past eight months. In that time, she had come to love him, not with the same intensity she had once loved Mitch, to be sure, but she loved Roger nonetheless. He was a fine, decent man, and she knew marrying him was the right thing to do. Why, then, did his ring suddenly feel heavy on her finger?

"I was surprised to see you in church this morning," she said, needing to break the heavy silence that had settled between them.

"I was a little surprised myself. Your old man preaches a hell of a sermon. All that fire and brimstone."

"Yes, he does." There was no mistaking the love, or the pride, in her voice. She glanced out over the creek, remembering the first time she had seen Mitch here. *This is my spot.* She smiled wistfully as she recalled that day.

"What are you thinking?" Mitch asked.

"Nothing, really. Just remembering."

"We had some good times here," he remarked, making her wonder if he, too, was reminiscing about those halcyon days gone by.

"Yes." It was here, in this very place, that he had taught her to swim. It was on this very rock that he had taught her how to kiss. . . . She shook the memory away. "I'd better go."

"Smithfield coming to Sunday dinner?"

"Yes." She took a deep breath. "Would you like to join us?" She said the words quickly, before she could change her mind. She could well imagine her father's shock, Roger's displeasure. But the words had been said, and she couldn't call them back. Didn't want to call them back.

"Why do I have the feeling you'd faint if I said yes?"

She lifted her chin and Mitch caught a glimpse of the spunky girl she had been.

"Will you come?" Alisha asked. She could feel a tide of color rushing into her cheeks but she refused to look away, refused to rescind the invitation. She could invite anyone she pleased to dinner. After all, it was her house, too, and she was the one doing the cooking! Besides, Mitch's presence at the table would certainly add a little excitement to their staid evenings.

"Well, thanks for the invite, but I don't think so. Sitting with your old man and your fiancé doesn't sound the least bit pleasant." He grinned at her. "Although, just seeing the expression on your old man's face might be worth it."

She laughed, and he laughed with her. Too long, she thought, it had been far too long since she felt this light-hearted, this alive. Why was it only Mitch who made her feel this way?

Why hadn't he sent for her? The laughter died in her throat as the question that had plagued her for the last five years teased the back of her mind. Why, why? *"I'll send for you, as soon as I get settled somewhere,"* he had said. *"Will you come?"* She could still hear his words in her mind, still hear herself asking, *"You promise, Mitchy?"* And his voice assuring her that he would.

What had happened to make him change his mind? Womanlike, she had assumed he had found someone else, but that didn't seem to be the case. She wished she had the nerve to ask him straight out, but she couldn't form the words.

"Well," she said at last, "I've got to go. Maybe you'll come to dinner some other time."

"Maybe." He took a deep breath. "Maybe I could take you out to dinner some night."

She should decline, politely. It would only cause trouble with Roger and her father if she were seen in Mitch's company, not to mention the gossip it would surely arouse.

She took a deep breath, prepared to refuse. "Yes," she said. "I'd like that."

"Tomorrow night?"

She nodded, her heart pounding. "Where?"

"I'll pick you up."

Alisha shook her head. "I'll meet you." She saw the protest rise in his eyes. "Please, Mitch."

"All right. The hotel dining room, at six?"

"I'll be there."

He watched her walk away, admiring the gentle sway of her hips, the way the brilliant rays of the afternoon sun seemed to follow her, surrounding her in a halo of golden light. He wondered what the odds were of her actually showing up at the restaurant tomorrow night. Probably not too good. Unless he missed his guess, she would change her mind as soon as she got home, maybe send him a brief note of apology.

Still it was something to look forward to.

Chapter 7

Her father and Roger discussed politics over dinner. Alisha said little. Being a woman, she wasn't expected to have an opinion on who would be the best candidate for governor, or the pros and cons of having the railroad come through town. Usually, such narrow-mindedness annoyed her, but tonight she was glad to remain silent while the men talked. She wouldn't have been able to concentrate on the conversation anyway. All she could think about was Mitch. He was back, and he was here to stay, at least for a while. And she was having dinner with him tomorrow night.

". . . hard to believe Garrett's back in town."

Alisha looked up at the mention of Mitch's name.

"People are calling him a hero," her father said. "If he hadn't intervened the other day, the robbers would have gotten away with near ten thousand dollars."

"He was always looking for a fight, as I recall," Roger said, his voice heavy with disdain. He looked at Alisha. "Isn't that right?"

"Was he?" She didn't want to discuss Mitch with her father or Roger. Standing abruptly, she picked up her dishes and carried them into the kitchen.

The men went into the parlor while she cleared the table and did the dishes. Standing at the sink, her hands immersed in dishwater, she tried to think of something, anything, besides Mitch Garrett, but it was impossible. She'd been unable to think of anything else since he came back to town. Had she truly thought of anything else since he went away? Dinner tomorrow night. What should she wear? She looked down at her dress. Long sleeves, high collar. Utterly dreary, she thought. All her clothes were drab and dreary. Everything in her closet was brown or gray or dark blue. She might as well be an old maid or a widow. She didn't own a single dress that was bright or cheerful or even pretty.

She thought about the soiled doves she sometimes saw coming out of the saloon. They rouged their cheeks and painted their lips and put kohl on their eyes and wore low-cut dresses in gaudy colors. She might not agree with their lifestyle, but people, especially the men, noticed them. And she very much wanted Mitch to sit up and take notice.

She rinsed the dishes, plucked a cotton towel from the back of a chair, and began to dry them. There was only one thing to do. She was going to buy a new dress. She had been saving money out of her wages to buy a new rocking chair for her father for Christmas, but suddenly a new dress seemed more important. Something red, she thought, giggling. Something wickedly low cut that would show off her bosom and her shoulders.

When the dishes were done, she poured three cups of coffee and placed them on a tray. She added the sugar bowl and creamer, a plate of sugar cookies she had baked earlier that day, and carried the tray into the parlor.

Her father and Roger both looked up at her and smiled.

Alisha smiled back, wondering what her father and fiancé would think if they knew she was planning to have dinner with Mitch Garrett tomorrow night.

Mitch stood outside the restaurant where he was supposed to meet Alisha. According to the courthouse clock, it was a quarter past six. He grunted softly. Well, he hadn't really expected her to show up.

He swore under his breath, more disappointed than he wanted to admit. He'd been looking forward to seeing her all day. To pass the time, he had taken a ride around the ranch. It was a pretty piece of land, especially the meadow near the south pasture. Towering pines bordered the lush green meadow that was watered by a narrow stream. It wouldn't take much to restore the ranch. A little money, a lot of hard work, and it would make a good place to settle down, raise some cattle and some kids. . . . He'd never thought much about being a father, maybe because his old man had been such a rotten one, but lately he'd been thinking it might be nice to have a son of his own.

He swore again. He'd been doing far too much thinking lately. He needed to get shed of this town right quick before he made a damn fool out of himself.

He blew out a sigh as the clock chimed the half-hour. Six-thirty.

There was no point waiting around any longer. He was about to head for the nearest saloon when he saw a woman clad in a sky-blue dress hurrying down the boardwalk.

A slow smile spread over his lips as he recognized Alisha.

"Sorry I'm late," she said breathlessly.

His gaze moved over her, slow and lazy and filled with appreciation. "It was worth the wait."

Heat flooded her cheeks. "Thank you."

He opened the door for her, followed her inside. It was a pretty fancy place for a town the size of Canyon Creek. The tables were covered with white cloths. Dozens of candles in silver wall sconces lit the room with a soft warm glow. Each table had a small vase of wildflowers. The dishes were china, the glassware looked like crystal.

Alisha held her head high as she made her way to an empty table near the back, well away from the windows near the street. She was sure it was only her imagination, but she couldn't help feeling that people were staring at her—pointing, gossiping behind her back, speculating on what Miss Faraday was doing dining with a man who was not her fiancé, her father, or a relative. A few of them recognized Mitch. She saw it in their eyes, heard it in the whispers that followed them to their table.

Mitch held her chair for her. He had picked up some manners somewhere along the way, she thought as she watched him take the seat across from hers, unfold his napkin, and put it in his lap.

She picked up the menu, glad to have something to do with her hands.

"What's good here?" Mitch asked.

"Just about everything," Alisha replied, not meeting his gaze.

"What are you having?"

"I'm not sure. The roast beef, I think. Although their

fried chicken is very good, too." She looked at him over the top of her menu. "I'll bet you have the chicken."

He grinned at her. "You'd win."

She grinned back. Mitch had always loved Chloe's fried chicken. Alisha had asked her to make it often, just so she could sneak some to Mitch.

The waitress came to take their order. At the last minute, Alisha decided on the chicken, too.

"You look real pretty this evening," Mitch remarked when the waitress had gone.

Alisha ran a hand over her skirt. "Thank you."

"Is that a new dress?"

She nodded. She had fully intended to buy a red one, had even tried one on, but at the last minute she had decided on this one. It was a soft shade of blue, pretty as a robin's egg.

"I always liked you in that color."

Was that why she had picked this dress? Had she subconsciously remembered that blue was his favorite color?

She met his gaze, wishing she could think of something to say, something clever, something witty. Something. But she couldn't think at all when he was watching her through those dark, dark eyes. No one else had ever looked at her the way he did, made her feel the way he did.

"I've decided not to sell the ranch after all."

She blinked at him. "What?" Oh, Lord, that meant he was going to be staying in Canyon Creek. Permanently.

Mitch nodded. Until that very moment, he had been planning to move on as soon as he sold the ranch. But seeing Alisha, being with her, he knew he couldn't leave. She might be engaged to Roger Smithfield, but she wasn't married yet. And in spite of everything that had happened, he still loved her, still wanted her.

"You don't look very happy about it," he remarked.

"I . . . I'm just surprised. I thought you hated it here. When you left, you said you'd never come back."

"Yeah, well, things change." He smiled at her. "What did you tell your old man?"

"About what?"

"About tonight. About having dinner with me."

"Oh." A fresh wave of heat flooded her cheeks. "I told him I was going to visit one of my students. To talk to his parents about his grades." It was something she did from time to time, so her father hadn't questioned her.

"I see."

She lifted her chin, her eyes sparking with defiance. "You didn't expect me to tell him the truth, did you?"

"No, I guess not. I don't suppose Smithfield would be too happy about your being here, either.

Alisha felt a sharp stab of guilt. "No." Roger was a good man. He was building them a house, planning for their future. Besides running his own carpentry shop, he worked part-time at the mercantile. Tonight, he was working late at the store, earning some extra money by taking inventory. She should be there, helping him. At any other time, she would have been.

"Why did you agree to have dinner with me, Lisha?"

"Why?" She blinked at him, a dozen answers scampering around in her mind. "Why shouldn't I?" she asked, unwilling to tell him the truth. "What's wrong with old friends having dinner together?"

"Friends?" He looked mildly amused. "Is that what we were? Just friends?"

Another wave of heat swept into her cheeks as she recalled the moonlit nights they had spent near the creek, the warm hugs, the long, lazy kisses, the hours they had spent making love . . . the promise he had not kept . . . the child she had lost.

The waitress arrived a short time later with their dinner. Alisha stared at her plate, her appetite gone. Taking a deep breath, she clenched her fists in her lap as she summoned the courage to ask the question that had plagued her for the last five years.

"Why, Mitch?" she asked. "Why didn't you send for me?"

He looked up from his plate. "What are you talking about?"

"You promised. You promised to send for me. Why didn't you? I waited and waited."

He put his fork down and leaned across the table. "I sent for you. Sent money for the train. And you wrote me back and told me you had married Smithfield."

"I never got a letter from you."

Mitch reached into his back pocket and withdrew a piece of paper. It was badly creased and stained. He unfolded it carefully and handed it to Alisha.

She took it from him with a growing sense of trepidation, her eyes widening as she read the faded words. The handwriting was unmistakable. She didn't want to believe it, didn't want to think that her father was capable of doing such a low-down, despicable thing, but the proof was in her hands.

"I didn't write this." Alisha dropped the letter on the table, not wanting to touch it a moment longer. Suddenly she felt empty inside, numb, as if everything she had ever believed in had suddenly been proven a lie.

"No? Then who did?"

"My father."

Well, Mitch thought, that explained a lot of things. Picking up the letter, he crushed it in his hand. He had kept that cursed letter all these years because he'd thought it had come from Alisha, because, painful as the words had been, the letter and his memories were all he'd had left of her.

A vile oath escaped his lips. He was tempted to march up to the Faraday house and confront the old man face-to-face, demand to know why Faraday had lied to him. Except that Mitch already knew the answer. He was the illegitimate, half-breed son of a gambling man. He hadn't been good enough for Alisha then, and he probably wasn't good enough for her now. But he was madder than hell.

"So," he said, reining in his anger, "where does that leave us?"

"What do you mean?"

"You promised to marry me."

"That was a long time ago. I'm not the same girl I was then." She shook her head. "Besides, I'm engaged to Roger."

"I asked you first."

"Mitchy . . ." She spoke her childhood name for him without thinking.

His expression softened. "No one else has ever called me that, you know. Just you."

"You don't even know me anymore."

"I know you," he replied quietly. "I've always known you." He leaned across the table again. "I know you better than you know yourself, better than Roger Smithfield will ever know you."

Did he still want her? Hope flared in her heart, a wild, sweet hope as she thought of what it would be like to be Mitch's wife. She savored it for one precious moment, and then shook her head. "My father would never approve. And Roger . . . he's been good to me. I can't hurt him."

He sat back in his chair, as tense as a cat ready to spring. "But you don't mind hurting me."

"You could have written me again," she retorted, feeling all her old hurt and anger welling up inside her as she recalled how awful it had been when she realized she was pregnant, how much easier it would have been to tell her father if Mitch had been there beside her, lending her his strength. "If you really loved me, you would have come back for me."

"For what?" He slammed his fist on the table, causing the cutlery to rattle. Water splashed over the edge of her glass, making a dark stain on the white damask tablecloth. "I thought you were already married."

Alisha glanced around the restaurant. Several people were staring in their direction. What had she been thinking when she agreed to meet Mitch here tonight? By tomorrow morning, it would be all over town that she'd had dinner with Mitch Garrett. What would her father say when he found out? What would Roger say?

She looked around the room, at the curious stares. She couldn't face them, she couldn't face Mitch. "I shouldn't have come here."

Throwing her napkin on the table, she stood up and hurried out of the restaurant. She paused on the boardwalk a moment, her heart pounding. She couldn't go home, not now. Her father would take one look at her face and know something was wrong.

Lifting her skirts, she ran across the street and down the narrow path that led to the creek.

Mitch swore under his breath as he watched Alisha run out the door. Unconsciously, he shoved the letter into his pants pocket. Rising, he dropped a couple of dollars on the table, then grabbed his hat and left the restaurant.

Darkness had fallen. Standing on the boardwalk, he glanced up and down the street. There was no sign of her. He stood there a moment, and then crossed the street toward the path that led to the creek. She would be there.

He followed the familiar path, remembering all the times he had traveled it in his youth, usually with Alisha at his side. He had walked her home from school, glad for any excuse to be with her. They had parted where the trail forked. She had gone left and he had gone right, across the creek, down the rutted road that led to the shack that had never been a home.

He rounded the bend and made his way toward the creek. She was there, as he had known she would be. Standing on the rock, silhouetted in the light of the moon, just as he had imagined her, night after night when he couldn't sleep, when thoughts of Alisha, of what he had lost, tormented his heart and soul.

She didn't turn, but he heard her voice clearly. "Why did you have to come back here?"

"You know why."

"Go away, Mitch. Please, just go away."

"Is that what you really want?"

"Yes."

He moved up behind her, almost but not quite touching her. He took a deep breath, filling his senses with the sight of her, the scent of her, the nearness of her. "Lisha . . ."

"No." She shook her head. "No, no." And yet even as she spoke, she was turning, yearning, reaching out for him.

His arms were ready for her, open and inviting, just as they had always been, and she stepped into his embrace, wary as a rabbit scenting danger, eager as a child reaching for a treat that had been too long denied.

"Lisha!"

His arms closed around her, crushing her close. She buried her face against his shoulder, her hands sliding up and down his back, restless and wanting. He was taller, broader, than she remembered.

"I've dreamed of this," she murmured, her voice muffled. "Dreamed of it and yearned for it."

She felt his lips move in her hair, felt his arms tighten around her, and then he was lifting her chin, gazing down into her eyes, and she knew he was going to kiss her.

Her eyelids fluttered down as his mouth closed over hers. As if by magic, the years fell away, and she was thirteen again, being kissed for the first time. It was as wonderful, as magical, as she recalled. At thirteen, she had been confused by the yearnings of her body, by the heat that had flowed through every particle of her being, by feelings she had not understood. At twenty-three, she knew what desire was, knew that one kiss would surely lead to another, and another. And feared that she was no more capable of denying him, of denying herself, now than she had had been at seventeen.

She pressed against him, reveling in the feel of his arms around her—arms that were stronger and more muscled than she remembered. She breathed in his scent, ran her fingers through the thick hair at his nape. How had she lived all these years without this, without him?

She closed her eyes, imprinting this memory in her mind.

And then, summoning every ounce of willpower she possessed, she drew away, her hands clenched at her sides. "That shouldn't have happened," she said. "It can't happen again."

"Tell me you didn't like it." His gaze bored into hers, demanding the truth. "Tell me you don't want me to do it again."

"It doesn't matter what I want. I'm promised to Roger. And I keep my promises."

"Is that right?" he asked, and there was no mistaking the barely suppressed anger in his voice. "What about the promise you made to me?"

She shook her head. "I'm sorry."

"Dammit, Lisha, I told you I would have come back for you, but I thought you were married."

"It doesn't matter now. I'm engaged to Roger, and I won't hurt him. He's been good to me." She knew about hurt, about the pain of broken promises and broken hearts. She wrapped her arms around her body to keep from reaching for him. "Please, Mitch, just go away and leave me alone."

"I'm not going anywhere," he muttered. "But if you mean what you say, I won't bother you anymore."

"I do mean it."

Mitch nodded slowly. "All right, if that's the way you want it. I hope you won't regret it."

"I won't," she said, but it was a lie, the worst lie she had ever told. She watched him turn and walk away, and it felt as though he was taking her heart and soul with him.

When he was out of sight she hurried home, trying to convince herself she had done the right thing in sending Mitch away. For a moment, she stood on the porch, staring down at the creek. He was crazy to think they could just pick up where they had left off five years ago, and she had been crazy to consider it even for a moment. She had promised to marry Roger, and she meant to keep that promise.

What about the promise you made me? Mitch's voice rang in her mind, his voice angry and hurt-filled.

With a sigh, she opened the door and stepped into the foyer. "I'm home, Papa."

"In here, Alisha."

She followed the sound of her father's voice into the den.

Her father looked up from the letter he was writing. "Roger came by a little while ago."

"Did he?"

"Yes. He said he was sorry he missed you. So," Russell said, dipping his pen in the inkwell on the corner of his desk. "How did it go? Did you get everything straightened out with Will and his folks?"

"What?"

Russell frowned. "Are you feeling well? You look a little pale."

"Papa, why did you write to Mitch and tell him I married Roger?"

There was a taut silence. The pen fell from her father's hand. Drops of ink spread over the neatly written letter.

"What?" Russell asked weakly. "What did you say?"

"You heard me. How could you do such a terrible thing? What gave you the right?"

"How . . . ?" Russell stammered. "Who?" He shook his head. "Where did you hear such a thing?"

"From Mitch. I went to dinner with him tonight."

Russell surged to his feet. "You did what?"

"I had dinner with him tonight."

"You lied to me."

She fought back the anger rising within her. "You know all about lies, don't you, Papa?" she asked quietly.

The color drained from her father's face, but he didn't deny it. "He was no good, Alisha. A half-breed with no future. I did what I thought was best for you, the same as any father would have done." He held his hands out, palms up, in a gesture of supplication. "Surely you can see that?"

"No, I can't see that. I loved Mitch, and he loved me."

"I made the right decision."

"Papa, I was old enough to make my own decisions."

"Old enough," he scoffed. "Why, you were still a child, barely seventeen."

"Mama was sixteen when she married you." Alisha shook her head, her faith in her father badly shaken. "I've always believed everything you taught me. How many of them have been lies, Papa?" she asked, her voice and her temper rising. "How many?"

Russell stared at his daughter, each word like a blow striking his heart. "Alisha, please . . ."

"How could you do such a dreadful thing?" she exclaimed. "You ruined my life! I'll never believe anything you tell me again," she declared as she turned and ran out of the room. "Never!"

"Alisha, wait!" Russell felt a stab of pain in his chest as he watched his daughter run out of the room. "Angela," he murmured as he slumped back in his chair. "Angela, what have I done?"

Chapter 8

He'd said he would stay away from her, and he had meant it, but it seemed that every time Mitch turned around in the next few days, Alisha was there. In the general store. Crossing the street. At the bank. Or maybe, subconsciously, he was seeking her out. All he knew was that seeing her every day was driving him crazy. And seeing her with Roger Smithfield was enough to tie his stomach in knots.

Smithfield. Always the teacher's pet in school. Always clean and neat, his shoes always shined, his blond hair slicked back. Never in trouble. Mitch would have died before he would have admitted it, but he'd always been a little jealous of Smithfield's scrubbed good looks. The girls had always fawned over Smithfield, all except Alisha.

Much to his surprise, Mitch found himself in church again the following Sunday morning. He hadn't intended to go and had, in fact, been more than a little late in arriving. The congregation was halfway through the second hymn when he slipped into the first vacant seat he came to. Glancing around, he found himself sitting across the aisle from Roger

Smithfield. Looking at the man, it was easy to see why Alisha wanted to marry him. Smithfield was tall and good-looking, with his wavy blond hair and winning smile. Mitch had seen the house Smithfield was building for Alisha. It was going to be the showplace of the county. No doubt she would be very happy there, in her new house, with her new husband. . . .

He shifted in his seat. What the devil was he doing here, driving himself crazy?

He didn't hear a word of Faraday's sermon. All he could think of was Alisha living in another man's house, cooking his meals, mending his clothes, sharing his life, his bed. . . .

When Russell Faraday stood to offer the Benediction, Mitch left the church and headed for the jail. Removing his badge, he tossed it on the desk, then wrote a short note to the city fathers telling them to find someone else for the job.

Going up to the house that would never be home, he packed his gear. He had always intended to visit his mother's people, and this seemed like a damn good time to do just that.

A light rain was falling when he stepped outside. His horse looked up at him and shook her head. With a grin, Mitch closed the front door, then descended the stairs. He patted the bay on the shoulder, then slid his rifle into the boot and swung into the saddle. He remembered his mother telling him that the Apache were usually in Apache Pass this time of the year. If he rode hard, he could be there in three or four days.

Settling his hat on his head, he lifting the reins and urged his horse into a lope. A long ride in the rain was just what he needed.

*   *   *

Alisha lifted her head as her father said the final amen. Taking her seat at the organ, she glanced quickly toward the back of the church, frowning when she saw that Mitch was gone. She told herself it was just as well; she had nothing more to say to him, but she couldn't suppress her disappointment. She liked having Mitch around, liked knowing he was there.

Roger was waiting for her when she left the church a few minutes later.

"Hello, Alisha," he said. "Right nice sermon your father preached today."

She smiled up at him. It was the same thing he said every Sunday. "Yes." She glanced around the church-yard, hoping to see Mitch loitering about.

"Mind if I walk you home?"

"Of course not." He asked that in one form or an-other, every Sunday, too. It had never bothered her be-fore. Why did she suddenly find it so annoying? And where was Mitch?

"Is your father feeling well?"

"What do you mean?"

Roger patted her shoulder. "Nothing. He just looks a little pale this morning."

"Does he?" She felt a stab of guilt, remembering the scene she had caused the night she'd confronted him. Her father had been unusually quiet and withdrawn ever since. Now that she thought about it, he had looked a little wan these past few days.

"I'm sure it's nothing to worry about," Roger said. He patted her shoulder again. "You haven't been out to see the house in the last few days. It should be fin-ished by the end of next week."

"That's wonderful."

"Shall we go look at it now?"

"If you like."

"I think you'll be pleased," Roger said, taking her hand in his.

Reversing direction, they walked through the town. Alisha nodded at the people they passed—old Mr. West sitting in a rocking chair in front of the barber shop, Mrs. Chamberlain, who was sweeping the board-walk in front of her shop, the Kensington twins, who were tossing a ball back and forth in the alley beside the sheriff's office.

They turned left at the corner of Front Street and First and followed the narrow, rutted road that led to the house they would share when they were married.

"Oh, Roger, it's lovely," Alisha exclaimed.

"You said you wanted yellow trim. I hope it's the right shade."

"It's perfect." The house was L-shaped, with a peaked roof and a red brick chimney. She slipped her hand from his and ran up the three stairs to the veran-dah. Opening the front door, she stepped into the foyer, then moved into the parlor. Roger was planning to quit his job at the store and devote all his time to his trade. The house was the first he had built entirely on his own, and he was hoping that when people saw what a good job he had done, they would want to hire him. He loved his work and took pride in his craft, and it was reflected in every room. The floors were made of oak, sanded and waxed to a high sheen. The walls were painted white.

She moved through the house, imagining how she would decorate each room. She paused in the bed-room they would share, feeling a twinge of unease as she imagined sharing a bed with Roger. Would he be disappointed when he learned she wasn't a virgin?

Should she tell him before the wedding? She wished she had someone to talk to, someone she could confide in. She had no close friends in town. Even though no one but her father and Chloe knew she had borne a child out of wedlock, speculation had run rampant when she and Chloe left town, ostensibly to visit family in the East. She had, on several occasions, considered asking Chloe for advice. Chloe had married Sylvester Quimby, publisher of the *Canyon Creek Gazette*, and moved into her own home the year Alisha turned eighteen.

"Alisha? Don't you like it?"

"It's lovely," she replied quickly. "I was just . . . just decorating it. In my head, you know? What would you think of doing the bedroom in blue? I saw a lovely spread at the mercantile."

Roger stepped up behind her, close enough that she could feel his breath moving in her hair.

"Alisha." She didn't resist when he placed his hands on her shoulders and turned her to face him. "I want to kiss you," he said. "Is it all right?"

"Of course."

He drew her into his arms and kissed her and Alisha closed her eyes, remembering another man's arms, another man's lips. Mitch had never asked if he could kiss her. There had been nothing hesitant in his manner, no uncertainty in his voice or his kiss. Mitch had always known what he wanted. What she needed. She remembered the nights she had met him down by the creek—starlit summer nights when the air was soft and warm and the crickets and tree frogs serenaded them, rainy winter nights when storm clouds hid the moon and the heat between them drove away the cold.

Guilt rose up within her. She had no business thinking of Mitch, especially now, when she was in Roger's arms. She had pledged her heart to Roger when she agreed to marry him. He deserved her affection and her loyalty.

"I'll try to make you happy, Alisha," Roger whispered.

"I know you will."

"I told Mr. Halstead over at the mercantile you'd be coming by to look at curtain material and the like." Roger draped his arm around her shoulder as they went into the kitchen. "Buy whatever you want for our house, Alisha, whatever you think we need. Mr. Halstead will put it on my account."

"That's very generous of you, Roger."

"I just want you to be happy."

"I am." The lie pricked her conscience. She seemed to be telling a lot of untruths these days—to her father, to Roger, to Mitch. To herself. "We should go," she said. "Father will be wondering what happened to us."

With a nod, Roger brushed a kiss across her forehead and released her. Hand in hand, they left the house.

It wasn't until the next night that Alisha heard that Mitch had left town. She stared at Roger, unable to believe the news. "Left? How do you know? Where did he go? When's he coming back?"

"I don't know," Roger replied with a shrug. "What difference does it make?"

"None, of course. I was just curious."

The next day, after school, she went by the sheriff's office. The shades were drawn, the door was locked. A sign in the window advised anyone needing help to contact Casey Waller or Fred Plumber.

She couldn't believe he would leave town without telling her. Unable to help herself, she made the long walk up to the Garrett house.

She was breathless when she reached the top of the rise. With one hand pressed to her side, she studied the place. In all the years she had known Mitch, she had never come here.

She knew the house was empty even before she climbed the steps and knocked on the door. She wondered what she would have said if he had come to the door. Moving to the left, she peered in the window, but it was too dark inside for her to see anything.

Overcome with curiosity, she tried the front door. It opened with a squeak. She battled her conscience for a moment, then stepped inside. The interior was dark and quiet. Her footsteps sounded extraordinarily loud as she walked down the short hallway to the parlor. The room was dark and oppressive. The air smelled musty, tinged with stale tobacco.

Leaving the parlor, she walked slowly from room to room. He was gone, there was no doubt about that. The house felt empty, abandoned.

Feeling heavyhearted, she left the house, shutting the door behind her. Why had he left town so abruptly? Where had he gone? Was he coming back?

She tried to tell herself it didn't matter. Whatever they had once shared, whatever tender feelings she had once felt for Mitch Garrett were dead and buried years ago and could not be resurrected no matter how she might wish it.

And yet she couldn't help but wonder what her life

would have been like if her father hadn't interfered, if Mitch had sent for her, if her baby had lived. . . .

Resolutely, she put such thoughts from her mind. There was no point going over it again, no point wondering, wishing. It was over and done, and she was glad he was gone again, apparently for good.

"Still lying to yourself, aren't you, Alisha Faraday?" she muttered as she hurried toward home. And knew she would always wonder how her life would have turned out if Mitch had ignored her father's letter and come back for her all those years ago.

Chapter 9

It was mid-afternoon four days later when Mitch reached the entrance to the Apache stronghold. He had removed his hat and shirt, hoping that any scouts who saw him would recognize him as one of their own.

He rode easy in the saddle, his hands well away from his guns. He had been riding up the mountainside about an hour when he felt a tightening between his shoulder blades and knew he was being watched.

Resisting the urge to look behind him, he kept riding. The trail grew narrower, flanked by the mountain on one side, and a sheer drop on the other. His horse snorted and shied as a rabbit sprang out from under a bush and darted up the path ahead. Mitch felt a sudden sinking in the pit of his stomach as the mare's hindquarters came perilously close to the edge of the trail.

Winding upward, the trail widened a little, hemmed in on both sides by the mountains.

A short time later, he came to a fork in the trail. He was pondering whether to turn to the left or the right when he heard the unmistakable sound of several rifles being cocked.

Slowly, he raised his hands to shoulder level. *"Ya a teh, shila aash,"* he said, hoping his voice didn't betray his nervousness. Greetings, my friend.

"We have no friends among the whites." The voice, speaking remarkably good English, came from behind him, high up and a little to his right.

"I am Otter, son of White Robe, daughter to Stalks the Bear." Mitch spoke the Indian name his mother had given him for the first time since childhood. She had called him Otter because he loved the water, because he had tried to swim whenever she bathed him.

There was a flurry of hushed whispers, and then the voice said, "Go to the left. Wait for us at the cottonwood at the bottom of the trail."

Releasing the breath he hadn't been aware he was holding, Mitch took up the reins and followed the left fork in the trail, which snaked back and forth for about a hundred yards.

A few minutes later the narrow path opened on to a stretch of flat ground and he saw a tall cottonwood standing like a sentinel at the head of another trail. Four warriors clad in clouts and moccasins stood near the tree. Three held rifles, one carried a bow and had a quiver of arrows slung over his shoulder.

Mitch reined his horse to a halt a few yards from the men. He had never seen any of his mother's people, but she had told him that the men were fierce warriors, trained from infancy to be hunters and fighters. She had told him that Apache men could go for days without food or water, and were warriors without equal. Now, studying the four men in front of him, Mitch knew she had not lied. They were stocky and barrel-chested, solid and muscular, with dark copper skin, thick black hair, and suspicious black eyes.

The warrior on the far right took a step forward. "Why have you come here?"

Mitch recognized the voice as the one he had heard earlier. "I was raised among the whites. I wish to learn the ways of my mother's people."

The warrior looked at Mitch with obvious distrust. "White Robe has never mentioned having a son of warrior age."

Mitch stared at the man, his breath trapped in his throat. It seemed his heart stopped for a moment before pounding in his ears. "What did you say?"

The warrior looked at him strangely. "White Robe did not mention she was expecting you."

"She's here?" Mitch asked hoarsely. "My mother is here?"

"Is that not why you have come here?"

"No." Mitch blinked rapidly, fighting back the tears that burned his eyes. "I thought she was dead. I wanted to meet her people, learn their ways."

"Come," the warrior said. "We will take you to White Robe."

Mitch searched his memory, trying to recall the Apache word for thank you. His mother had often spoken to him in her language until his father had put a stop to it. Sadly, Mitch had forgotten most of what he had learned.

"*Ashoge*," Mitch said.

With a nod, the warrior gestured for Mitch to follow. The other three men turned and went back up the trail to guard the entrance to the stronghold.

She couldn't be here, Mitch thought as he followed the warrior through a narrow pass. She was dead.

A short time later, the pass widened on to a wide green valley surrounded by tall cliffs. Mitch stared at the tipis spread in concentric circles on the valley floor, at the men and women immersed in their daily tasks, at the children running half-naked along the stream that meandered through the center of the valley. Stared, and felt a stirring deep within his soul, a calling to that part of him that he had resisted for so long.

He had never been here before, yet it all seemed achingly familiar, like the echo of a song long forgotten, the last vestiges of a dream that eludes the memory upon waking.

He took a deep breath, drawing in the scents around him—the smoke from a cookfire, the smell of roasting meat, sage and earth and pine. There was a sweet aroma to the very air itself, and it smelled like home.

When they reached the village, the warrior stopped in front of a large tipi located in the shade of an ancient pine. "This is White Robe's lodge."

"*Ashoge*," Mitch said. He sat there for a moment, trying to compose himself, telling himself it couldn't be his mother, it was just a woman who had the same name.

Dismounting, he ground-tied the bay, then rapped on the lodge flap.

His heart was pounding like a drum as the flap was pulled back and he saw his mother standing in the opening.

Mitch shook his head. "I don't believe it. He told me you were dead."

The woman looked at him, clearly not recognizing him.

"It's me," he said. "Mitch."

She leaned forward a little, her gaze moving over

him. "Otter," she murmured, her expression and voice mirroring her disbelief. "No. It cannot be. He told me you had died of a fever."

"When did he tell you that?"

"I went back to visit you a few months after I left your father. I hoped he might have changed. I missed you, and thought perhaps I would stay with him. He said I was not welcome there, and that you had died of smallpox."

She stepped back, motioning for him to enter her lodge.

"I guess he lied to us both," Mitch said, ducking inside. "If he wasn't already dead, I'd kill him."

"He is dead then?"

"Yeah, got himself killed in a poker game. Somebody caught him with a fifth ace."

White Robe let out a sigh that might have been regret, but Mitch didn't think so. Relief would be more like it.

He thought of all the years he had missed with his mother because of his old man's lies, and knew he had never hated his father more than he did at that moment. "I never understood how you got hooked up with him in the first place."

"He was very handsome, and I was very young." She shrugged. "It is bad luck to speak of the dead. Let us not speak of him anymore."

White Robe's gaze moved over the son she had not seen in almost fourteen years. "How tall you have grown." Hesitantly, as if afraid he might disappear at her touch, she reached up to cup his cheek.

"*Shi ma.*" He whispered the Apache words for mother, his voice ragged with emotion as he took her in his arms. He held her tight for a long while, his tears falling unashamedly.

She shuddered as she took a deep breath, and he felt her tears on his chest.

"Otter." White Robe murmured his name over and over again. When her tears dried, when she felt she could let him go, she took a step backward. "You look much like your grandfather," she remarked. "I wish you could have known him. He was a brave man. Come, sit. Are you hungry?"

Mitch smiled as he sat down. He hadn't seen her in years, and the first thing she wanted to do was feed him. "Later, *shi ma*. Sit down and tell me ..." He grinned at her. "Tell me everything."

She sat beside him, unable to stop staring, reaching out to touch him from time to time, as if to assure herself he was really there.

"I was never happy in that house. I knew you were not happy either, and that is why I decided to leave there. To leave him. I did not know he would refuse to let you go with me. When he said you could not go, I told him I would stay, but he was angry then, and he said he no longer wanted me."

Mitch nodded. He remembered that day, remembered his father's anger, his mother's tears. She had pleaded with Con to let her stay, but he had thrown her out of the house and locked the door, screaming that he would kill her if he saw her again. "Go on."

"I did not want to leave you, *ciye*."

"I know."

"But I was afraid of him, and so I came home and lived with my parents. My father was killed by the soldiers two years later. My mother died soon after." She paused a moment. "I have a good husband now, and another son."

"Are you happy?"

She nodded, her expression softening.

"So, I have a brother. How old is he?"

"Four summers." she replied, pleased when Mitch took the news of her new family in stride.

Mitch laughed. "Well, I always wanted a little brother," he said, squeezing his mother's hand. "Thanks, *shi ma.*"

"What of you, *ciye*? Has life been good to you?"

"I can't complain."

"Have you found a woman?"

He thought briefly of Alisha, then shook his head. "No. I reckon I never will."

"You are young yet."

He grunted softly. He didn't feel young, just old and rode hard.

"How long will you stay?"

"I don't know. Till you throw me out, I reckon. I've got no place to go, and no one waiting for me when I get there."

She smiled at him, her dark eyes glowing. "Then you will stay here with us until you are an old, old man." She stood up, her fingers ruffling his hair. "Elk Chaser and our son, Rides the Buffalo, will be home soon, and they will be hungry." She smiled at Mitch again. "And surprised."

Mitch watched his mother as she prepared a large pot of venison stew. She had gained a few pounds, there were a few strands of gray in her hair, but other than that, she had changed little since he had seen her last. There was still a sparkle in her eyes and she still smiled easily.

He looked around the lodge, taking it all in. It was large and roomy. Three bedrolls were spread near the rear of the wickiup. There was a small fire pit in the center of the lodge for cooking and keeping the lodge warm in winter, pots and cooking utensils stacked nearby. Several buckskin bags that he guessed contained clothing and the like hung from the lodge poles. There were a couple of willow backrests.

His mouth began to water as the lodge filled with a fragrant aroma.

A short time later a man and a young boy entered the lodge. The boy was grinning ear to ear as he held up the carcass of a rabbit.

"*Enjuh!*" White Robe said as she took the rabbit. "You did well, Rides the Buffalo."

The boy nodded, obviously proud of his accomplishment. He stopped smiling when he saw the tall stranger standing near the back of the lodge.

White Robe took a deep breath. "This is Otter," she said, her gaze moving from her young son to her husband. "I hope you will make him feel welcome in our lodge by speaking to him in his own language."

Surprise flickered in Elk Chaser's eyes. "Has he come back from the dead?"

"Sit down, my husband," White Robe said. "I will tell you about it after you eat." She smiled at Rides the Buffalo as she took the rabbit carcass from his hand. "I will prepare this for you tomorrow."

White Robe served the men first, then Rides the Buffalo, and then herself.

Elk Chaser said little, but Mitch was aware of the older man's scrutiny as White Robe explained that she had taught her husband and son to speak English because she didn't want to forget it. She told him there were three or four other Apaches in the stronghold who also spoke English and Mitch remarked that he had met one.

When the meal was over, White Robe told Elk Chaser how Con had lied to both her and Mitch.

"It doesn't make sense," Mitch remarked. "He never cared for either one of us."

"He was a proud man. A jealous man," White Robe said. "I was his woman. You were his son. He believed in keeping what was his."

Mitch snorted softly. "I guess it would have been all right if he'd thrown you out."

"Yes," White Robe replied. "My leaving offended his pride. Just as your leaving would have."

"Well, it's all in the past now."

White Robe looked at her husband. "I have invited Otter to stay with us."

Elk Chaser nodded. "You are welcome in our lodge."

"*Ashoge*," Mitch said.

Rides the Buffalo had listened intently to the conversation between the adults. Now, he tugged on his mother's skirt. "He is your son?"

"Yes."

"We are brothers, then?"

"Yes."

Rides the Buffalo smiled at Mitch. "Hello, my brother."

"Hello." Rides the Buffalo was a cute kid, Mitch thought. His skin was a mite on the fair side for an Apache, there was a slight wave in his hair, his eyes were brown. If he hadn't known Elk Chaser and his mother were the boy's parents, he would have thought the boy had some white blood in him somewhere.

Rides the Buffalo pointed at the Colt holstered on Mitch's hip. "Will you teach me to shoot?"

Mitch glanced at his mother. "If it's all right."

White Robe nodded, and Mitch grinned at the boy. "Maybe you'll show me how to use a bow."

Rides the Buffalo's eyes widened in astonishment. "You do not know how to use a bow?"

Mitch shook his head. "Not really. I made one when I was a boy, but I never had anyone to teach me how to use it." He held out his hand. "Deal?"

The boy stared at Mitch's outstretched hand and frowned. "Deal? I do not understand this word."

"It means we agree."

With a grin, Rides the Buffalo put his hand in Mitch's. "Deal."

Chapter 10

"Miss Faraday? Miss Faraday?"

With a start, Alisha realized that Bobby Moss was calling her name. "Yes, Bobby, what is it?"

"It's time for lunch."

"Is it?" She glanced at the small heart-shaped watch pinned to the bodice of her dress, surprised to note that it was twenty after twelve. "Class dismissed."

With a sigh, she watched her students hurry into the cloakroom for their lunch pails. As usual, Bobby Moss was the first one out the door. In many ways, he reminded her of Mitch. Like Mitch, Bobby hated school, hated to be cooped up indoors, especially on days like this, when the sun was shining and the fish were jumping. Bobby played hooky at least once a week during the winter, more often during the spring and summer. She had long since stopped telling his parents. She knew she should report Bobby's habitual truancy, but she also knew that his father would punish him severely. Bobby was thirteen, and a bright boy. He never caused any trouble in class. He studied hard and always passed his tests, usually with the highest score in his age group. She knew it was wrong to keep silent, but Bobby had enough trouble at home as it was, and she didn't want to cause him any more. As long as he continued to do well, she saw no reason to cause the boy any grief by mentioning his frequent absences.

She ate her midday meal at her desk, her thoughts, as always these days, centered on Mitch. She couldn't go on like this, thinking about him all the time. It was interfering with her teaching. Like today. She hadn't heard the church clock chime the hour. No telling how long Bobby had called her name before she heard him. But that wasn't the worst of it. Last night, when Roger kissed her, she had found herself wishing it was Mitch holding her in his arms. And then she had pretended it *was* Mitch. To her horror, she had almost called Roger by Mitch's name when she said good night.

There was no question about it. She had to put Mitch out of her mind.

If she only knew how.

Alisha was still thinking about Mitch, or rather, trying *not* to think about Mitch, when she got home after school. She put her coat in the closet; placed the stack of papers she was going to grade after dinner on the table in the kitchen.

"Papa?" Running a hand over her hair, she went into the parlor, expecting to find her father reading the newspaper, but he wasn't there. "Papa?" She went into his study, but he wasn't at his desk, either.

Thinking he must have gone to visit one of his parishioners, she went into the kitchen to make dinner.

She was peeling potatoes when she heard a crash from the back of the house. Wiping her hands on her apron, she left the kitchen. "Papa, is that you?"

She looked in the parlor, in his bedroom, in her own,

but saw nothing. Wondering if she was hearing things, she headed back to the kitchen. She was passing her father's study when she heard a low groan.

Pausing, she glanced inside. At first, she didn't see or hear anything, and then she heard a scraping noise, and her father's voice whispering her name.

"Papa?"

"Here."

Hurrying into the room, she walked around the desk, gasped when she saw her father lying on the floor. "Papa! What happened?"

She knelt beside him, wondering how long he had been lying there. "Papa?" His face was chalk-white, his breathing shallow and uneven. "Don't move, Papa, I'll go get the doctor."

She started to rise, but he grabbed her hand. "No . . . no . . . time . . . listen to me. . . ."

"It can wait."

"No." His hand clutched hers. "Lied . . . to you."

"It's all right. I know. Rest now."

She tried to free her hand from his, but he held on tenaciously. "Baby . . . not . . . dead."

"Papa, we can talk later. You need a . . ." The words died in her throat. "Baby? What baby?"

"Yours."

She stared down at him, everything else momentarily forgotten. "What are you saying?"

"Sent it . . . away . . . baby."

"Away? Where? *Why*?"

"Gave it to . . . McBride. Told him . . . to . . . take care of it."

James McBride was an old friend of the family. He and her father had attended the seminary together. His church was in Dawes City, the town where Alisha had gone to wait out her pregnancy. Alive. Her son was alive. He would be four years old now, hardly a baby any more.

"How could you?" Alisha exclaimed. "How could you do such a terrible thing?"

"Thought . . . it was for . . . the best." His eyes closed and he took a deep shuddering breath. "Forgive . . . me."

Forgive him? How could she ever forgive him for what he'd done? He had lied to Mitch, lied to her. Robbed them of their child. She wanted to yell at him, to strike out at him, but he moaned softly, bringing her back to the present. His face was pinched and gray, and fear shot through her. She would get to the bottom of this later. Right now, her father needed help, and quickly. "I'm going to get the doctor."

His hand fell away from hers, and she scrambled to her feet. Grabbing a blanket from the back of the sofa, she covered him. Then, lifting her skirts, she ran out of the house and down the road toward the doctor's office.

Her baby was alive. The wonder of it, the joy of it, rose up within her, only to be smothered by the memory of her father's pale face. "Oh, God," she prayed, "please don't let him die." No matter what he'd done, he was her father, and she loved him.

She pounded her fist on the doctor's door, hurriedly explained that her father needed help immediately, then turned and ran all the way back home.

Her father had lied to her. Her baby, her son, was alive.

When she reached the house, she ran into the den and knelt at her father's side. "Papa?" She shook his shoulder lightly. "Papa!"

His eyelids fluttered open and he summoned a weak smile. "Please," he said, his voice barely audible, "don't . . . hate . . . me."

"Papa? Papa!" She shook his shoulder again as the spark of life slowly faded from his eyes. "Papa, don't leave me! I forgive you, Papa," she said, sobbing. "Please don't leave me."

She looked up, her vision blurred by tears, as the doctor rushed into the room. He quickly examined her father, checked for a pulse, for a heartbeat, then slowly shook his head. "I'm sorry, Miss Faraday."

She nodded, hardly aware that he was lifting her to her feet, helping her to the sofa, telling her not to worry, he would take care of everything.

But all she could think of was that her father was dead, and her son was alive.

Chapter 11

Never had the house seemed so big, or so quiet. Alisha stood at her bedroom window, staring out into the darkness beyond. Doctor Stoner had arranged to have her father's body taken to the undertaker. She had sent a wire to James McBride asking if he would come and conduct the funeral service. He had sent his condolences, and advised he would be there tomorrow night. The service would be the following morning.

The good women of the Ladies Aid Society had immediately gone to work. They had brought her enough food to feed an army, and promised more would be forthcoming. Her father had been the town's sole spiritual advisor for twenty-five years, and had been loved by one and all. Even those who did not attend church had come to him for help and advice. He had never turned anyone away.

She heard a knock at the front door and knew it was Roger, come to make sure she was all right.

She blinked back her tears as she went downstairs. She wasn't all right. She doubted if she would ever be all right again. Her whole world had turned upside down. Her father was dead, but her son was alive. *The*

Lord giveth and the Lord taketh away. Blessed be the name of the Lord.

Her emotions were raw, torn between sorrow at her father's sudden death, outrage that her father had lied to her yet again, and joy beyond measure at the discovery that the son she thought had died at birth was still alive.

She forced a smile as she opened the door. "Hello, Roger," she said. "Come in."

"How are you?" he asked.

"I'll be all right."

She went into the parlor, and he followed her.

"Alisha . . ."

She heard the love and concern in his voice, saw it reflected in the gentle depths of his gray eyes, and it was her undoing. With a sob, she went into his arms. She needed someone to hold her, someone to tell her everything would be all right. She wanted Mitch, needed Mitch, but he wasn't here and she didn't know where he'd gone.

Roger held her tight, his hand stroking her back as he soothed her tears with soft words of comfort. But she found no comfort in his arms, or in his words, and she knew, in that instant, that she could never marry Roger Smithfield. She didn't love him the way a woman should love the man she was going to spend the rest of her life with, and she never had. Before Mitch came back into her life, she had been prepared to settle for less, but not now.

When her tears subsided, he led her to the sofa and sat down, drawing her down beside him. "Alisha, I know this may not be the right time, but . . ." He took her hands in his. "I think we should think about getting married next month instead of in June."

"Next month?" She looked at him, astonished. How could he talk about changing the date of the wedding now, with her father lying cold and still at the undertaker's?

"I know, I know," he said quickly, "but this house belongs to the church. They'll be getting a new pastor soon, and you'll be needing a place to live. If we get married next month, you can move into the new house, with me."

"Roger—"

"Just think about it. I know some folks will say it's unseemly, our getting married so soon after your father's passing, but I'm sure most of them will understand."

"I can't think about it now." She stood up, needing to put some space between them. "I'm really tired, Roger."

"Of course." He stood up. "Try to get some sleep. I'll see you tomorrow."

Alisha nodded.

Roger kissed her cheek, murmured good-bye, and left the house, quietly closing the door behind him.

"Oh, Mitchy," she whispered tremulously. "Why aren't you here? I need you so."

"The earth is the Lord's, and the fullness thereof; the world, and they that dwell therein. For he hath founded it upon the seas, and established it upon the floods. Who shall ascend into the hill of the Lord? Or who shall stand in his holy place? He that hath clean hands, and a pure heart . . ."

Reverend James McBride paused in reading the Twenty-fourth Psalm and looked out over the mourners. "We can, all of us, be certain that our brother, Russell, has ascended the hill of the Lord and taken his place with the saints. . . ."

Clad in a high-necked black bombazine gown and a veiled black bonnet borrowed from Chloe, Alisha stood beside Roger while Reverend McBride offered a glowing eulogy, recounting Russell Faraday's life and accomplishments, his generous nature, his willingness to spend his life in tireless service to others.

Alisha glanced around. It looked like the whole town had turned out to bid a last farewell to her father. He would have been pleased and embarrassed by such a show of affection from the members of his flock.

She shifted her weight from one foot to the other, her thoughts not on what James McBride was saying, but on the talk she would have with him later that night. He was the only one who knew what had happened to her child, and as he bowed his head and prayed over the earthly remains of Russell Matthew Faraday, Alisha offered a prayer of her own that her son was still alive and that, somehow, she would find him.

It seemed as though the whole town came to her house after the service. They offered Alisha their condolences, spoke fondly of her father as they reminisced about the part he had played in their lives. Mrs. Neibich recounted the time Russell had sat up all night with her husband, keeping him company while she was in labor with her first child. Mr. Thomas mentioned how grateful he had been for her father's words of comfort and counsel when his daughter ran away to marry a no-account, traveling salesman.

Alisha listened and nodded and made polite responses to each of them, and all the while she was thinking of her son, wondering what Mitch would say when he found out.

It was near dusk when the last mourner took his leave. Roger left a few minutes later. She knew he was hurt that she hadn't asked him to stay, but she needed to talk to James McBride, and she needed to talk to him alone.

With a sigh, Alisha closed the door behind Roger. Removing her bonnet, she took several deep breaths, then went into the parlor where Reverend McBride was waiting. He was short where her father had been tall, his blond hair graying at the temples. His eyes were kind as he smiled at her.

"Can I get you anything, Reverend?" she asked.

"No, child. Come," he said, patting the seat on the sofa beside him, "sit down a spell. You look a mite peaked."

Alisha smiled wanly as she sat down. "It's been a long day."

"Yes. I shall miss my old friend. He was a good man."

"Yes, he was." Alisha folded her hands tightly in her lap. "I need to ask you something, and I want you to tell me the truth."

"Well, of course," James McBride replied, his tone slightly indignant.

"What happened to my baby? Where is he now?"

The good reverend stared at her, his mouth agape.

"Papa told me, just before he . . . before he passed on, that my son is alive."

James McBride exhaled deeply, then nodded. "It's true."

"Where is he? Do you know? Is he all right?"

"He's with the Apache, Alisha. He was a fine,

healthy baby." McBride shrugged. "I don't know if he's still alive."

"What Apache? Where?"

"There was a mountain man in town the night your son was born. I asked him if he knew of any Indians in the area. He said there was a tribe camped at Apache Pass, that they would take the boy in and raise him as one of their own."

Alisha nodded, her mind racing. Her baby was alive, and living with the Apache. Was it coincidence or the hand of God that had sent her baby to Mitch's people?

"Thank you, Reverend."

"I'm sorry, Alisha. There were many times when I wanted to tell you, but I had given your father my word that I would never speak of it."

She shook her head. "How could you keep such a secret from me all these years?"

"Your father thought it was for the best, and so did I."

"And neither of you thought to ask me?"

"You were hardly more than a child yourself."

"I was seventeen!"

James McBride held his hands out, palms up. "I'm sorry, Alisha. I hope one day you'll find it in your heart to forgive me. And to forgive your father. We both did what we thought was best for you at the time."

"What about my son?" Rising, she began to pace the floor, her agitation growing as she thought of her son being raised by Indians. At first, knowing her son was with Mitch's people had seemed like a blessing, but now she thought about what it really meant. He would never learn to read or write or do his sums, never read the Bible or attend church. He would grow up wild and savage, never knowing who his real mother was. "Did either of you think about what was best for him?"

James McBride stood up, his expression somber. "At the time, your father's only concern was for you. Perhaps he was misguided in his decision, perhaps not. But it's over and done now. You need to put the past behind you, Alisha. There's nothing to be gained by brooding over that which cannot be changed."

"Put it behind me!" she exclaimed, her anger escalating. "My son is alive, and you tell me to put it behind me? I can't do that." She blew out a deep breath. "Thank you for coming, Reverend."

"Alisha . . ."

She walked to the door.

"Good night, Reverend."

He followed slowly, his expression troubled. "Good night, child."

She watched him take up his coat and leave the house, and then, alone for the first time that day, she sat down and cried, weeping for the child she had thought dead, for the lies her father had told that had kept her and Mitch apart, for the life they might have had together.

She cried until she was empty inside, until she had no tears left. Her father was gone. Mitch was gone. But her son was alive, and somehow she would find him.

Chapter 12

◄◆►

Mitch stared in amazement at Rides the Buffalo. Only four years old, yet the kid was already well on his way to becoming a warrior. When Mitch had decided to visit his mother's people, he'd had a vague idea of becoming a warrior, but he knew now that becoming a true warrior wasn't something a boy learned at a certain age, it was something that started at birth. It was more than skill with weapons, more than the ability to hunt and track. It was a way of living and believing, an innate sense of pride, of self.

Mitch shook his head as he watched Rides the Buffalo. The boy knew how to throw a knife, how to use a bow. He knew how to track and kill small game, how to find food and water, how to hide from an enemy, how to build a wickiup. He was already an expert horseman.

Mitch blew out a sigh as he watched his little brother place an arrow in the center of a target made of deer hide, then loose three more arrows in a handful of seconds, each one striking the target.

"Nice shooting," Mitch exclaimed.

Rides the Buffalo handed his bow and an arrow to Mitch. "Now you."

The bow, made of mulberry wood, was boy-sized. The arrow, made of willow, was about two-feet long, fletched with turkey feathers. Should have been easy, Mitch thought. He had made a crude bow and arrow when he'd been a kid, had even managed to bring down a rabbit or a bird from time to time, yet he sent four arrows flying, and missed the target four times.

"Perhaps you need a bow more your size."

Mitch turned to see Elk Chaser walking toward him, a grin on his face. "I doubt if it will help," Mitch replied good-naturedly. "I don't think the fault lies in the bow, but in my skill."

"I think you are right," Elk Chaser agreed as he handed Mitch his own bow.

It was a good, sturdy weapon made of bodark wood. Strong yet flexible, it was easily five feet in length. He accepted an arrow from Elk Chaser. It was made of willow, fletched with two eagle feathers. The bowstring was made of deer sinew.

After five tries with only one hit, Mitch handed the bow back to Elk Chaser. "I can see I will need a lot of practice."

Elk Chaser looked at Rides the Buffalo. They exchanged solemn looks, then laughed out loud.

"Come," Elk Chaser said, grinning. "Let us eat."

That evening, Mitch walked down to a quiet place near the river. Standing on the bank, he gazed at the reflection of the moon that shimmered like molten gold on the surface of the slow-moving water.

He had never felt such a sense of homecoming, of belonging, as he had since he'd entered the rancheria. The people had made him feel welcome. Their language, a language he had not heard since childhood, sprang easily to his lips. Faces he had never seen before looked familiar, and he had to keep reminding himself that he had never been here before.

He stared up at the sky, the urge to pray strong within him, though he had not uttered a prayer in more years than he cared to admit. When his mother left his father, he had prayed for her return, prayed fervently as only a frightened and lonely child can pray, and then the old man had told him White Robe was dead, and Mitch had stopped praying.

But now, with his mother nearby and the soft sounds of the night all around him, he felt the need to pray, to offer his thanks to the Great Spirit for returning his mother to him after all these years.

Did he even remember how to pray?

"Ashoge, Usen," he murmured. "Thank You for returning my mother to me. Thank You for bringing me home to this place. Thank You for my brother. . . ."

Mitch grinned into the darkness. Earlier, he had asked Elk Chaser how Rides the Buffalo had gotten his name.

"It happened like this," Elk Chaser began. "It was summer. My son had watched the hunters one day as they moved among the buffalo, covered with buffalo hides to disguise their scent and shape. He is brave, my son, and so, one day, he takes his buffalo skin and creeps up to the edge of the herd that is grazing nearby. Being a small warrior, he is hardly noticed as he slips in among the herd. Hidden beneath his robe, he makes his way to the center. Watching the buffalo closely, he imitates the movements of a buffalo calf.

"But then, being only a small boy and not able to see much from the ground, he decides to climb up on a rock. This gives him a different view of the buffalo. He remains motionless on the rock, smiling at his feat of courage. Soon, a large bull moves near the rock, so close that my small warrior reaches out to touch the curly hide. The bull, being full of years, does not notice.

"Being brave, but foolish, my son climbs onto the buffalo. Lying flat on the animal's broad back, he pulls his robe over him.

"Slowly, the herd begins to move. My son does not know that hunters clad in buffalo hides have moved in among the herd.

"Just before the attack is to begin, one of the warriors notices the boy on the back of the old bull. Acting quickly, he cuts the bull from the herd and just before the other warriors begin their attack, he pulls my foolish son from the back of the buffalo. Startled, the buffalo lunges forward, knocking the warrior and my son to the ground.

"The warrior is angry, but my son, who is too young to be afraid, or to realize the danger he was in, begins to laugh, and soon the warrior begins laughing with him.

"That night, my son has a new name. He is Rides the Buffalo."

"It is a good story," Mitch remarked, smiling. "And a good name."

And a good life, he mused as he turned and gazed at the lodges spread across the floor of the valley. Yet even as the thought crossed his mind, Alisha's image rose before him, her eyes sparkling, her lips curved in a smile of welcome.

Alisha . . .

Swearing softly, he turned away from the river, determined to put her out of his mind, out of his heart.

Chapter 13

Alisha placed her teacup on the table beside the sofa, counted to ten, and looked over at Roger, who was standing near the hearth, his arms folded across his chest, a scowl on his face.

"I'm going, Roger, and nothing you can say will make me change my mind."

"You're upset. You're not thinking clearly. Dammit, Alisha, you can't go traipsing off into the desert looking for a bunch of savages."

Alisha stared at Roger, somewhat taken aback by his use of profanity. In all the years she had known him, she had never heard him swear, but she refused to be swayed. "I can, and I will. Can't you see? I have to go."

Exasperated, Roger began to pace the floor.

Alisha took a deep breath. He had taken the news that she had an illegitimate son surprisingly well, but when she told him she was going to try and find the boy, he had looked at her as if she had lost her mind. They had been arguing for the last forty minutes to no avail. Roger had declared that she was being foolish and stubborn. Maybe he was right, but, right or wrong, she was going after her son. She had already missed the first four years of his life. She wasn't willing to miss one day more than she had to.

Roger took a deep breath. "Alisha, you have no one to look after you now. As your future husband, I insist that you stay home, where you belong. There's a trader in town. I saw him over at the restaurant this morning. If you're determined to find your son, I'll hire him to look for the boy."

"Hiring a guide is a good idea," Alisha said, "an excellent idea." She had thought of it herself, of course. She wasn't foolish enough to consider crossing the desert alone. Still, she was willing to let Roger think it was his idea. "But I'm going with him."

"Alisha, I can understand how you feel. Truly, I do, but I must forbid it."

"Forbid it?" She stared at him. "Forbid it?" She took a deep calming breath. "You're not my husband yet, Roger. And I am going, as soon as possible."

"Is that your final word on the matter?" Roger asked quietly. "You won't change your mind?"

"I can't."

"Very well. If you won't reconsider, I think I shall have to call off our engagement."

"Call it off?"

Roger nodded. "I'm sorry, but I don't think I could tolerate a wife who will not heed my counsel."

She felt a twinge of regret, and a wave of relief. "I'm sorry, Roger."

"So am I," he said, appearing surprised that she stood her ground. "Good-bye, Alisha," he said stiffly, and taking up his hat, he left the house.

As soon as Roger left, Alisha put on her gloves and bonnet and hurried into town. It took her over an hour to find the man she was looking for, and when she did, she wondered if she was making a huge mistake.

Red Clements was a short, squat man with long, limp brown hair, squinty brown eyes, and a nose that had been broken more than once. Alisha judged him to be in his late thirties, but his face was so lined and brown from the sun, it was hard to tell. He wore a greasy buckskin shirt and trousers and carried an enormous knife on one hip and a huge pistol on the other.

"You loco, girl?" Clements exclaimed when she told him that she was looking for a guide to take her to Apache Pass.

She had assured him she was not. Like Roger, Red Clements tried to talk her out of making the journey. He enumerated his reasons, counting them off on his fingers: the Comanche and the Apache were on the warpath, there were wild animals, it wasn't seemly for a single young woman to be traipsing around with an old reprobate like him, it looked like rain, he had just come back from a long journey and needed a rest.

Alisha refused to be put off. She listened patiently to his objections and when he finally ran out of reasons, she offered him twenty-five dollars, and when he still refused, she offered him fifty. It seemed fitting, ironic even, that the money left to her by her father be used to find her son. It was the fifty dollars that changed the man's mind.

Clements studied her a moment. "What kind of business does a little gal like you have with the 'Paches?"

"I have family there."

Clements shook his head vigorously. "I'm not going into Apache Pass to try and rescue no captives. Not for fifty bucks. Not for a hundred bucks! I value my scalp more'n that." He turned to walk away.

"They aren't captives."

Clements wheeled around to face her again. "No?"

It was obvious she didn't have any Apache blood, and just as obvious he was wondering what kind of relatives she could have there.

"If they aren't captives, what are they?" Clements asked.

Alisha thought about it a moment, then smiled. "They're . . . they're guests, of course."

"Uh-huh." Clements looked at her oddly a moment, then shrugged. "You'll have to pay for our supplies, too," he said. "Is that gonna be a problem?"

"No, not at all," Alisha replied, though she thought that the fifty dollars should have covered the price of their supplies, as well. Still, she would gladly have paid three times that amount, if she'd had it, for the chance to find her son.

"We'll leave tomorrow mornin'," Clements advised. "I'll pick up some grub. You got a horse?"

"No."

He grunted softly, as if he had expected that answer. "You want I should get one fer ya?"

"Yes, please. How long will it take us to get there, to the Indians?"

Clements scratched his head. "Usually takes me 'bout three, four days, but I expect you'll slow me down a mite." He looked her up and down. "I reckon it'll take us at least five days, maybe six." He grinned. "Maybe seven."

"I don't intend to slow you down, Mr. Clements. Let's plan on four days."

He chuckled. "Well, we'll see 'bout that, won't we? I'll be by to get ya at first light. Be ready."

"I will. Thank you, Mr. Clements."

"You won't be thankin' me tomorrow night," he muttered. "You'll be wishin' you'd stayed here, where you belong."

"Tomorrow morning, Mr. Clements," she said. "I'll be ready."

Alisha spent a good part of the rest of the day packing up her father's belongings. He'd had little in the way of worldly possessions—his clothing, a shelf of books, a well-worn Bible, which she kept, along with his silver-backed pocket watch. The house and most of the furnishings belonged to the parish. She blinked back her tears as she left her father's bedroom and closed the door. She would donate his clothing and books to the church.

She went through her own clothing, putting what she would be taking on her journey to one side and packing the rest in boxes. She would ask Chloe to keep them for her until she returned.

Despite her fear and grief, she grew more excited with each passing minute. She was going to find her son! Mitch's son. She wondered how tall he was, if he was chubby or thin, if he looked like Mitch. No doubt he had Mitch's dark hair. What color were his eyes? She wondered how old he had been when he took his first step, said his first word. She had missed so much. After his birth, she had felt empty, bereft. Her arms had ached to hold the baby she had never seen. In the first few days after his birth, she had awakened several times each night, certain she heard a baby crying in the house. Never had a day gone by that she hadn't thought of her child, yearned for him. Many a night, she had cried herself to sleep, knowing that the empty place he had left in her heart would never be filled.

Her son, born out of her love for Mitch. She couldn't stop smiling as she thought of him, of seeing him. She had no doubt that she would find him. No doubt at all.

She went to bed early, but she was too excited to sleep, and when, in the wee small hours of the morning, she finally dozed off, it was to dream of her son, running toward her with outstretched arms, crying, "Mama, Mama, I knew you would come. . . ."

Red Clements knocked on her door shortly after dawn the following morning. "You ready?"

"Yes."

He looked her up and down, one brow raising as he took in her starched, white shirtwaist and brown twill skirt. "I don't suppose you got any . . . uh . . . trousers?"

"Of course not."

"How many petticoats you got under there?"

A flush rose in her cheeks. In deference to the journey, she was wearing only one petticoat instead of the three she usually wore. It was bad enough that she felt almost naked without him asking such a forward question. "Please don't be impertinent, Mr. Clements."

"What? Oh, sorry, ma'am." He shook his head. "It's just that them skirts are gonna get mighty dirty. You got a hat?"

"No." It wasn't quite the truth. She had several hats, but none of them were suitable for an arduous trip in the desert.

"That's what I figured." He handed her a hat that was similar to his own, only much cleaner. "That your gear?" he asked, gesturing at the string bag on the floor inside the front door.

"Yes." She put on the hat, securing the cord under her chin.

Reaching down, Clements hefted the bag, then looked at her, one eyebrow raised. "What you got in here?"

"Just a few changes of clothing and my . . . uh . . . personal things."

He grunted softly, then turned and went to where he'd left the horses. He stopped beside a tall, raw-boned horse that was the color of mud. Flipping open his saddlebags, he dumped her gear inside.

He glanced at her over his shoulder. "You do know how to ride, don't you?"

"Of course." Alisha replied brightly. She didn't think it would be wise to tell him that she hadn't ridden in years, not since she was a little girl, and that she hadn't been very good at it then.

"This here's Sophie. She ain't much to look at, but she's got a nice easy gait, and plenty of speed and bottom."

Alisha nodded. She didn't know what bottom was, but, judging by Clements's tone of voice, it was a worthy attribute in a horse.

"Come here and mount up. Like as not we'll have to adjust them stirrups."

She fixed a smile on her face as she approached the horse, which was even bigger close up. Taking hold of the saddle horn with her left hand, she put her left foot in the stirrup, gave a little hop, and pulled herself into the saddle. It was, she thought as she settled her skirts around her, like sitting on top of a mountain.

Clements adjusted the stirrups, handed her the

reins, then mounted his own horse, a wiry buckskin
with one blue eye and one brown eye. Taking up the
reins, Clements glanced over his shoulder. "Ready?"

"Ready," Alisha replied, hoping she didn't sound as
apprehensive as she felt.

With a nod, Clements clucked to the buckskin.

Sophie needed no urging. With a shake of her head,
the mare followed the buckskin's lead. Alisha felt a
surge of excitement. At last, she was on her way! She
was ready for some adventure in her life, she thought.
She was tired of living the staid life of a schoolteacher,
tired of always being on her guard, of never being able
to say what she was really thinking. Except for the trip
to Dawes City when she was pregnant, she'd never
been anywhere. Ever since Mitch left Canyon Creek,
her life had been as dull as dishwater. Of course, going
to Apache Pass wasn't quite the same as taking a trip
to Boston or New York City, but at least she was going
somewhere.

Soon, the town was far behind them, and there was
nothing to see but miles of flat ground, gray-green
sage, and spiny cactus. Now and then a jackrabbit
sprang into view. Once, she saw an eagle gliding on
the air currents, but, other than that, there was little to
see but Clements's back.

After three hours in the saddle, some of her excitement waned. The mare did, indeed, have a nice easy
gait, but after three hours with only one brief stop to
rest the horses, Alisha was ready to call it a day. Her
thighs hurt. Her back hurt. Her shoulders hurt. Her
backside hurt. However, when Clements asked how
she was doing, she forced a cheerful note into her
voice and assured him that she was fine, just fine.

It was a vast, quiet land. It made her feel small, insignificant. Lonely, somehow. It was hard to imagine that anyone, even Indians, would choose to live in such an inhospitable place. She knew all manner of creatures made their home in the desert—lizards and Gila monsters and other creepy crawly things, like scorpions and spiders.

She remembered that Mitch had once told her that Apache Pass wound its way between the Dos Cabezas Mountains on the north and the Apache stronghold on the south.

To pass the time, she tried to recall everything she knew about the surrounding area. In 1854, the Pass and the surrounding area had become part of the United States as part of the Gadsden Purchase when twenty-nine million acres of ground had been purchased from Mexico. In 1857, the Butterfield Overland Mail built a stage station near Apache Spring. Butterfield employees had been the first whites to live in Apache Pass. The Butterfield transported mail and passengers from St. Louis, Missouri, to San Francisco.

Alisha smiled. She had always wanted to go to San Francisco, but the price of a ticket was over a hundred dollars, far too expensive for a schoolteacher. . . .

Schoolteacher! She suddenly realized that, in the shock of her father's death and the excitement of learning her son was alive, she had neglected to let anyone on the school board know she was leaving town. Well, she thought, it was too late to worry about it now.

At noon, Clements reined his horse to a halt. "We'll rest a bit," he said.

Feeling as though she had been riding for days instead of hours, Alisha lifted her right leg over the horse's withers and slid to the ground, but her legs refused to support her and she landed on her fanny, hard.

She glared at Clements, who was trying not to laugh but it was no use. He laughed until tears ran down his cheeks, and then, still chuckling, he offered her a hand up, which Alisha disdained. With a little humph of pique, she grabbed hold of the stirrup and pulled herself to her feet, realizing, as she did so that she needed some privacy, and very quickly.

She looked around, hoping for a large shrub, a bush, a tree. There was nothing, only flat ground and stunted clumps of sage and mesquite and cactus as far as the eye could see.

Resolutely, she started walking toward the largest cactus.

"Hey!" Clements hollered. "Where do you think you're going?"

"I need to . . . to, ah . . . I just need to!"

"Ah," Clements said. "Well, watch out for snakes!"

Snakes! Standing behind the cactus, she cast a hasty glance around. *You can do this*, she told herself. *You can do whatever you have to, endure any hardship. Just think about your son.*

When she returned to where Clements waited, she saw that he had unsaddled the horses and was offering them handfuls of grain. When the horses had been fed, he reached into his saddlebag and pulled out two hunks of beef jerky.

Alisha accepted one with a wan smile. Taking a bite was like stepping backward through time as she recalled a warm summer day when Mitch had brought several hunks of jerked beef to the river. She had stared at it, not sure what it was, until he explained that it was jerked beef, and that his mother had made

it. He had told her that the Indians made it out of buffalo or venison. He had wolfed his down like it was
candy. She had thought it tasted like sun-dried leather.

It still tasted like leather, she mused as she bit off a
piece.

An hour later, they were riding again.

By the time Clements made camp for the night, she
was certain she would never walk again.

Chapter 14

Mitch sat beside Rides the Buffalo, listening as his mother told the story of how fire came to be. It was a familiar story, one she had told him when he'd been about the same age. Last night, she had told the story of how Coyote stole the buffalo from Humpback.

Mitch settled against the backrest, his legs stretched out in front of him. The sound of his mother's voice, soft and low, as she began the story, took him back to his own childhood.

"In the long ago time, before there was fire," White Robe began, "animals and trees talked to each other. Of all the beasts, Fox was the most clever, and he tried to think of a way to create fire for the world. One day he went to visit the Geese because he wanted to learn to fly. The Geese promised to teach him if he would fly with them. They put wings on Fox, but warned him he must not open his eyes while flying.

"When the Geese flew, Fox flew with them. One time, darkness fell quickly as they were flying over the village of the fireflies. Suddenly, the glare from the fireflies made Fox forget he was supposed to keep his eyes closed, and he opened them! And do you know what happened?"

Rides the Buffalo shook his head.

"Fox began to fall. He landed inside the fireflies' village, where a fire constantly burned in the center. Two fireflies came to see Fox, and gave him necklaces of juniper berries.

"Fox hoped to persuade the fireflies to tell him how to find his way out of the village. They led him to a cedar tree and told him the tree would bend down at his command and catapult him over the wall, if that was his wish.

"Fox said he would think about it. That night, Fox found a spring where the fireflies got their water. He also discovered colored earth with which to make paint. He painted himself white and went back to the village where he suggested they have a dance.

"The fireflies thought that would be fun, so they gathered wood for a fire. Secretly, Fox tied a piece of cedar wood to his tail. Then he made a drum, maybe the first one ever made, and beat it vigorously with a stick. Slowly, he moved closer to the fire.

"Fox pretended to be tired from beating the drum and he gave it to some fireflies. Fox quickly put his tail in the fire, lighting the bark, and said, 'It is hot here. I must find a cool place.'

"Fox ran to the cedar tree, calling, 'Bend down, bend down!'

"The cedar tree bent down so Fox could grab hold and then it straightened up and Fox jumped over the wall. He ran and ran, with the fireflies chasing after.

"As Fox ran, the bushes and wood on either side of his path caught fire from the sparks falling from the bark tied to his tail.

"When Fox got tired, he gave the bark to Hawk, who carried it to the brown Crane. He flew southward, scattering sparks everywhere he went. And that is how fire came to the earth."

Rides the Buffalo clapped his hands, pleased with the story. Rising, he bid his father good night, gave his mother a hug, smiled at Mitch, and crawled into bed.

"I think I'll go for a walk," Mitch said. Rising, he gave his mother a hug. He had found himself hugging her a lot in the last two days. Making up for lost time, or maybe just proving to himself that she was real.

He stood outside a moment, listening to the quiet sounds of the night. He didn't really want to go for a walk, but he felt the need to give his mother and Elk Chaser some time alone.

With a sigh, he walked down to the river. Sitting on the bank, he gazed up at the sky. As always these days, he found himself thinking of Alisha, wondering what she was doing, if she missed him as much as he was missing her.

A falling star caught his eye, reminding him of the nights they had spent together, how she had always made a wish on a falling star, and insisted he make one, too.

"Lisha," he murmured. "I wish you were here."

Alisha gazed up at the starlit sky. She hadn't been afraid this afternoon. Why was she afraid now? Mr. Clements had assured her that there was little danger that the Indians would bother them at night, something about a belief that their souls would wander forever in darkness if they were killed at night. She hadn't given any thought to the danger of Indian attack that afternoon. She had been far too excited about the prospect of seeing her son to think of anything else. Only now did she realize the danger she was in. She could be killed by Indians and no one would know. And even if they reached the Apache village safely, there was no guarantee that they would be welcome.

She shook her fears aside. She was here now, and she wasn't turning back. Her father was dead. Mitch was gone. She had nothing to live for except her son. If only Mitch was there beside her, she wouldn't be afraid. She had never been afraid of anything when he was beside her. Where was he now?

She watched a falling star streak across the heavens. Mitch used to make fun of her because she had always made a wish when she saw a failing star. She had always insisted he make a wish, too, even though he thought it was girlish nonsense.

"Oh, Mitch," she whispered, "how I wish you were here."

Chapter 15

Alisha shifted in the saddle, wishing Mr. Clements would decide it was time for a rest. She hadn't expected a day in the saddle to leave her feeling so sore all over. Of course, spending the night on the hard, cold ground probably had a lot to do with it, too. When she got up that morning, muscles she had never known she had screamed in protest.

"Have you been to the Apaches' camp often?" she asked, hoping conversation would take her mind off her aches and pains.

"Never been to the stronghold in 'Pache Pass, but I got me a wife amongst the Jicarilla."

"You're married to an Apache woman?"

"Yeah. She's a pretty li'l thing. Name's Mountain Sage."

"Oh." Alisha contemplated that for a few minutes. If Mr. Clements had an Indian wife, then she had probably spent the last night worrying over nothing. The Indians weren't likely to attack them, not when Clements was married to one of their women. "Do you have children?"

"Three," he said with obvious pride. "Two boys, and a girl."

"You don't live with them?"

"Not all the time. Got me a wife and a couple kids in St. Louis, too, ya see."

Alisha stared at Clements. "You have *two* wives?"

He shrugged. "It ain't uncommon. Lots of mountain men and traders have Injun wives."

She was too stunned to speak.

"It ain't as bad as it sounds. I take good care of 'em both."

"Do they . . ." Her voice came out in a high-pitched squeak and she cleared her throat and tried again, "Do your wives know?"

"Mountain Sage knows. I ain't never told Dorothy, though." He grimaced. "Ain't no way she'd ever understand, ya know, being brought up the way she was and all."

"And your Indian wife doesn't mind?"

"Nah. It's common for warriors to have more than one wife."

"But that's sinful."

"Injuns don't think so. 'Pache life is hard. A woman needs a man to protect her, and since there's usually more women than men . . ." Clements shrugged. "It's just practical, ya know?"

"Who looks after Mountain Sage when you're in St. Louis with . . . Dorothy?"

"Her kin. 'Pache men go live with the woman's family when they get married. From then on, his obligation is to support and protect 'em. When I go huntin', Sage always give a part of my kill to her ma."

"I see," Alisha said, though she didn't see at all.

"The 'Paches are good people. They're honest. They

don't steal from their own. They pay their debts. They got a good sense of humor, they're loyal. Cheerful most of the time. Women are hard workers. The men are fierce fighters."

"Are they good to their children?" she asked, thinking of her son.

"Yeah. 'Paches loves kids. Young'uns are rarely punished, or even scolded. Little girls play house, ya know, with dolls and such. The boys play, too, 'ceptin' they play at being men. 'Pache boys grow up fast. I seen four and five year olds already well on their way to being warriors."

"Warriors!" Alisha exclaimed. "At four?" Her son was four. Was he already learning how to hunt and fight?

"Injuns start 'em out young. 'Pache boys are considered men by the time they're twelve or thirteen."

Alisha fell silent as she contemplated this last bit of news. She had boys in her class who were twelve and thirteen. A couple of them were tall and mature for their ages, but they weren't men yet. Not even close. "That's incredible," she murmured.

"Yep. Ain't easy, becoming a 'Pache warrior. The elders make the novices take long runs carrying heavy loads on their backs. They have to learn how to live off the land. They test 'em by having them take a mouthful of water, then run for a couple of miles without swallowing it. The elders test their willpower and endurance by making them go without sleep for long periods of time." Clements shook his head, but his voice was filled with admiration when he spoke again. "It ain't easy, being a 'Pache warrior, but there ain't no fighters that can equal 'em, that's fer damn sure."

Alisha stared at Clements, more convinced than

ever that she had to find her son. She didn't want her baby to be subjected to such barbaric trials and rituals. She didn't want him learning to kill, praying to strange gods.

For the first time, she thought past the moment when she would see her son for the first time. She would be a stranger to him. How would she explain who she was? Her son had been living with his adoptive parents since the day he was born. What if he didn't want to leave them? What if they wouldn't let him go? What would she do, in their situation? Would she be able to part with a child she had raised from infancy just because a woman showed up claiming to be the child's mother?

Clements cocked his head in Alisha's direction. "Somethin' eatin' at ya, missy?"

"I just realized I'm probably on a fool's errand."

"How so?"

Alisha shook her head. She couldn't explain her past to this uncouth man, couldn't humiliate herself by telling him that she had given birth to an illegitimate child. At least he had married the mothers of his children.

"Well, I don't know as how it will be any comfort to ya, but most everyone I ever met has been a fool at one time or 'nother," he drawled.

"Yes," Alisha said uncertainly. "I guess that's true."

"Iffen ya ever want to talk about it, I'm a pretty good listener." Clements grinned at her. "Man with two wives don't have much choice."

"How soon will we get there?"

Clements stared ahead a few moments. "'Nother two days, I'd say."

Chapter 16

Mitch sighted down the shaft of the arrow, took a deep breath, let out half of it, and released the bowstring. He felt himself grinning ear to ear as the arrow hit the target scant inches from the arrow of Rides the Buffalo.

"*Enjuh!*" Rides the Buffalo exclaimed. Good.

Elk Chaser nodded. "You have learned quickly."

Mitch nodded. The crude bow and arrows he had fashioned as a child were nothing compared to Elk Chaser's weapons. He had been surprised at how much strength it took to draw the bowstring. While hunting with a handful of warriors the day before, he had been mightily impressed by their skill. Elk Chaser had brought down a deer five hundred feet away.

It had taken hours to stalk the deer. Once found, the Apache had crawled on the ground, careful to keep weeds and brush between them and the deer so they would not be seen. Always careful to stay downwind.

Of course, Mitch was nowhere near the marksman Elk Chaser was. Hell, he wasn't even as good as Rides the Buffalo. But he was getting better every day.

Besides deer, there were herds of antelope and elk on the prairie which spread below the mountains.

Wild turkeys lived in the forests and along the streams. Eagles were hunted for their feathers, which were used to fletch arrows, for ceremonial fans and decoration.

"We will have to fashion you a bow of your own," Elk Chaser remarked.

"I'd like that," Mitch replied. He winked at Rides the Buffalo. "Maybe my little brother will help me."

Rides the Buffalo nodded solemnly. "I will."

Mitch returned the bow he had been using to Elk Chaser. It was a powerful weapon, strengthened with layers of sinew on the back which had been applied so carefully they were scarcely visible. Elk Chaser's arrows were more than three feet long.

When he'd been a child, Mitch's mother had often told him stories of her people, of how the men could camouflage themselves with dirt and plants so that they were virtually invisible. An Apache warrior could travel from fifty to seventy-five miles a day over the roughest terrain. As a boy, Mitch had been awed by the tales she told him. As he grew older, he decided she must have been exaggerating. But after seeing Elk Chaser and the other men on the hunt the day before, he knew his mother hadn't been exaggerating. The Apache had learned to live in perfect harmony with the world around them. Yesterday morning, while tracking a small herd of deer, he had watched the men, noting the way they paid heed to the smallest things— the position of a stone that had been overturned, horse droppings on the trail, the way a twig or branch had been broken. He remembered, too, the stories his mother had told him of brave fighters, both men and women.

Mitch felt a stirring of old anger as he thought of all

he had missed. Had his father let him go with his mother, he might have grown up to be a warrior. It was too late now. He might learn the ways of the Apache, he might embrace their beliefs and immerse himself in their lifestyle, but he would never be a true warrior.

Mitch grinned as Rides the Buffalo fired four arrows in quick succession, each one striking the heart of the target. He might never be the warrior his little brother would, but he was determined to learn all he could while he had the chance.

Alisha blew out a sigh. It had been a long five days. She was hot and tired and sticky and wanted to take a bath and wash her hair more than she wanted anything else in the world, except for seeing her son.

She looked down at her clothes. Her shirtwaist, once white and crisp, was now limp and covered with a fine coat of dun-colored dust. The hem of her skirt was dirty and ripped on one side where it had caught on a cactus. The hem of her petticoat was also dirty and torn.

Clements had said they would reach the entrance to Apache Pass late that afternoon. She was thinking of that now, excitement fluttering in her belly like a hummingbird's wings as she tried to imagine those first few moments when she would meet her son face-to-face for the first time.

Alisha nodded as Clements remarked that they would be stopping to rest the horses soon, almost tumbled over her horse's rump when, suddenly and without warning, Clements lashed her horse on the rear with the end of his reins, hollering for her to ride like hell.

Alisha grabbed hold of the saddle horn with both hands, holding on for dear life as Sophie lunged forward. At the same time, she heard a hideous high-pitched wail that sent cold chills down her spine. Glancing over her shoulder, she saw a half-dozen Indians coming up fast behind them. She saw Clements draw his rifle, heard the sharp, rolling report as he fired at the pursuing Indians. The warrior in the lead tumbled off his horse.

She heard that hideous shriek again and knew it had to be a war cry of some kind, knew that she would never see her son, that she was going to be killed right here.

Tears stung her eyes as she slammed her heels into Sophie's sides. "Faster!" she cried. "Faster, Sophie!"

The high-pitched shrieks of the Indians were punctuated with the roar of gunfire and then, only moments after the attack began, there was an ominous silence.

Alisha glanced over her shoulder again. Four Indians were chasing her. There was no sign of Red Clements.

Fear such as she had never known curdled in her belly, making her feel suddenly faint. She clung to the saddle horn, praying that Sophie wouldn't fall, that she could find a place to hide.

Time lost all meaning, and there was only the sting of the wind in her face, the bitter taste of fear in her mouth. And the sure knowledge that she was going to die.

Sophie's hide was covered with frothy yellow lather, her sides heaving like an overworked bellows, when the Indians caught up with them. In a move Alisha wouldn't have believed if she hadn't seen it, one of the warriors rode up beside her and jumped from the back of his horse onto the back of hers. Reaching around in front of her, he jerked the reins from her hand and brought Sophie to a halt. Tossing the reins over the mare's head, he slid off the mare's rump, then reached up and dragged Alisha from the saddle.

Alisha could scarcely breathe, she was so frightened. Heart pounding, she tried to offer a last prayer to God, but she couldn't think, couldn't speak, could only stare into the dark eyes of the man who stood in front of her.

I wish I could have seen my son before I die, she thought sadly. *I wish I had told Mitch I still love him. . . .*

Mitch checked the cinch on his saddle, made sure his canteen was full, checked the supplies in his saddlebags. Yesterday's hunt had been for warriors only. Today, Elk Chaser and three other men were taking their sons and grandsons hunting. They would be gone for several days. Elk Chaser had asked Mitch if he would like to go along, and Mitch had quickly agreed, eager to learn everything he could about the People and their ways. He had expected it to take two or three months for him to feel at ease among the Apache, but such was not the case. These were his mother's people, his people. Everything he had learned, everything he had seen, seemed vaguely familiar, as if the spirits of his ancestors were whispering in his ear, telling him that the ancient legends he was hearing were true, recalling to his mind the old stories his mother had told him as far back as he could remember and beyond.

They rode out just after dawn, five men, and eight boys between the ages of four and ten. Men and youth alike were clad in breechclouts and moccasins. Elk

Chaser had given Mitch a pair of moccasins. They were a remarkable piece of footwear, fitted to protect the wearer's feet and legs from thorny plants and poisonous reptiles. They reached halfway up Mitch's calf, and had tough soles that turned up at the toe. Like the others, he also wore a breechclout. His mother made it for him soon after he arrived so that he would blend in with the others. A strip of red cloth tied around his forehead kept his hair out of his face. No one looking at him now would guess he was not pure Apache, unless they were close enough to see that his eyes were blue and not black.

Mitch grinned at Elk Chaser as they forded a dry streambed. Even as a boy chasing rabbits, he had loved the anticipation of the hunt, the excitement of the chase, the kill. It was humbling, knowing that Rides the Buffalo, who was the youngest of the group, was more adept at hunting with a bow than he was. He took a small measure of comfort in the fact that, with a rifle or a pistol, he was any man's equal.

They rode for several hours. In addition to hunting, the boys were learning to track, to recognize landmarks, to determine the time of day by the position of the sun.

Mitch urged his horse up the side of the ravine. It was a beautiful day, warm and clear. The cactus were in bloom, and there was nothing to see for miles in any direction but cactus and desert and gray-green clumps of sage. In the distance, an eagle drifted on the air currents.

Mitch saw the bright red splash of color at the same time as the others. Without being told, the boys fell back a little while the men rode forward, their weapons at the ready.

The body was sprawled facedown on the low side of a small rise. It had been stripped naked, save for the bottom half of a pair of red long johns. A patch of dark-brown blood had dried around the shaft of the arrow in the man's back. A second arrow protruded from the meaty part of his left arm.

The warriors dismounted a few feet from the body. Leaving their horses, they searched the ground for sign, nodding and talking rapidly.

"Comanches," Elk Chaser told Mitch. He held up both hands, fingers spread. "At least ten of them. They rode off that way," he said, pointing toward the south. "They have taken whoever was riding with this man."

"How long ago?" Mitch asked.

"Late yesterday."

Mitch nodded, feeling a wave of pity for the man who had survived. Either he would be forced into slavery, or tortured to death. Looking at the body, Mitch decided the dead man was the better off of the two.

Satisfied that there was no longer any danger, the warriors vaulted onto the backs of their horses.

Mitch looked at Elk Chaser. "You're not going to bury him?"

Elk Chaser shook his head. Like all Apache, he had a great horror of the dead. The Apaches buried their own as soon as possible, and always during the day. Interment was in a cave or crevice, if such a place was available; otherwise, they buried their loved ones in the earth, covering the grave with brush and dirt and rocks to keep coyotes and other predators away.

Mitch had seen such burial mounds from time to time. He watched as Elk Chaser mounted his horse and started to ride after the others. It seemed a shame to leave a body lying in the desert to rot, but he had little choice. He had nothing with which to dig a hole, nothing with which to cover the body.

He was about to turn away when he heard a low moan. Frowning, he nudged the body in the side with the toe of his moccasin. And the body twitched.

Muttering an oath, Mitch rolled the man over, and found himself looking into a pair of pain-glazed brown eyes.

"Damn, you're alive."

"Water . . ."

"Elk Chaser!" Mitch called. "Wait!"

Moments later, the warriors were gathered around the wounded man again. The boys stood together in the background, pointing and whispering.

The warrior known as Kills Twice grunted softly. "Let us kill the *pinda-lick-o-ye*, and go."

Fear flickered in the eyes of the wounded man, and he reached out toward Mitch. "Help . . . me. . . ." he gasped, and then went limp.

"You all go on with the hunt," Mitch said. "I'm taking him back to camp."

"*Duunndil'edida!*" Elk Chaser exclaimed. "Do not be foolish. He will not be welcome there."

"Well, hell, I can't just leave him out here to die." Mitch glanced at Kills Twice. "Or to be killed."

"He is the enemy. It is the Apache way to kill their enemies." Kills Twice smiled. "*Usen* has delivered him into our hands. Let us finish him now and move on."

Mitch's gaze locked with that of Kills Twice. "I'm taking him back to camp."

Kills Twice stared at him a moment, then shrugged. Calling to his son, Kills Twice swung onto his horse's back and rode away. The other warriors followed.

"You must blindfold him when you are near the entrance to the rancheria," Elk Chaser said.

"I will."

"There are many who will be angry because of this. The Blue Coats killed four of our men and two of our women this past winter."

Mitch nodded. "I understand."

Elk Chaser clapped him on the shoulder, then mounted his horse and followed the others.

Muttering an oath, Mitch knelt beside the man and broke off the shafts of both arrows so that only a few inches remained protruding from the wounds, then he lifted the unconscious man and laid him facedown over the saddle. Vaulting onto the horse's rump, he reached forward and picked up the reins. Riding behind the saddle was not the most comfortable place to ride, to be sure, but it beat the hell out of walking.

It was late afternoon when they reached the entrance to the rancheria. The wounded man hadn't regained consciousness but, remembering Elk Chaser's stern admonition, Mitch removed his headband and used it to blindfold the man.

When he reached the top of the narrow trail, he called to the warriors guarding the entrance, then made his way into the encampment.

Everyone he passed turned to stare at the body draped over the saddle, only to turn away when they saw it was not one of their own.

Mitch found his mother sitting in the shade in front of her lodge, sewing. She looked up, astonishment flickering in her eyes, when she saw the man sprawled facedown across his saddle.

"He needs help," Mitch said. Dismounting, he slung

the unconscious man over his shoulder and carried him into his mother's lodge.

White Robe looked after Mitch's horse, then entered the lodge. She quickly stirred the coals in the fire and tossed in a handful of sweet grass to purify the air.

Knowing he would only be in the way, Mitch stood back while his mother examined the wounds.

"Come," she said. "You must hold him down while I remove the arrows."

Mitch knelt in front of the man, his hands firmly planted on the man's shoulders, while his mother straddled the man's legs. She removed the arrow in his arm first, electing to push it all the way through, rather than try to draw it out. She quickly washed the wound, packed the holes with green tree moss, and bound the arm in a strip of cotton cloth.

The arrow in the man's back had to be cut out. Even unconscious, the man thrashed and moaned as she worked the head of the arrow from his back. When the arrowhead had been removed, she washed and bandaged the wound as she had the other one, then stood up.

"I will make broth. He will need lots of liquid to replace the blood he has lost. If he lives."

"*Ashoge, shi ma,*" Mitch said. Rising, he gave his mother a kiss on the cheek.

Leaving the lodge, Mitch walked down to the river. Squatting on his heels, he watched the water splash and tumble over the rocks, his thoughts on the white man. Who was he? What was he doing out here? He looked vaguely familiar. Someone he'd seen on the streets of Canyon Creek, maybe.

He grunted softly, the thought of Canyon Creek bringing Alisha quickly to mind. He should have

taken the time to tell her good-bye, he mused ruefully.
Wished her well in her forthcoming marriage.

Picking up a rock, he hurled it into the river, watching the ripples spread out in ever-widening circles. He
should have just grabbed her and run. Let her scream
and holler all she wanted about promises and honor.
She had promised to marry him long before she became engaged to that pretty boy Smithfield. What did
Smithfield know about her? Had he been the one to
hold Alisha and comfort her when her mother died?
Had he been the one Alisha had always turned to for
comfort? Had Smithfield taught her to swim? Given
her her first kiss? Taught her what it meant to be a
woman? Dammit, why hadn't he stayed and fought
for her? He had never given up on anything he wanted
in his life. He wanted Alisha Faraday and by damn, he
was going to go back and fight for her. When the
wounded man could travel, he would take him to
Canyon Creek, and then he'd find Alisha and make
her admit the truth—that she loved him, not Smithfield.

He grinned, pleased with the thought of carrying
her away. He should have done it long ago. She could
protest all she wanted, he thought, but he would make
her happy. She would forget about Smithfield soon
enough. He'd see to that.

He imagined what it would be like to spend the
night with Alisha at his side, to see her face first thing
in the morning, hear her whisper his name in the quiet
of the night.

"Lisha." Whispering her name, he turned and went
back to his mother's lodge.

*   *   *

The stranger was awake when Mitch entered the wickiup.

"Obliged to ya," the man said. He groaned softly as he struggled to sit up, his face going pale with the exertion. "Damned Comanch," he gasped. "What the hell was they doin' . . . ?" He paused for a breath. "So far from home anyways." He offered Mitch his hand. "Red Clements."

Mitch shook the man's hand. "Mitch Garrett." He sat down. "Sorry about your friend."

"My friend?" Clements exclaimed. A look of horror passed over his face. "The woman!" he said with a low groan. "Lord in heaven, they got the woman."

Mitch felt a sudden sense of trepidation. "What woman?"

"I was guidin' a pretty li'l gal. She paid me fifty bucks to bring her to the 'Paches." Gritting his teeth, Clements threw off the blanket and tried to stand up. He swore as he fell back on the blankets. "I've got to go after her."

"You're in no shape to go anywhere."

"Got to. Damn!"

"Who was she?" Mitch asked, his stomach clenching. "This woman?"

"Name was Faraday. Alisha Faraday."

Mitch stared at the man. What reason could Alisha have for wanting to come here? She wouldn't have come looking for him, even if she had known he was here.

"Why?" Mitch asked. "What business did she have here?"

"Said she was lookin' for someone."

Mitch stood up, his mind whirling. Alisha had been

captured by the Comanche! Damn. He had to go after her. Now!

Mitch glanced over his shoulder as his mother entered the lodge carrying a load of wood. "*Shi ma,* would you please pack some food for me?"

"Where are you going?" She dumped the wood beside the fire pit and added a few sticks to the fire.

"He was guiding a woman here," Mitch explained quickly. "I'm going after her. There's no time to explain now. Please, just pack me enough food for a couple of days."

"You must wait," White Robe said. "Wait for Elk Chaser. He will know what to do."

Mitch paced the lodge. "I can't wait!" Alisha, in the hands of the Comanche. What would they do to her? If she was still alive, she would be terrified . . . if . . . He pounded his fist into his palm. He couldn't think like that. He had to believe she was still alive or he'd go insane. Oh, Lord, Alisha . . . *Please let her be all right.* "I've got to go after her."

"Your ma's right, boy. You won't be no help to that gal iffen you get yourself kilt trying to save her."

"Elk Chaser won't be back for a couple of days. I can't wait that long." Mitch turned to his mother. "Do you think any of the other men would go with me?"

"Why are you so concerned for this woman?" White Robe asked.

"It's Alisha. You remember her? The preacher's daughter."

"Ah," White Robe said, a knowing look in her eye. "Yes, I remember her."

"You know her?" Clements asked. "Was she coming here to see you?"

Mitch shook his head. "I don't think so. There's no way she would have known I was here."

White Robe frowned. "Why else would she come here?"

"I don't know." Mitch looked at Clements. "Did she tell you why she wanted to come here?"

"Claimed she had family here."

"Family?" Mitch frowned. "What family?"

"She didn't say. I thought it was passing strange that a lady like her would have kin living with the 'Pache. . . ." Clements looked up at White Robe. "No offense meant, missus."

White Robe nodded.

Clements took a deep breath. "Give me a few minutes to pull myself together, Garrett, and I'll side ya."

"I'm obliged for your offer, Clements, but you won't be on your feet for at least a week," Mitch replied. "I can't wait that long."

"*Ciye . . .*"

"I've got to go, *shi ma.*" He had to go after Alisha now, had to feel like he was doing something. He couldn't just sit and wait. He'd go crazy. Even though he knew striking out on his own was a damn-fool thing to do, he couldn't wait for Elk Chaser to return, couldn't wait until Clements was able to travel. He was a fair tracker, and he knew the general direction the Comanches were headed. And there was a chance, however slim, that one man, acting alone, would be more effective than a dozen warriors.

"Tell Elk Chaser where I've gone," Mitch said.

"*Ciye*, wait." White Robe stuffed several chunks of jerky and a dozen ashcakes in a buckskin bag and thrust it into his hands, along with a canteen that was stamped with the insignia of the U.S. Cavalry.

"*Ashoge, shi ma.*" He hugged his mother, grabbed his weapons, and left the lodge.

It only took a few minutes to cut his horse out of the herd, a couple more to saddle the bay. And then he was riding southeast, toward the land of the Comanche.

Chapter 17

Fear. It was the dampness on her palms, the cold sweat trickling down her spine, the sick feeling deep in the pit of her stomach. She stared at the rawhide thong that bound her wrists together. Why hadn't she listened to Roger when he told her to stay home? If she hadn't insisted on making this journey, Red Clements would still be alive. Regret filled her heart when she thought of Mr. Clements's families. She choked back a sob. His wives and children would never know what had happened to him. Her friends and students would never know what had happened to her.

She glanced at the warriors riding on either side of her. What a ninny she had been. She had lived her whole life in the Southwest. She knew how dangerous the Indians were. She had read numerous accounts of stagecoaches and outlying ranches being attacked by marauding Indians. The Apaches had been on the warpath for the last seven years, ever since Cochise had been accused of kidnapping a local rancher's child and stealing the rancher's stock.

She had only been sixteen at the time. She remembered how upset Mitch had been when the local paper described the incident, calling Cochise a murdering savage. Though Mitch had never met Cochise, he had a great respect for the Apache chief. And later, it had been proven that Cochise and his Apaches had been innocent.

Alisha wiped the sweat from her brow. She had known the journey to Apache Pass would be dangerous, but, in the excitement of learning that her son was alive, she had foolishly disregarded it. And now she was about to pay the ultimate price for her foolishness. She didn't know if these Indians were Apaches or not, but it made no difference.

She gazed into the distance. There was little to see but desert and sage and cactus, a bold blue sky, a blazing sun.

She wondered how long it would take for the Indians to reach their village, and what would happen to her when they arrived. Would they rape her? Torture her? Scalp her? She had read of the atrocities committed by the Indians but, safe and secure in her sheltered life, it had all seemed distant and unreal, something that happened to other people. Until now.

She glanced at the Indians beside her again, and thought of Mitch. He was half Apache. If he had been raised by his mother's people instead of by his father, he would have been a warrior, like these men, clad in buckskins and feathers, and they would have been enemies. She thought of her son, being raised by the Apache. Clements had said that a boy of four was already well on his way to being a warrior. She tried to imagine her son as a grown man, a warrior on the warpath, attacking innocent women and children, burning ranches, stealing cattle.

Lost in thought, it took her a minute to realize that

the Indians had stopped. She was surprised to see that the sun was slipping below the horizon. The warriors dismounted and began setting up camp. One of the men dragged her off the back of her horse and gave her a push. She stumbled forward, tripped on a rock, and fell. With her hands bound, she was unable to break her fall. She cried out as her head struck the ground.

With a look of disgust, the warrior who had pushed her grabbed her by the shoulders and hauled her into a sitting position. Lifting a waterskin from the back of his horse, he took a long swallow, then thrust the container into her hands.

She stared at the waterskin, repulsed by the idea of putting her mouth where his had been.

"*Hibitu!*" he said, and gestured for her to drink.

Closing her eyes, she lifted the waterskin and took a swallow. The water was warm and slightly brackish, but it quenched her thirst.

"*Tobo? Ihupiitu!*"

She gasped, water trickling down her chin, when he jerked the waterskin from her hands.

It took only a few minutes for the Indians to set up their night camp and soon a small fire brightened the gathering dusk. The men sat around the fire, talking and laughing while they ate. The warrior who had offered her a drink thrust a hunk of dried meat into her hands, then went to sit with the others.

Fear did not make for a hearty appetite, neither did the food she had been offered, but she forced herself to eat. Mitch had once told her that no matter what the circumstances, survival must always be the first order of business. She would keep up her strength just in case she found an opportunity, however unlikely that seemed at the moment, to escape.

An hour later, the warriors rolled up in their blankets and went to sleep, save for two who stood cloaked in the shadows of the night, keeping watch.

Alisha shivered as a cool evening breeze blew over the land. The Indians had offered her food and drink, but no blanket to turn away the cold. Huddled into a ball, her bound hands numb, she closed her eyes and tried to sleep. But sleep would not come. Morbid thoughts and fears of the fate that awaited her when the Indians reached their destination crowded her mind, keeping sleep at bay.

How slowly time passed when one was cold and alone and afraid.

To take her mind from her desperate situation, she thought about Mitch. He had always been there to save her when she got into trouble in the past, she mused. Of course, most of the time, he had been the one who got her into trouble in the first place, like the time they had gone hiking in the foothills. She had been about ten at the time. It had been a beautiful warm summer day. Mitch had fallen a little behind her because she had run ahead to gather a bunch of flowers growing wild on the hillside. . . .

Humming softly, she bent down to reach for a bright yellow bloom growing between two small rocks.

"Lisha! Don't move!"

She stopped and glanced over her shoulder at Mitch, wondering what was wrong. And then she heard the unmistakable warning rattle. Looking down, she saw the snake coiled less than a foot away. She stared at the diamond-shaped head, the forked tongue darting in and out, the tail with its ugly rattles. Her first instinct was to run, screaming, down the hill.

"Don't move, Lisha." Mitch's voice was soft and low this time, soothing. "Don't move. He's just as afraid of you as you are of him."

Somehow she doubted that. The snake didn't look scared—only mean and ugly, with its beady, black eyes and scaly skin.

"Listen to me, Lisha. I want you to back up, very slowly."

She shook her head, afraid to move, afraid to breathe. She had once seen a trapper who had been snakebit. He had staggered into town, his leg all black and swollen. The doctor had cut off the man's leg in an attempt to save his life, but the poor man had died anyway.

"Lisha, Lisha."

She looked into Mitch's eyes and some of her fear melted away.

"Trust me. I'll get you out of there. One step at a time," he said. "Slowly. Now."

Heart pounding with fear, certain the snake would strike the minute she moved, she took a small step backward.

The snake's tongue darted in and out, testing the air.

She took another small step backward, dislodging a rock that rolled down the hill.

The snake's tail vibrated faster, the whir of its rattles sounding like dry bones in a tin cup in the stillness that seemed to have settled around her.

"It's all right. Come on, Lisha. Come here to me."

Slowly, small step by small step, she followed the sound of Mitch's voice. He would save her. Heart hammering in her breast, she backed away from the snake. Weak with relief, she fell into Mitch's arms. . . .

How she longed to be in his arms now, she thought, to tell him that she loved him, that the child born of their love for one another was alive and living with the Apaches.

She looked up at the night sky. Never had she felt so alone, and yet she wasn't alone.

Please, God, please help me. I know You're up there. I know You can hear me. Please, God, please help me get out of this mess so I can find my son. And please bless Mitch. I love him so much. . . .

A sense of peace filled her heart. With a sigh, she closed her eyes and slept.

Mitch sat cross-legged on the ground, gnawing on a piece of jerky. He'd ridden back to the place where he'd found Clements and picked up the trail of the Indians. He wasn't the world's best tracker, but the Comanches weren't making any effort to hide their trail and he'd had little trouble following them until darkness swallowed up their tracks, forcing him to stop for the night.

He tried not to think about how afraid Alisha must be, refused to even consider that the Indians might have killed her. He'd go crazy if he thought that. No— she was alive and well, and he would find her. He had to believe that. He could well imagine her fear. She'd have no reason to believe anyone knew where she was, or that Clements was alive.

And yet, over and above everything else, he wondered why she had been traveling to Apache Pass in the first place. Clements had told him she claimed to have family there. Clements had seemed lucid enough, but maybe he'd been out of his head with pain and fever. Lord knew he was badly hurt. Mitch grunted softly. Surely if Alisha had family living with the Apaches, she would have mentioned it to him long ago. While growing up, they had spent a good deal of time talking about his mother's people, both of them curious about the Apache way of life.

Family. He was still puzzling over what that could mean when he crawled under his blanket and went to sleep.

White Robe sat outside her lodge, sewing the sole to a moccasin she was making for Otter, when Elk Chaser and the others returned to the stronghold. Laying her sewing aside, she ran toward her husband.

Elk Chaser smiled, pleased that she had missed him though he had been gone but two days and a night.

Rides the Buffalo jumped off his pony and ran toward his mother. "A deer, *shi ma*, I killed a deer."

"*Enjuh*," she replied distractedly. "That is good." She hugged him quickly. "You must tell me all about it later. But first I must speak to your father."

Hearing the concern in his wife's voice, Elk Chaser dismounted and tossed the reins of his horse to his son. "Look after our horses, *ciye*."

Rides the Buffalo started to say something but a stern look from his father stilled his tongue. Taking up the reins to his own horse as well, he turned and walked toward the river.

"Something troubles you, my wife."

"Yes," she said, and quickly explained what had happened while they walked to their lodge. "And so," she said, "he has gone on his own to find her."

Elk Chaser nodded. It would have been wiser to

wait for help, but he understood Otter's impatience. From what White Robe said, Otter had deep feelings for the white woman.

"I will find Diyehii and Cheis and we will go after him."

"*Ashoge*, my husband. I will have food for your journey prepared when you return."

With a nod, Elk Chaser went to find Diyehii and Cheis.

Alisha gazed into the distance, the countryside as foreign to her eyes as the language of her captors was to her ears. It was like being caught in a nightmare from which she could not escape.

That morning, she had been roused from a troubled sleep while the sky was still dark. A warrior who had managed to convey to her that his name was Mukwooru had offered her food and drink, allowed her a moment of privacy, then lifted her onto the back of her horse. Taking the reins, he had vaulted onto his own mount. That had been hours ago. She wondered how much longer it would take to reach their village, though she was in no hurry. Wondered what they had been doing so far from home in the first place.

But, over all, was the mind-numbing fear of the future, of what fate awaited her when they reached their destination.

She glanced at Mukwooru, riding beside her. He was only a little taller than she was, though he was heavily muscled. He had long, black braids, dark copper skin, and a face as hard and unyielding as stone. He wore a buckskin shirt, a breechclout, and a sort of boot, painted blue, that reached from his foot to his hip. A single eagle feather was tied in his hair.

She quickly turned her head away when he caught her staring. She looked down at her bound hands, overcome by a feeling of despair. Even if the Indians didn't kill her, she would never see her son, never see Mitch or any of her friends again. Faced with the possibility of living with Indians for the rest of her life, she thought she would rather they killed her. Better that than live with a people she would never understand, who would never understand her. *Give me liberty, or give me death!* She smiled as the words of Patrick Henry flitted through her mind. Bobby Moss had played the part of Patrick Henry in the Fourth of July pageant last year. . . .

She sighed, wondering who the school board had found to teach school in her absence. She would miss teaching, just as she would miss Bobby and Becky and Lucinda and all her other students.

But it was Mitch she would miss most of all. She blinked back her tears, thinking of all the years they had lost—years they might have spent together if her father hadn't interfered.

"Oh, Papa," she whispered. "How could you have done such a thing?"

But for her father's lies, she and Mitch would have been married now, living together, raising their son. They might have had other children.

The Indians made camp at dusk. Thoroughly weary, she sat down where Mukwooru indicated, accepted the food and drink he offered her. By the almost-jovial mood of the men, she surmised that their journey would soon be over. Once they reached the Indian village, there would be little chance for her to escape. And even if she did, where would she go? She wouldn't last more than a day or two out in the wilderness on her own.

Despair and discouragement weighed heavily upon her and she tried to fight them off, tried to find a ray of hope in the morass of hopelessness that perched on her shoulder like a carrion crow. But, try as she might, she could see no way out of her present situation. She was hopelessly lost in this hostile land, hopelessly ill-prepared to survive in this barren desert the Indians called home.

She gasped as a young man grabbed her by the arm and hauled her to her feet. The other warriors gathered around, their expressions curious, or amused, or lustful, as the young man lifted a lock of her hair and let it fall through his fingers. He said something that made the other men laugh, and then he slid his hand over her breast. Several of the men called to him, apparently urging him on.

With a cry, Alisha jerked away, her heart pounding with terror as she realized her worst fear was about to come true.

The warrior growled something at her and then, his face etched with fury, he slapped her across her face, hard enough to make her ears ring. Clutching her left shoulder with one hand, he began to fumble with the buttons on her shirtwaist.

She stood there a moment, her cheek throbbing. *Oh, Lord*, she thought, *please help me. I'm so afraid.*

And like the answer to a prayer, the words of one of her father's favorite psalms whispered through her mind. *O Lord, my God, in thee do I put my trust: Save me from all them that persecute me, and deliver me; Lest he tear my soul like a lion, rending it to pieces, while there is none to deliver.*

She stared at the men surrounding her. She wouldn't give up. She wouldn't surrender without a fight. No matter how bad things seemed, there was always hope. Mitch had taught her that.

She wouldn't just stand there and do nothing, wouldn't surrender her virtue.

A murmur ran through the group as the warrior unfastened her shirtwaist and pushed it aside, exposing her shoulder. It was now or never. Taking a deep breath, she drove her knee into the warrior's groin as hard as she could.

The air whooshed out of the young man's lungs as he doubled over, his hands clutching his groin.

There was an explosion of laughter from the other men as the warrior dropped to the ground and rolled back and forth, his face a mask of agony.

One of the other men said something to his companions, then started toward her. It was then that Mukwooru shoved his way into the crowd, his face dark with anger. He spoke to the warriors gathered around, pointing at Alisha and then at himself, and though she couldn't understand what was being said, it was obvious that he was telling his companions that she belonged to him.

The other men drifted away, muttering amongst themselves, while Mukwooru led her to his bedroll and pushed her down.

She stared up at him, her hands clenched, wondering if he was going to finish what the young warrior had started. Mukwooru stared at her for several moments, his eyes hot, and then he turned and walked away.

Alisha sank down on his blankets, relief washing

through her. "Thank you, Lord," she whispered fervently. "Thank you, thank you, thank you!"

Later, as she lay on the ground looking up at the stars, she remembered another Bible verse that had always given her comfort. *The Lord hath heard my supplication; the Lord will receive my prayer.*

Please, God, she prayed as she drifted to sleep. *Let it be so.*

Chapter 18

Mitch reined his horse to a halt. Leaning forward, he patted the bay's neck while he scanned the ground for sign. He offered a silent prayer of thanks that the Comanches' trail was still easy to follow, that, judging from the footprints he had seen earlier, Alisha was still alive, thank God.

He would find her, or die trying, he thought. And once he found her, he was never letting her out of his sight again. He was going to wed her and bed her and she wasn't going to have a damn thing to say about it. He had spent the last five years thinking about her, wanting her, *needing* her, and he damn well meant to have her. . . .

He swore softly, and then laughed. As if he'd ever been able to make Alisha do anything she didn't want to. Of course, he'd never really tried because, growing up, they had always seemed to drift toward the same things. . . . She had liked hunting and swimming and hiking in the hills, the same as he had. He had taught her to ride on an old plow horse that had belonged to his father. Alisha had been eight or nine at the time, and more than a little afraid of the horse. It had taken him about three days to get her up on that old mare, but once she overcame her fears, she'd done pretty well. Of course, having only the one horse, they'd had to ride double. Not that he had cared. At that age, most boys shunned the company of little girls unless they were teasing them, but Alisha had been his best friend, his only friend. Growing up, he had beat the tar out of more than one bully who had been mean to her until the boys at school learned to leave her alone or face the consequences.

With a sigh, he urged the bay into a trot, hoping that, like the knights of old in the stories Alisha used to read to him, he would arrive in time to rescue his lady fair.

He rode all that day and into the evening, hoping to cut the Comanches lead, and just when he was about to call it quits for the night, he saw the faint glow of a campfire.

He quickly reined the bay to a halt, afraid the mare might betray his presence if she caught the scent of other horses. Dismounting, he tethered the bay to a clump of scraggly brush. He crawled forward on his hands and knees for several yards, then dropped down on his belly, inching as close as he dared to the camp. In the light of the flames, he could make out the forms of a dozen warriors squatting around the fire. Alisha sat a little apart from the men.

Though he couldn't see her face clearly, Alisha looked none the worse for wear, as far as he could tell. At least she was alive.

Clinging to that thought, he crawled back to where he had left the bay. He loosened the saddle girth a little; then, with a blanket draped over his shoulders, he ate a little of the food his mother had prepared for him.

His mother. It was still hard to believe that she was alive. He wished now that he hadn't waited so long to visit her people. All these years he'd thought her dead, and she had been living with the Apache, getting married, having another child. He grinned as he thought of his little brother and then frowned as he turned his thoughts back to Alisha. He had to get her away from the Comanches now, before they reached their village. Trying to sneak her out of their camp would be suicide. Trying to pick the Indians off one at a time would only alert them to his presence. What he needed was a diversion.

He grunted softly. There was plenty of dry grass and brush in the area. It was risky, but at the moment, it was the only thing he could think of.

Judging from where the Comanches were now, and the course they had been following, he had a pretty good idea of the direction they would take when they broke camp. With luck, he would be able to get ahead of them, unseen.

Alisha wrinkled her nose as she caught the scent of smoke. She'd been half asleep. Now, she looked up as Mukwooru reined his horse to a halt. Her own mount stopped beside the warrior's. A fierce wind had started blowing a short time ago. Since Mukwooru was leading her horse, there was no need for her to watch where she was going, and she had been riding with her head down and her eyes closed to keep the wind from stinging her face. Now, she heard the warrior mutter what sounded like a curse.

The other warriors gathered around Mukwooru, all talking quickly. It was then that Alisha noticed a heavy layer of smoke in the distance.

Looking closer, she saw that the grass was on fire. Fanned by the wind, it was coming in their direction. Alisha looked at the smoke, wiped her eyes, and looked again. It wasn't possible, but she would have sworn she had seen a man riding in the midst of the smoke, dragging a clump of burning brush behind his horse. She tried to get a better look, but the smoke was too thick now. Her horse danced beneath her, its ears twitching uneasily as the acrid smell of the smoke grew stronger.

Mukwooru silenced the warriors. He spoke to them, his tone urgent as he gestured at a dry creek bed about a hundred yards in the distance.

With a wild cry, the warriors whipped their horses, heading toward the creek bed, which was their only possible refuge from the fire. With luck, the flames would jump the creek bed and leave them unscathed.

Alisha grabbed hold of the saddle horn as Mukwooru urged his horse into a run, forcing hers to do the same. She glanced over her shoulder. Thick clouds of blue-gray smoke hovered over the prairie. She could see the flames now. Hot, red tongues of fire that danced and slithered over the ground, greedily devouring the dry prairie grasses. A jackrabbit sprang out of a clump of sage, bounding away.

She screamed as her horse plunged over the sandy embankment, sliding on its haunches before it gained its feet again.

The other warriors quickly dismounted. Forcing their horses to lie down so that they were below the level of the creek bed, the men lay across the necks of their mounts to keep the animals from rising.

Mukwooru dropped the reins to Alisha's horse as he dismounted, then turned and handed his horses's reins to one of the other men to keep the animals from bolting. Seeing what might be her only chance to escape, Alisha leaned forward in the saddle, one hand clutching the pommel while she grabbed her horse's reins. Heart pounding, she slammed her heels against Sophie's flanks as hard as she could.

It was a big risk, one that might very well cost her her life, yet it might also be the chance she had prayed for. Knowing she would rather die than spend the rest of her life as a captive, she urged the mare onward.

The horse, already spooked by the scent of smoke, sprang forward, its shoulder slamming into Mukwooru, knocking the startled warrior off his feet.

She heard Mukwooru's shout as Sophie scrambled up the embankment. Holding the reins in one hand and the saddle horn in the other, she hung on for dear life as the mare raced across the prairie, heading for the tree line, away from the Comanches, away from the fire which chased her like a living, breathing thing. She had to reach the trees, had to find a place to hide. It was the only chance she had.

"Run, Sophie!" she cried, drumming her heels against the mare's sides. "Run!"

They were almost at the tree line when Alisha heard a shout. Glancing over her shoulder, she saw Mukwooru riding out of the smoke toward her.

Time slowed, stood still, and she knew he was going to catch her.

Mitch glanced over his shoulder. The fire behind him was spreading across the prairie, fanned by the wind. Dropping the rope secured to a clump of burning brush, he rode on, then stopped again and looked back to see if his plan was working. He had taken a big gamble in setting the prairie grass on fire, but then, he'd never been afraid of risks, until now. He had been certain the Comanches would take shelter in the dry creek bed rather than try to run for the trees, which were farther away, and they'd proved him right. He felt a surge of satisfaction, then smiled, his heart swelling with pride and relief when he saw Alisha's horse breaking from the creek bed. But the smile quickly died when he saw one of the Comanche warriors set out in pursuit.

Mitch spurred his horse, his heart leaping into his throat. This was something he hadn't planned on.

His horse was digging up the ground with every stride as they raced toward the ravine where the rest of the Comanche had taken refuge. He bent low over his mount's neck, felt the big bay gather itself, and then they were sailing over the creek bed.

He heard the surprised shouts of the Indians as the bay cleared the ravine. Glancing back, he saw the warriors pointing in his direction, heard their angry cries as they vaulted onto the backs of their horses and poured out after him like angry ants whose nest had been destroyed.

But he had no time to worry about them, not now, not when Alisha was in danger. Looking ahead, he sought a route that would take him around the fire and into the trees.

Elk Chaser stood out of sight, unmoving, as he watched one of the Comanches emerge from the smoky haze that covered the prairie and ride toward the trees. He was safe enough, for now. The trees might catch fire, but they would not burn as quickly as the dry grasses of the prairie. The heavy foliage would slow the fire's onslaught.

The Comanche lashed his horse unmercifully, his determination to catch the woman evident in every line of his body. He slowed his horse as he entered the tree line.

Elk Chaser held his breath as a rabbit scurried through the underbrush. The movement, slight as it was, drew the Comanche's attention. Reining his horse to a halt, he dismounted and walked toward Elk Chaser's hiding place.

Knowing the Comanche expected to find the woman cowering in fear, Elk Chaser grinned as he stepped out into the open. He had only a moment to appreciate the look of astonishment on the Comanche's face, then, with a harsh cry, he sprang forward.

The other man was younger, swifter, and he quickly ducked out of the way. Spinning around, the Comanche lunged forward, his own war club lifted high. Elk Chaser was ready for him and they came together, clubs swinging.

Elk Chaser grunted as his foot slipped on a sprinkling of pine needles and he went down on one knee. Hands locked on the ends of his war club, he held it over his head to ward off the Comanche's attack.

A long, ululating cry filled the air as Cheis and Diyehii ran forward to help Elk Chaser. With the ease of long practice, Diyehii put arrow to bowstring and let it fly. The arrow caught the Comanche in the chest, driving him backward, until he was lost in the smoke.

Elk Chaser gained his feet, then peered into the distance. The fire was at the trees now. There was no chance of riding through it, no hope of finding Otter, or the girl he had come to rescue.

He was lamenting the fact that he would have to tell White Robe that her oldest son was truly lost to her this time, when he heard the sound of horses approaching.

Fearing the Comanches had found them, he motioned for Diyehii and Cheis to take cover.

Like shadows hiding from the sun, the three warriors ducked into the underbrush just as a pair of horses burst into view through the heavy smoke.

Elk Chaser sprang from cover, frantically waving his arms as he recognized White Robe's son. "Otter," he called. "Over here!"

Surprised to see the man, Mitch jerked hard on the reins to keep from running him down.

"I see you found the woman," Elk Chaser said.

Mitch nodded. He had intercepted Alisha in her wild flight from the Comanche. There'd been no time for more than a quick kiss, but he'd seen the love in her eyes, the trust when she followed his lead without question. "Mount up and ride like hell," he said as he spurred his horse forward. "They're right behind us!"

Elk Chaser, Cheis, and Diyehii quickly mounted their horses and took off after Mitch and the woman. Elk Chaser heard the war cries of the Comanche, noted the change in their voices as they came upon the body of their fallen comrade.

Elk Chaser urged his horse forward, away from the Comanche, away from the flames. Foxes and deer, rabbits and quail fled before him, seeking refuge from the approaching inferno.

It wasn't a wide stretch of woods and before long, they cleared the trees into the prairie beyond. Mitch had counted on the trees slowing the fire, giving them time to escape to the clearing on the other side. He looked back once to make sure Elk Chaser and the other two warriors were behind him, and then he rode for the foothills until they came to a draw that wound through a stretch of hard, rocky ground which would make tracking them difficult. Right now, his only concern was getting Alisha to safety.

Elk Chaser slowed his horse, looking back. Cheis and Diyehii were coming up fast behind him, and behind them, the Comanches.

"Let us hold them here," Elk Chaser said, thinking to give White Robe's son and the woman time to get away.

"*Ai!*" Cheis agreed.

Elk Chaser was reaching for his bow when the arrow found him. He doubled over, his breath leaving his body in a harsh gasp of pain, as the slender shaft buried itself in his back. His horse bucked and squealed as an arrow pierced its hindquarters.

"You go ahead, with your son," Diyehii called. "Cheis and I will try to hold them off."

"No," Elk Chaser said, biting off each word as he fought against the pain in his back. "I will stay and fight."

"Go!" Cheis yelled. "You are wounded. You cannot fight!"

Elk Chaser knew Cheis was right. He could feel himself weakening; it was an effort to stay in the saddle. He would be of little help now; if his friends were worried over his safety, they might not give their full attention to the battle at hand. The draw was narrow. With luck, Diyehii and Cheis would be able to pick off the Comanches one by one.

Clutching the saddle horn with one hand, Elk Chaser urged his horse after Otter.

Mitch slowed his horse to a trot, then reined the animal to a halt. Moments later, Alisha rode up beside him. "Are you all right?" His gaze moved over her. "They didn't . . ."

"No."

Dismounting, Mitch lifted her from the saddle and drew her into his arms. "Damn, I've been worried sick."

"I missed you." She ran her hands over his face, down his arms, as if to assure herself he was really there. "I was so afraid I'd never see you again."

He grinned at her, relieved beyond words that she was all right. "You're my woman," he said, dropping a kiss on her nose. "You should have known I'd come after you."

"How did you know where to look?"

"We found Clements. He told us."

"He's alive?" Surprise and hope brightened her face. She had grown quite fond of the man.

"He was, last I saw him."

"Thank the Lord. I was sure he was dead."

Mitch hugged her tight. "We'd better go. I just wish I knew where the hell we are."

"You don't know?"

He shook his head ruefully. "I've never been in this part of the country before. Near as I can tell, that's north. The rancheria should be that way. Right now, we need to find a place to hide, and right quick."

At the sound of hoofbeats, Alisha glanced over her shoulder, gasped when she saw an Indian riding toward them. She released a sigh of relief when she recognized him as the Indian Mitch had spoken to earlier.

Mitch started to ask Elk Chaser where the other two warriors were when Elk Chaser slumped forward and Mitch saw the arrow protruding from his back.

Mitch swore under his breath. As he handed the bay's reins to Alisha, then hurried to Elk Chaser's side. Reaching up, he placed his hand over the warrior's heart, relieved to feel the faint rise and fall of the man's chest.

"Is he dead?" Alisha asked.

"No." Mitch glanced around as he heard gunshots from the far end of the draw. Damn! Apparently at least one of the Comanches had a rifle. "We've got to get out of here. Come on."

Walking beside Elk Chaser's wounded horse to make sure the warrior didn't slip off the animal's back, Mitch headed down the draw. As they reached the end of the draw, the sandy bottom gradually turned to hard, rocky ground that wouldn't hold a print. And then, like the answer to a prayer, he spied what looked like a cave cut into the side of a low hill.

"Wait here." Handing the reins to Alisha, he scrambled up the rocky hillside to check it out.

Chapter 19

The cave was long and narrow and just high enough to allow the horses inside. Mitch lifted Elk Chaser from the back of his horse and lowered him gently to the ground.

Turning, he lifted Alisha from Sophie's back, then led all three horses toward the rear of the cave.

"Is he going to be all right?" Alisha asked. She took off her hat and tossed it aside, then ran a hand through her hair.

"I don't know. He's unconscious." Which was probably a blessing, Mitch thought, all things considered.

"What do you think happened to the others?"

Mitch hesitated, wondering if she wanted the truth.

"They're dead, aren't they?"

"I'd say that's a good guess."

"What if they find us, the Comanche?" She glanced toward the entrance, her fingers restlessly worrying a pleat in her skirt.

"Let's not worry about that now. Why don't you take a look in Elk Chaser's war bag and see what he's got in there?" he suggested in hopes of taking her mind off the danger they were in.

Alisha nodded. "All right."

Mitch knelt beside Elk Chaser. The warrior was unconscious, his breathing slow and shallow. A fine sheen of sweat coated his brow. Drawing his knife, Mitch slit Elk Chaser's shirt up the back, exposing the wound.

The arrow was solidly embedded in the warrior's back. Had it been a little more to the left, had it penetrated a little deeper, it would have pierced his heart.

Mitch swore softly, wondering whether he should try to remove the shaft. There was little bleeding now, but all that would change as soon as he started digging the arrowhead out.

He looked up as Alisha knelt across from him. "Find anything we can use?"

"Some jerky, and a flint." She pointed at the small buckskin bag dangling from a thong around Elk Chaser's neck. "What's that?"

"His medicine bag."

She looked at him, a question in her eyes.

"It contains his personal medicine."

"What kind of medicine? Is he sick? I don't understand."

"It's not that kind of medicine. It holds objects that represent his power." Mitch thought a minute. "Sort of like a Catholic wearing a cross, or someone carrying a rabbit's foot."

"Good luck charms, you mean?"

Mitch nodded. "I guess you could call it that." He slipped the thong over Elk Chaser's neck. Every Apache always carried a bit of hoddentin with him, and Elk Chaser was no exception. There was a small pouch of it inside the bag, together with a piece of turquoise and a blue feather.

Mitch put the hoddentin sack to one side, and closed the medicine bag. Hoddentin was a kind of powder made from tule. His mother had told him that hoddentin was made by the shaman and was believed to possess powerful medicine. A pinch of it was thrown toward the sun at planting time to insure a bountiful harvest, or as an offering when a war party set out. It was sprinkled on the bodies of the deceased. It was eaten by the sick, and said to restore the strength to one who was exhausted.

Perhaps it would staunch the bleeding if they removed the arrow from Elk Chaser's back.

He looked up at Alisha. "You know anything about doctoring?"

"Not really." She glanced at the arrow protruding from Elk Chaser's back. The sight of it made her stomach roil. "That should probably come out."

"Yeah."

There was no point in putting it off any longer. The arrow had to come out; infection was sure to set in otherwise.

"What are you going to use for bandages?" she asked.

"I was thinking about your petticoat."

Alisha nodded. While he ducked outside to gather some brush for a fire, she removed her petticoat, wishing, for the first time on this godforsaken trip that she had worn more than one. After tearing off the ruffle, she tore the rest into strips.

Ten minutes later, they were ready. Mitch withdrew a long-bladed knife from the sheath on his belt and held it over the fire he'd built near the rear of the cave.

"You aren't going to cut the arrow out with that, are you?" Alisha asked, shuddering.

"It's all I've got."

She glanced at the knife sheathed on Elk Chaser's belt, and sighed. It appeared to be of a similar size.

Neither of them spoke as they waited for the blade to cool.

"All right," Mitch said. "You sit by his head and try to keep him still while I cut."

Alisha took a deep breath, then knelt beside Elk Chaser's head.

"This might be a good time to say a prayer," Mitch remarked as he straddled Elk Chaser's legs.

A low moan rose in Elk Chaser's throat and he began to thrash about.

"Hold him!" Mitch exclaimed, and she put her hands on Elk Chaser's shoulders, using her weight to hold him down. He didn't blame her for looking away. It wasn't a pretty sight. He swore when his knife slid into healthy flesh.

"What's wrong?" She looked at him, then at the bleeding wound.

"Damn knife slipped," he muttered. He wiped his palms against his pant leg, took a deep calming breath.

She nodded, then closed her eyes as she turned back to the task at hand.

After what seemed like hours, but was probably no more than twenty minutes, the arrow was out.

Mitch soaked up the blood with the ruffle off her petticoat. When the bleeding had slowed, he packed the wound with hoddentin, then cut a length of petticoat, folded it into a thick square and placed it over the wound. A long piece of Alisha's petticoat held it in place.

Mitch sat back, wiping the sweat from his brow. "Well, I've done all I can. The rest is up to him."

"What do we do now?"

It was a good question, Mitch thought. He only wished he had a good answer. Elk Chaser's horse couldn't travel, so if they decided to make a run for it, one horse would have to carry double, which would slow them down. Even if Elk Chaser's horse was sound, they'd have to travel slow with frequent stops. Still, all other concerns aside, Mitch was afraid that moving Elk Chaser now would kill him.

"Shouldn't we do something for his horse?"

Rising, he went to look at Elk Chaser's horse. The horse snorted and shook his head at his approach.

"Easy, fella," Mitch said. "I just wanna have a look."

"Is he going to be all right?"

"Come here, Lisha." His childhood name for her came easily to his lips, reminding him of warm, care-free days by the river.

She came to stand beside him. "What are you going to do?"

"I'm gonna cut a few inches off the shaft to ease some of the strain. I'm afraid he might scrape it against the wall and drive it in deeper."

"Why don't you take it out?"

Mitch glanced around the cave. "Not in here. It's too dangerous. I don't want you getting kicked, or run the risk of Elk Chaser getting stomped by a bronc loco with pain. Here." He handed her the horse's reins. "Stand beside his shoulder. You won't get kicked there. And keep a tight hold on him. He isn't gonna like this. Easy fella," he said, moving up alongside the horse. "Easy now."

Taking hold of the shaft, Mitch broke it in two, so that only a few inches protruded from the horse's rump.

The horse squealed and lashed out with its hind legs. Mitch grabbed hold of the bridle. "Hey, now, quit that." He looked at Alisha over the horse's back. "Get Elk Chaser's medicine bag and sprinkle some of that hoddentin around the arrow, will you?"

With a nod, she did as he asked. "What are we going to do about getting out of here?"

"I don't know." Mitch patted the horse on the shoulder, then walked to the cave's entrance and peered through a narrow crack in the brush he had used to camouflage the cave. All seemed quiet, and then, in the distance, he saw a rider quartering the ground. So, the Comanches were looking for them. "We sure enough need help, but we aren't likely to find any out here."

"Then you've got to go and find some."

She had followed him to the mouth of the cave, and now he glanced at her over his shoulder. "And leave you here alone? Not a chance." He didn't think he'd ever let her out of his sight again.

"What else can we do? Elk Chaser's horse is wounded, but even if it wasn't, Elk Chaser's in no condition to travel anyway."

"I'm not leaving you here alone."

"We can't leave him here alone, either. And I'd only slow you down. You'll be able to travel much faster alone, won't you?"

He nodded in reluctant agreement.

"I think you should go for help."

"Dammit, Lisha, I'm not gonna ride off and leave you here alone."

"I'll be all right." She put on a brave smile. "I'm not afraid."

He didn't like the idea of leaving her, but she was

right. If he rode straight through, he could reach the rancheria early tomorrow morning and be back the following night. She had enough food and water to last until then. If the worst happened and the Comanches found the cave, they weren't likely to kill her. He glanced at Elk Chaser. The Comanches would kill the old warrior for sure, but it was a risk Mitch would have to take. They couldn't just sit here, doing nothing.

"You know I'm right," Alisha said. "Don't you?"

He grunted slowly as he drew her away from the cave's entrance. "When were you ever wrong?"

"I was wrong to let you go," she whispered.

"I was wrong to leave you."

"Mitch, I missed you so much. You'll never know how much."

"I know." He drew her into his arms. "Don't you think I missed you, too? There wasn't a day I didn't think about you. Dammit, I wanted to come back and make you love me."

"I wish you had."

"So do I. When this is over, I'm not letting you out of my sight again."

"I'll hold you to that, don't think I won't."

"Dammit, Alisha, I don't want to leave you here."

She didn't want it, either, but it was the only way, and they both knew it. "We'll be fine." She ran her hand over his cheek, feeling the faint scrape of bristles against her fingertips. "Hurry back to me."

"You know I will." He held her tighter, loving the way she felt in his arms, the way her body molded so perfectly to his. "If they find you, do whatever they say, understand? Don't make them angry. Don't give them any cause to kill you. Just wait for me. I'll come for you, I promise."

She looked up at him, her eyes filled with love and trust. "I know."

"There's some food in my saddlebags. Not much, just jerky and ashcakes."

"Ashcakes?" She grimaced. "It's not what it sounds like, is it?"

"No. They're made of ground mesquite beans, tallow, and honey. There's enough food and water to last the two of you a couple of days."

"We'll be fine," she said, and her voice hardly quivered at all.

"Lisha." How was he going to leave her? It seemed cowardly, somehow, to ride off and leave her behind, and yet he knew it was their only hope. Damn. If anything happened to her, he'd never be able to live with himself.

"I love you, Mitch," she said fervently. "I've always loved you."

He swore a short, pithy oath, and then he kissed her. And everything else ceased to exist. The years fell away and nothing in the world mattered except the fact that she was back in his arms, where she belonged. She clung to him, her body trembling, her lips warm under his.

"I won't fail you, Lisha," he said solemnly.

She nodded, and he knew she was making a valiant effort not to cry.

"Here." He opened his saddlebags and pulled out his extra Colt. "Keep this handy, just in case."

She grimaced as she took it. "It's heavy."

He looked at her for a long moment, then went to

the cave's entrance and peered out. All was clear, for the moment.

He checked the cinch on his saddle, made sure the rifle was in the boot, then picked up the reins. If he was going, he'd best do it now before he changed his mind.

He turned to tell her good-bye, and she was there, at his side. He gazed into her eyes, praying that he was doing the right thing. He kissed her one more time, for luck, and then led his horse out of the cave.

Outside, he rearranged the scrub brush over the opening until he was satisfied that the Comanche couldn't find the entrance, and then he swung into the saddle and headed north.

Chapter 20

Alisha watched Mitch leave the cave, and all her vaunted courage went with him. But then, he had always been her strength. She clutched his pistol to her breast, her mind flooding with memories of Mitch . . . Mitchy holding her, comforting her, fighting her battles, teaching her to swim, to hunt. Mitch, kissing her hurts, drying her tears, making her laugh. Mitchy . . . she couldn't think of her past without thinking of him. He was an integral part of every memory, good and bad.

Mitch . . .

"Hurry," she whispered. "Please hurry."

A low moan caught her attention and she glanced over her shoulder to see Elk Chaser.

"Fire . . ." he muttered.

"What?"

"Fire . . . put it . . . out."

"Why?"

He drew in a deep breath. "Comanche . . . smell . . . smoke."

"Oh!" Hurrying to the rear of the cave, she threw handfuls of dirt on the flames, shuddered as the cave went dark save for the tiny slivers of light that infiltrated the brush that covered the cave's entrance.

She stared at Elk Chaser, now just a dark shape lying on the floor of the cave.

"No, don't!" She scooted toward him and placed a restraining hand on his shoulder. "Don't move. You're badly hurt."

"Where is . . . Otter?"

"Otter?" She frowned a moment. "You mean Mitch? He went for help."

"Water . . ."

His voice sounded weak and raspy and she wondered what she would do if he died. The thought of being alone in the dark with a dead body sent a cold chill down her spine. Uncapping Mitch's canteen, she held it for Elk Chaser while he drank and drank.

When he finished, his head lolled forward. She capped the canteen and put it aside, then quickly checked his pulse, praying that he hadn't died.

She breathed a sigh of relief as she felt the faint pulse in his wrist.

Needing something to do, she went to where the horses stood head to tail near one wall of the cave.

"Hi, Sophie." She scratched the mare's ears, wondering how she was going to care for the horses while Mitch was gone. She couldn't take them outside. "Bet you'd like to get rid of that saddle, wouldn't you girl?"

Fumbling with the cinch, she finally managed to get it undone. She hadn't expected the saddle to be so heavy. Reeling under the weight, she dropped it on the ground.

Elk Chaser's horse snorted softly as she approached him. "It's okay," she murmured. "I'm not going to hurt you."

She held out her hand and the horse sniffed her palm and then, to her surprise, he licked her. His tongue was warm and wet.

"I'll bet you're thirsty, too, aren't you? But I don't have anything to . . ." She patted the horse's neck. "Wait a minute."

Going to the cave's entrance, she picked up her hat and filled it with water. "Only a little," she said, as the horse began to drink. "I don't know how long it's going to have to last."

Mitch leaned low over his mount's neck, urging the horse to go faster, faster, please, just a little faster.

He thought about Alisha, sitting in the cave with night coming on. For all her bravado, he knew she was frightened. She had always been a little afraid of the dark. Of course, she might have outgrown that by now. She had blossomed into a beautiful young woman, and he felt a sharp pang at the years that had been lost to them. No more, he vowed, no more. He had found her again, and he would never let her go.

He knew a moment of relief as he saw a familiar landmark in the distance. And then, from the corner of his eye, he saw a rider coming up fast. He cursed softly. It was one of the Comanches.

The Indian rode as if he was part of the horse. Legs gripping his mount, the warrior drew an arrow from the quiver slung over his back, sighted down the shaft, and let it fly.

Mitch swore as the arrow found its target. His horse stumbled and went down, the shaft protruding from its neck a few inches above the shoulder. Mitch rolled free and gained his feet as the warrior rode toward him. Before the Comanche could fit another arrow to

his bow, Mitch pulled his gun and fired, and the warrior toppled over his horse's rump, dead before he hit
the ground.

The horse, a stocky calico gelding, had been well
trained. It snorted and sidestepped a few feet to the
side, but stayed near its rider.

Holstering his weapon, Mitch walked slowly toward the horse. "Easy, now," he murmured. "Easy,
fella."

The horse backed up a step, foxlike ears twitching
back and forth.

"Easy, now," Mitch murmured, trying to keep the
anxiety out of his voice, afraid he'd spook the horse
and send it running for home. "Easy, fella." Moving
slowly and carefully, he reached for the reins.

He led the Indian pony back to where his own horse
lay thrashing on the ground. Drawing his weapon,
Mitch put the animal out of its misery, then swung
aboard the Indian pony and headed north.

Alisha stood near the entrance of the cave, peering
through a narrow opening in the brush. In the distance, she could see a pair of Indians quartering back
and forth. At first, she thought they were the two
Apache warriors who had been with Elk Chaser. She
had almost called out to them but something had
warned her to keep still, and when two other riders
joined them, she knew they were Comanches, and
they were looking for her.

Elk Chaser moaned softly and she hurried to his
side and placed her hand over his mouth. "Be quiet,"
she whispered, and he nodded.

Never had time passed so slowly. Gradually, the inside of the cave grew darker until she couldn't see her hand in front of her face.

She gave Elk Chaser a drink, then offered him a piece of jerky, but he pushed it away.

When he slept again, she went to stand by Sophie, comforted somewhat by the horse's warmth.

"He'll come back," she said. "I know he'll come back as soon as he can." She blinked rapidly, fighting the urge to cry. "Hurry, Mitch. Please, hurry."

He hovered between life and death, and he knew it. His body felt heavy, racked with pain. It hurt to breathe, and he was thirsty, so thirsty.

It would be easy to surrender and let death win. His spirit was ready to go, ready to escape its house of pain and follow the path to the Afterworld.

No sooner had this thought crossed his mind, than he felt his spirit leave his body and he found himself standing in front of a cave. A mulberry tree grew near the cave and a guard stood beside it. The guard made no move to stop him, and he went into the cave. It was large, without much light, but he walked forward until he fell down a narrow passage. Down, down, he fell, and the passage grew wider and lighter, until it was like daylight, although there was no sun. The passage grew wide, then narrower and then ended in a narrow path. Two huge snakes were coiled here. They hissed at his approach, but he showed no fear, and they let him pass. Further on, he came to two grizzly bears, but, like the snakes, they let him pass by because he showed no fear. He followed the narrow passage and came upon two mountain lions crouched in the path, but he spoke to them, and they turned aside and let him pass by. And then, as the trail widened again, he came to a forest and beyond the forest there was a wide green valley. He stood on a ridge and gazed down into the valley. There were many lodges and horses and buffalo. A lake shimmered like blue glass in a field of green, spring grass. He saw people he knew, and they all looked happy and well fed. Joy swelled within him at the thought of joining those he knew and loved, but when he went to join them, he could not.

And then a man dressed in white buckskins materialized before him, and called him by name.

"You must go back," the warrior said. "We are not ready for you."

"No." Elk Chaser looked out over the valley, and saw his mother and his father and his younger sister who had died of the white man's coughing sickness when she was only nine summers. And he saw Blue Willow, who had been killed by the Blue Coats three months after he took her for his wife.

"If you stay," the warrior said, "one who now lives will die."

He looked at the valley, at the horses and clear streams, at his family and friends, and everything within him yearned for the peace and plenty spread before him.

He took a step forward, one arm outstretched. . . .

And then the vision was gone, and he was back in his body, burning with fever.

Alisha held the canteen to Elk Chaser's mouth. For a moment, she had been certain he was dead. He drank greedily, then drifted off again. Taking a scrap of petticoat, she soaked it with water, then laid it across his brow.

Soaking another scrap, she began to sponge his arms

and legs and chest, praying all the while that he would
live, that Mitch would soon return. She mourned her
father, and grieved for the son she had never seen, for
the years of his life that she had missed, and always, in
the back of her mind, she prayed for Mitch, that he
would make it safely back to the Apache, that he
would return before it was too late, before Elk Chaser
died, before the Comanches found the cave.

She fell asleep with his name, like a prayer, on her
lips.

Chapter 21

Mitch slowed his lathered horse. At any other time he would have felt guilty for pushing the animal so hard, but not now. The horse's well-being paled in comparison to saving Alisha's life.

He waved to the two warriors standing guard at the entrance of the rancheria as he urged his weary mount down the narrow trail that led to the valley.

Heads turned as he rode toward his mother's lodge. Several of the men pointed at his horse as he rode by, apparently recognizing the war markings painted on the horse as Comanche. Several warriors followed in his wake. When he dismounted, the men gathered around.

"Where is the husband of White Robe and the men who rode with him?" a warrior known as Fights the Wind asked belligerently. He stood before Mitch, his dislike for White Robe's son evident in his voice and his eyes.

"We were attacked by Comanches," Mitch said. "My mother's husband was badly wounded. I don't know about the other two."

White Robe stepped out of her lodge, her smile of welcome fading when she saw that Mitch was alone.

Mitch handed his horse's reins to a young boy who was passing by. "Cool him out for me, will you?"

The boy looked up at Mitch, obviously not understanding his words. White Robe repeated them in Apache, and the boy took the reins and began walking the horse back and forth.

She watched the boy a moment and Mitch knew she was gathering her courage. She took a deep breath, then turned to face him. "Where is my husband?"

As gently as possible, Mitch told his mother how he had found the Comanches who had attacked Red Clements and taken Alisha, and all that had happened afterward.

"You must take me to my husband immediately," White Robe said, and turned to enter the lodge.

"No," Mitch placed a restraining hand on his mother's arm. "There may still be Comanches in the area. I will not put you in danger." He glanced at the men who had gathered around. "*Shi ma*, ask the warriors if they will go back with me." He could have tried to ask them himself, but his Apache was not yet fluent enough for speech-making, and there was no time to waste.

White Robe repeated Mitch's question in Apache for the benefit of those who didn't understand English.

Fights the Wind understood all too well. He stepped forward. "We will not follow you, white man!" he declared in English. "Two of our best men may be dead because of your foolishness, and our brother is badly wounded. Perhaps, he, too, has gone to join his ancestors."

Several of the men nearby nodded in agreement.

"The white woman is nothing to us," Fights the Wind went on, emboldened by the support of those around him. "If you wish to risk your life by going back for your woman, so be it. But we will not go with you. We will not follow a white man."

Mitch swore softly, angered by Fights the Wind's harsh words. Still, he could not blame the man for feeling as he did. Mitch had only been in the village a few weeks. He was not a warrior. He was not a proven leader. Still, he had expected more support.

White Robe marched into the center of the crowd. "I do not believe what I am hearing!" she exclaimed. "My husband is in need of help, and you . . ." she gestured at the warriors gathered nearby, "you who call yourself men would turn your back on him because he went to help my son? My son is Apache. He is my seed. His woman was captured by our enemies, and he went to her aid. Would any of you do less? Would any of you refuse to help a brother in need? I am ashamed of all of you this day. You are not men! You are not warriors! You are scared children." She held out her hand. "You, Yellow Raven, give me a weapon. I will go with my son."

Yellow Raven took a step backward, and White Robe lowered her arm.

Red Clements poked his head out of the wickiup. "Hell," he said as he stepped outside. "I'll side ya iffen these men ain't got the stomach fer it."

White Robe looked around, her scorn-filled gaze resting briefly on the face of each of the warriors. "It is a sad day for our people when only a woman and a wounded white man are willing to ride to the aid of one who is in need."

A tall warrior known as Spirit Walking stepped forward. "I will go."

Another man reluctantly joined the first. "I will go."

"And I."

"I, too, will go," said a fourth. He gestured at Mitch. "But I will not follow this man. He is not a war leader." The warrior's gaze rested on Spirit Walking. "Spirit Walking has proven himself in battle. I will follow him."

Nods and murmurs of assent rippled through the crowd.

Mitch felt a surge of hope. He didn't care who led the damned party as long as they got going, and soon. He was acutely aware of every passing moment, afraid that he would get back to Alisha too late, that the Comanches would have found her, killed her and Elk Chaser both. He had an image of riding back and finding Alisha lying dead in the cave, her body cold and lifeless.

White Robe smiled as she went to stand beside Mitch. "I will prepare food for your journey."

"Hurry!" He was overcome by a sense of urgency, a horrible fear that he might already be too late. He never should have left her, would never be able to live with the guilt if anything happened to her.

"You will need a fresh mount," White Robe remarked.

"I'd appreciate the loan of a horse myself," Clements said.

"Forget it," Mitch said. "You can hardly walk."

"Maybe so, but we ain't walkin'." He held up a hand, silencing any further argument from Mitch. "I can ride and I can shoot, and I got me a score to settle with them damn Comanch, ya know."

"Yeah," Mitch said. "I reckon you do, at that."

White Robe smiled at Clements. "I shall be pleased to lend you a horse," she said. Turning, she called Rides the Buffalo to her. "Go quickly and catch up two of your father's best horses."

With a nod, Rides the Buffalo ran off toward the horse herd.

The warriors who had agreed to go with Mitch hurried off to their lodges to gather their belongings and collect their horses and weapons.

In less than an hour, they were ready, eleven warriors, mostly young men eager for battle, one wounded, old trader, and Mitch.

"Safe journey, my son," White Robe said as Mitch swung onto the back of a long-legged calico stallion. "And to you, too," she said, smiling at Clements.

"Thank you, ma'am," Red said. Gritting his teeth, he hauled himself onto the back of a sturdy buckskin gelding and rode toward the warriors.

"I'll bring Elk Chaser home, *shi ma*," Mitch said. "I promise."

White Robe drew Rides the Buffalo to her side. "I know you will."

"Don't worry," Mitch said. He gave her a smile and a wink, then went to join the other warriors, who were riding for the trail out of the stronghold.

Mitch was surprised to see Fights the Wind in the group. He wondered briefly if the surly warrior was there to help, or to put an arrow in his back when no one was looking. He knew the man only by name, yet there was no mistaking the warrior's animosity. His eyes burned with hatred and distrust.

They rode out of the valley single file, quiet as the

hot wind blowing over the face of the desert. Thirteen men. Mitch hoped it wasn't a bad omen.

Alisha wrapped her arms around her knees and stared toward the entrance of the cave. She had lost track of the time. Funny how the hours seemed to race by when you were having a good time, and how slowly the minutes crawled by when you were lonely and scared or enduring something painful.

She glanced over at Elk Chaser. He seemed to be resting comfortably. She had sponged him with cold water several times, made sure he had plenty to drink, kept him covered so he didn't catch a chill.

Afraid to think of what the future might hold, of what might happen if Mitch didn't make it back, she closed her eyes, searching her mind for a pleasant memory. She smiled as the present slipped away, swallowed up in the rosy golden glow of the past, of the first time Mitch had made love to her. . . .

She ran through the foliage that grew alongside the river, a wide smile curving her lips. She didn't dare turn around.

"Go on, run!" Mitch called. "But it won't do you any good!"

She didn't answer, just kept running, her heart pounding.

"Push me in the river, will you?" he growled.

She laughed, remembering the surprised look on his face, his arms windmilling as he tried to keep his balance, the huge splash as he hit the water.

She had laughed as he slowly gained his feet, then shrieked as he lunged toward her, only to slip and fall again.

"You'll be sorry when I catch you!" he hollered, and she had turned and bolted for the woods.

She knew she couldn't outrun him, knew he would catch her. And suddenly what had started out as a joke turned ominous somehow, and it was no longer a game. He would catch her!

Fear added wings to her feet and she flew over the ground, afraid without knowing why. But she was no match for him, could never hope to outrun him.

She shrieked as his hand closed over her shoulder, halting her wild flight. She struggled and lost her balance and they both fell, rolling over and over in the soft, springy grass. And then he was lying on top of her, his hands pinning her shoulders to the ground, his chest heaving, his dark eyes hot as he stared down at her.

She looked up at him, breathless. Afraid, without knowing why.

Long moments stretched between them. Drops of water fell from his wet hair and bare chest and dripped onto her cheeks and breasts. Her skirts grew damp where he straddled her legs. She was aware of the strength of his hands on her shoulders. He held her lightly, yet she was powerless to escape.

"I'm sorry," she whispered.

He shook his head. "Don't ever be sorry with me, Lisha," he said quietly.

And he lowered his head and kissed her.

He had kissed her before, but never like this. Perhaps it was the thrill of the chase and the fact that he had caught her. Whatever it was, this kiss was like no other, filled with a different kind of passion than ever before. Without taking his mouth from hers, he slid to the ground beside her, his arms wrapping around her, molding her body to his.

He was hungry for her, dying for her, couldn't get enough of her. His mouth was warm yet firm, and she opened for him willingly, not fully realizing how it affected him until she felt the tremor in his arms, heard the sudden change in his breathing. His tongue caressed her lower lip, then slipped into her mouth. A flame of desire sprang to life deep in the core of her being. His tongue was hot and slick, and she pressed herself against him, her whole body tingling with desire, aching for more, so much more.

"Lisha . . ." His voice was rough, yet tender. "Lisha, do you know what you're doing to me?" Swearing softly, he rolled away from her and sat up.

She stared at his back a moment, then sat up, wanting to touch him, wanting him to kiss her again. "Tell me," she whispered, but she did know. They had spent many an hour in each other's arms, but he had never done more than kiss her. She knew he wanted her as a man wanted a woman, but he had always held himself in check, and she knew it was because he loved her, because he didn't want to hurt her. It had only made her love him more.

He groaned low in his throat. "You must know how I feel." He swore again. "I want you so damn bad, it hurts. Hurts like you can't believe."

She stared up at him. "It hurts?"

"You have no idea."

"I don't want you to hurt, Mitchy," she whispered.

Turning, he pressed his forehead against hers, his whole body trembling, and in that moment she loved him more than ever before, loved him desperately, completely.

"Mitch."

He drew back and looked into her eyes.

"I love you." It was the first time she had said it aloud.

"Lisha . . ."

He kissed her then, ever so tenderly, ever so gently.

"I hurt, too," she said. "Can you make it go away?"

"I can," he said, his voice ragged. "I want to. But I'm afraid you'll hate me for it after."

"Why would I hate you?"

He laughed softly. "Because you're a good girl, Alisha Faraday. And you deserve someone a hell of a lot better than I am."

"No." She cupped his cheek in the palm of her hand. "I could never hate you. Never . . ." Her hand slid down his neck, along his shoulder, over the rigid muscle in his arm. He sucked in a breath as her fingers drifted over his chest, slowly, slowly, moving down, down, to cover that part of him that made him a man.

He groaned and caught her to him, crushing her against him as his mouth covered hers. Slowly, he lowered her to the ground, his body covering hers, his heat flowing into her, filling her, arousing her, until she writhed beneath him, filled with an urgency that was frightening and exciting.

His breath fanned her cheek, hot as the passion rising between them. She slid her hands across his chest, reveling in the touch of his bare skin beneath her hands. She gasped when she felt his hands on her breasts and he smiled down at her, his dark eyes hot and filled with love.

"Fair's fair," he said.

She couldn't speak, couldn't think, as his hands moved over her, teaching her what pleasure was, arousing her until she thought she might die of it. He kissed her out of her clothing, then shed his trousers, and she knew she had never seen anything more beautiful in her whole life than Mitch lying beside her. His hands were big and brown against her pale skin, magical hands that worshipped and adored her and made her feel beautiful, desirable.

He rose over her, his long black hair brushing the tops of her breasts, and she saw her own uncertainty and fear mirrored in the smoky depths of his eyes. "Lisha . . ."

He was giving her a chance to change her mind, but there was no going back, not now. She wanted him desperately, knew she would wither and die without him, and she wrapped her arms around his neck and drew him to her, and with that kiss of surrender, there was no turning back. . . .

The cry of a wolf startled her out of her reverie and she realized she was crying, crying for the beauty of the love they had shared, for the years they had lost, for a magical time that could never be recaptured. She cried for her mother, who had died too soon, and for her father, and for the child she had never seen, cried for the boy Mitch had been and the man he had become, cried all the tears she had held inside.

"Woman?"

She dashed the tears from her eyes at the sound of Elk Chaser's voice. "Yes, I'm here." Gaining her feet, she went to kneel beside him. "Do you need something?"

"No one should grieve alone," he said, and reaching up, he took her hand in his. "Do not be afraid. He will come back."

She couldn't see his face in the darkness of the cave, but the assurance in his voice soothed her fears, chased away her regrets.

With a sigh, she rested her back against the wall of the cave and then, her hand still in his, she closed her eyes and slept.

Chapter 22

Mitch had always heard the Apache were the best horsemen in the whole Southwest. He'd been told by an old mountain man that a white man would ride a horse until it dropped, and then an Apache would come along, get on the same horse and ride it another ten miles.

Now, he believed it. Hard as the ride was, Red Clements never complained. The old man was made of wang leather and iron, Mitch mused.

He had thought he made good time returning to the rancheria, but it was nothing compared to the pace set by the warriors on the ride back to the cave.

It was late morning the following day when they reached the area near the cave. Though all looked peaceful, a prickling along the back of his neck had Mitch feeling uneasy. Apparently sensing his apprehension, his mount turned skittish.

The warriors also picked up on it.

"It's too quiet," Fights the Wind remarked. He reined his horse to a halt and drew an arrow from the quiver slung over his back.

"*Ai*," Spirit Walking agreed.

Fights the Wind looked over his shoulder at Mitch. "Where is the cave?" he asked.

"Not far," Mitch said.

With a nod, Fights the Wind urged his horse forward. The warriors spread out behind him, riding single file.

Mitch and Red Clements brought up the rear.

They had only gone a few yards when a dozen Comanche warriors came boiling out of a fold in the ground, their war cries shattering the stillness.

The Comanche war cries were punctuated with the rising war cries of the Apache as Fights the Wind kicked his horse into a gallop. The other warriors chased after him.

Mitch and Red Clements hung back. There was a certain raw beauty in the fighting, Mitch thought as he watched the battle rage, a kind of barbaric symmetry as the warriors came together. Dust filled the air, punctuated with war cries and the sound of a club striking flesh. Mitch drew his Colt as a Comanche warrior came thundering toward him. The warrior plucked an arrow from the quiver slung over his back, nocked an arrow to the bowstring. He fired as the warrior drew back the bowstring, and the warrior toppled from the back of his horse.

Mitch looked over at Clements. "Let's go," he said. "The cave's that way."

"I'm right behind ya," Clements said.

Mitch urged his horse into a gallop, skirting the edge of the battle. The Indians could fight it out, he thought, his only concern now was for Alisha.

They were nearing the cave when they came upon two warriors grappling in the dirt, both struggling for possession of the knife between them. Mitch recognized Fights the Wind. The Apache had been badly wounded. Blood poured from a deep gash in his right shoulder, weakening him. He grunted as the Comanche jerked the knife from his hand. Knowing death was near, Fights the Wind stared up into his enemy's face, his expression defiant as he began to sing his death song.

A look of astonishment spread over Fights the Wind's face as blood suddenly spurted from the Comanche's chest and he toppled facedown in the dirt.

"Nice shot," Clements remarked.

"Thanks." Mitch slid from the back of his horse and knelt beside Fights the Wind. Removing his kerchief from his neck, he quickly wrapped it around the wound in the warrior's arm.

Fights the Wind looked away as Mitch tied off the ends of his kerchief. It was not the Apache way to offer thanks to any but the Great Spirit. To do so was considered weak. The only expression on the warrior's face was one of shame that a white man had saved his life.

"Red, look after him, will you?"

"Sure."

Swinging into the saddle, Mitch put his heels to his mount's flanks, his only thought to find Alisha.

"Please, God," he prayed. "Please let her be all right."

Chapter 23

Alisha stood up at the sound of hoofbeats. Snatching up the gun Mitch had left for her, she went to stand beside the entrance of the cave, the sound of her own heartbeat pounding loudly in her ears.

Please, she thought, please let it be Mitch.

She held her breath as the hoofbeats slowed. There was a moment of silence. The sound of footsteps.

"Alisha? It's me."

The brush was dragged away from the mouth of the cave and she hurled herself into his arms.

"I guess you missed me," he said wryly, and wrapped his arms around her.

He was here, at last. She held him tight, her face buried against his shoulder. Relief washed through her. It filled her heart, clogged her throat, and blurred her vision.

"Hey, don't cry," Mitch whispered. "Everything's all right."

She held him tighter, assuring herself that he was there, really there. She had thought of him day and night, reliving every day, every moment she could remember. And now he was here, holding her tight, and it was as if the five years they had been apart had never existed. She loved him, had always loved him. Nothing had changed that.

"How's Elk Chaser?" Mitch asked.

"I think he's better." She sniffed back her tears. "He sleeps a lot."

"Well, sleep's good for him," Mitch said.

He glanced toward the entrance of the cave as he heard the sound of riders approaching. Taking Alisha by the hand, he led her to the shadows in the back of the cave. Drawing his gun, he put her behind him, and waited.

"Hey, Mitch, you in there?"

"Yeah, Red."

Moments later, Clements entered the cave. Seeing Alisha, he removed his hat. "Howdy, little lady. Never thought I'd see you this side of the pearly gates."

Alisha smiled at him. "I'm glad to see you're all right, too."

"The fighting over?" Mitch asked.

"Over and done," Clements replied. "I always heard them 'Paches fought like the devil hisself. They kilt all the Comanch, only lost one warrior. 'Nother couple are wounded. Nothin' serious."

"Let's get out of here," Mitch said. "Lisha, pick up whatever you want to take along. Red, can you look after the horses? I'll take care of Elk Chaser."

Minutes later, they were outside. Mitch had suggested a travois for Elk Chaser, but the old warrior had insisted he could ride, and now he sat astride one of the Comanche ponies, his face an impassive mask.

The warriors had gathered around him, speaking in low tones. The dead Apache had been wrapped in a blanket and placed over the back of his mount. Red

Clements held the reins to Elk Chaser's wounded horse.

Mitch lifted Alisha onto Sophie's back. "Are you sure you're all right?" he asked.

Alisha nodded. "I'm fine."

His gaze moved over her. Her shirtwaist, once white, was a dingy gray. Her hair fell in a tangled mass over her shoulders and down her back, there were dark smudges under her eyes from lack of sleep. He had never seen a prettier sight in his whole life.

A short time later, they were riding back the way they had come.

Death hung heavy over the scene of the battlefield. The Comanche dead lay sprawled where they had fallen. Several vultures had gathered around the bodies. The birds looked up as the riders approached. One of the birds, heavily laden with entrails, flapped its great black wings and took to the air.

"Alisha, don't look," Mitch warned, but it was too late.

Her face went white as she choked back the bile in her throat.

He offered her a drink from the waterskin looped around his saddle horn, but she shook her head and looked away.

Mitch glanced at the battlefield. It was a grim sight, the scavenger birds fighting over the bodies, the stench of blood and death hovering in the air.

They made a wide berth around the field of carnage. The Apache abhorred death. As soon as they reached the rancheria, the dead warrior would be buried quickly in a remote cave or crevice of rocks, along with all his possessions. According to custom, his name would never be mentioned again. Those who assisted in the burial would purify themselves in sagebrush smoke.

But he could not think of death now. He reined his mount closer to Sophie, reached out and touched Alisha's arm.

She turned and their gazes met and held, and he knew that as soon as they reached the rancheria, they were going to have to have a long talk about their future.

They camped that night near a shallow stream sheltered within a stand of young trees. Elk Chaser immediately rolled into his blankets and went to sleep. A short time later, Red Clements sought his own bedroll.

Alisha sat close to Mitch, comforted by his nearness. She wasn't afraid of anything as long as he was there, beside her. As far back as she could remember, he had been her strength, her courage. He had dried her tears, made her laugh when she thought she would never laugh again, helped her learn to explore the woods in the dark, to see the world as he saw it.

What would he say when she told him that they had a son? A dozen times that night she had started to tell him, but somehow the time had never seemed right.

Earlier, she had taken Red Clements aside to ask him if he had seen any children in the village that looked like they might have white blood.

He had looked at her curiously, but, to his credit, he hadn't asked any questions. "Sorry," he'd said with a shrug of apology. "I didn't get a chance to look around much. But if he's there, I reckon you can find him."

If he's there. That was the big question. A lot could have happened in the last four years. His people could have moved to another village. She shied away from the possibility that her son might be dead. Life was always hardest on the very young and the very old.

"What is it, Lisha?" Mitch asked. "What's bothering you?"

"Nothing."

"Come on, I know you better than that. Something's troubling you. Whatever it is, you can tell me. You know that."

She blew out a sigh that seemed to come from the very depths of her soul. Maybe she should just get it over with and tell him now. What difference would it make? It was never going to get any easier.

She glanced at the Indians who were gathered around the fire, recounting the battle. "Can we go someplace where we can be alone?"

Mitch looked at her a moment, wondering at her request, and then nodded. "Sure, darlin'."

Mitch told one of the warriors that they were going for a walk. Then, taking Alisha by the hand, he led her into the shadows, away from the light of the fire.

Moonlight filtered through the slender oaks and willows that grew along the stream. A faint breeze teased the leaves of the trees; the water whispered secrets to the rocks as it tumbled and swirled along its way. Overhead, the stars came alive in the sky, winking at the moon.

Alisha walked beside Mitch, acutely aware of his hand holding hers. It felt so right to be with him. She had loved him more than half of her life. Her happiest times, and her saddest, had been shared with him. He had fathered her child. . . .

Her mind raced as she tried to find just the right words to tell him that he was a father.

Mitch gave a little tug on her hand, and she realized he had stopped walking.

"I don't think we should go any farther," he said.

He was right, of course. There was no telling what dangers lay ahead in the darkness.

Slowly, he drew her into his arms. His hold was light, giving her the opportunity to pull away.

"Lisha?"

She leaned into him, her answer in her upturned face.

His kiss was gentle, tinged with uncertainty, yet hot and eager, filled with years of unfulfilled desire.

Her hands slid up his back to lock around his neck as she pressed herself against him. Her body had no memory of the five years they had been apart. It molded to his as it always had, eagerly, willingly, female to male, perfectly matched and mated. She had been made for this man, and no other. She had believed it five years ago; she believed it now.

He slid his tongue over her lower lip, and heat exploded deep in the core of her being, spreading through her limbs like wildfire, leaving her breathless and limp and wanting more, so much more.

"Mitch . . ."

"I'm sorry." He let her go and drew back, his breathing as ragged as her own. "What's on your mind, darlin'?"

She took a deep breath and the words, held in for so long, came out in a rush. "We have a son."

He looked at her as though she were speaking a foreign language. "What?"

She hadn't meant to blurt it out like that, but the words had been said and there was no way to call them back. "A son, Mitch. We have a son."

"Where is he? Why the hell didn't you ever tell me this before?"

"I didn't know."

A low sound of disbelief rose in his throat.

"It's true. I mean, I knew I had a baby, but my father told me it was stillborn. I never saw him, the baby. Never. All these years I thought he was dead, and then, just before my father passed away, he told me he had lied, that the baby was still alive."

Mitch shook his head. "You had a baby and you never told me?"

"I thought you'd left me, that you didn't want me. I thought . . ."

"Go on," he said brusquely. "What did you think?"

She clasped her hands tightly. "I thought you had lied to me about loving me. You never wrote. You never came back." She looked up at him, eyes wide with defiance. "Why didn't you come back?"

"Because I thought you were married to Smithfield! I told you that."

"Let's not argue, Mitch, please."

He swore a vile oath. It was a good thing her old man was already dead, he thought bitterly, because right now he could easily kill the man with his bare hands.

He took a deep, calming breath. "So where is he now, the baby?" He laughed bitterly. "Hell, I guess he's not a baby anymore. So, where is he? Our . . . our son?" As soon as he asked the question, he knew the answer. "That's why you had Clements bring you here. You think our son might be with my mother's people."

"I don't know, but it seemed like a good place to start. All I know is that a friend of my father's gave the baby to a mountain man who said he was going to leave the baby with the Indians at Apache Pass."

Well, that explained what she was doing out here. Mitch closed his eyes for a moment, putting his anger behind him, and then he drew Alisha into his arms again and tucked her head under his chin.

"I'm sorry, Lisha. I'm sorry I wasn't there for you. I would have been there if I'd known, I swear it."

She swallowed past the lump in her throat. "I know."

"I'll never leave you again. Never. I swear it."

"Mitch. Oh Mitch."

She wrapped her arms around his waist and held on tight. She didn't want to cry. She had already shed enough tears to last a lifetime, but it was no use. The tears came, unbidden, as the ice around her heart melted, as all the old hurts dissolved, like dew beneath the morning sun.

"I love you," she whispered. "I've always loved you. Even when I tried to hate you, I loved you."

"Shhh." He brushed his lips across the top of her head. "It's all right, darlin'. You had every right to hate me. I never should have left you."

"Promise me," she said, looking up into his eyes. "Promise me you'll never leave me again."

"I swear it on the life of my mother."

"Oh, Mitch, tell me, tell me that you love me."

"I love you, darlin'. I always have. Always will."

Happiness bubbled up inside her, warmer than sunshine, sweeter than sugarcane. Blinking through her tears, she stood on tiptoe and kissed him, sighing with pleasure as he drew her body against his, crushing her breasts against his chest.

When he finally let her go, she felt like laughing and

crying and shouting all at the same time, but all that emerged from her throat was a deep sigh of contentment.

Mitch was back, and everything was going to be all right.

Chapter 24

Hand in hand, they walked back to the fire. Most of the Indians were sleeping. Two of the warriors stood in the shadows, keeping watch.

Mitch spread his bedroll, then looked at Alisha. With a shy smile, she stretched out on the blankets, a sigh of contentment escaping her lips as Mitch crawled in beside her and cradled her in his arms.

"I've dreamed of this," he whispered.

"Me, too." She glanced at the warriors sleeping near the fire. "Of course, I had a different setting in mind."

Mitch laughed softly. "Really?" He lifted a wisp of hair from her cheek and twirled it around his finger. "Want to let me in on it?"

"Well, I thought we'd be alone, for a start. Maybe by the creek back home."

"And what would we do there, by the creek back home?"

Stifling the urge to laugh out loud, she said, "Swim, of course."

Mitch did laugh, and the soft sound of his laughter filled her heart and soul with joy.

"I love you," she murmured. "I wish we were alone."

"We will be," he promised. "As soon as I can arrange it."

She woke a little after dawn, her head pillowed on Mitch's shoulder, their legs entwined. She studied his face a moment, noting the shadow of a beard along his jaw. How handsome he was, and how she loved him.

She watched him sleep for a few more minutes and then, feeling dirty and sticky after so many days without a bath, she slid out from under the covers and padded down toward the stream. She nearly jumped out of her skin when one of the warriors standing guard stepped into her path.

She pointed to herself, and then the stream, and he nodded and stepped back into the trees. And disappeared from her sight. No matter how hard she tried, she couldn't see him.

She had heard it said that an Apache could hide himself so completely you would never know he was there until you felt his knife at your throat. Now she believed it.

At the stream, she found a secluded place and after looking around to make sure she was out of sight of anyone passing by, she stripped off her clothing and waded into the shallow water.

It was cold enough to make her teeth chatter, but she was determined to be clean. Remembering something Mitch had once told her, she picked up a handful of sand and scrubbed it over her arms and legs. She rinsed her hair three times, then hurried out of the water. Wrapping her arms around her body, she stood in a patch of sunlight, her thoughts immediately turning toward Mitch.

She had spent the night in his arms. The thought

brought a smile to her face. It had been wonderful to fall asleep in his embrace, to wake beside him. . . . Mitchy . . . a wondrous feeling of happiness spread through her. She laughed, then clapped a hand to her mouth to stifle the sound, which seemed unusually loud in the stillness of early morning.

"Want to share the joke?"

At the sound of his voice, she glanced over her shoulder to see Mitch striding purposefully toward her. "Go away!"

He stopped less than a yard away, one brow arching as his gaze moved over her. "And leave the prettiest sight I've seen in years?"

A rush of heat engulfed her from head to toe. "Mitch . . ."

"You didn't used to mind my looking."

There was a note of wistfulness in his voice that went straight to her heart.

His gaze met hers as he stripped off his shirt, his moccasins, his leggings, until he wore only his clout.

"What are you doing?" she exclaimed.

"Thought I'd take a bath, too."

He was a study in masculine perfection—broad shoulders, wide chest, flat stomach, long, long legs. His desire for her was evident, and she felt her heart begin to race as he closed the distance between them.

"The water's that way," she said, pointing toward the river.

He stopped just short of touching her, a question in his eyes.

"We shouldn't," she said.

"I know."

She took a deep breath, knowing if she said the word, he would leave. It was a quick battle, right and wrong warring with her need to be in his arms, to feel him all around her, to be a part of him.

He nodded almost imperceptibly, as if he knew what she was thinking. "It's all right, Lisha," he said quietly. Leaning forward, he kissed her forehead, then turned toward the river. A cold swim was just what he needed.

"Mitch."

He paused, but didn't turn.

"Don't go."

He went very still. "Are you sure?"

"I'm sure."

Slowly, he turned to face her. "We don't have to, not now." As much as she had enjoyed their lovemaking in the past, he knew she had always felt guilty about it afterward. Guilty about facing her old man, about going to church, guilty for doing what she'd been taught all her life was a sin. He couldn't begin to imagine the torment she must have gone through when she found out she was pregnant. "We can wait," he said. "Until we're married."

"Married?" He smiled at the note of surprise in her voice. "Are we getting married?"

"Don't you think we should? We have a son, after all."

Tears glistened in her eyes. "Oh, Mitch, I love you so much."

He had to touch her, had to hold her, or die. He drew her into his arms, a sigh issuing from deep in his throat as her body pressed against his. It was the sweetest kind of torment, holding her close, knowing that, as much as he wanted her, he'd have to wait.

"Will you marry me, Alisha?"

"You know I will." She looked up at him, tears shining in her eyes. "Just name the day."

"Is tomorrow too soon?"

"Tomorrow? We can't be back at Canyon Creek tomorrow. And even if we could, I can't go home now. Not until we find our son."

"I wasn't thinking about Canyon Creek. I was thinking about getting married back at the rancheria."

Alisha blinked up at him. "You mean have an Indian marry us?"

Mitch nodded. "You don't like the idea?"

"But it wouldn't be legal, would it?"

"We can get married again when we get back to Canyon Creek if you like."

She thought about it a moment, then smiled. "I'll marry you anywhere, anytime."

"I'm gonna hold you to it this time," Mitch said with a grin, his swim forgotten. "Come on, let's get dressed. The sooner we get going, the sooner we can tie the knot."

It was almost sundown by the time they reached the encampment. Elk Chaser, Clements, and Fights the Wind looked ready to collapse. It had been a hell of a trip for all three of them, Mitch thought, yet none had complained.

As soon as they reached the edge of the village, the wife of Fights the Wind came flying across the ground, followed by her two young sons. Taking the reins of Fights the Wind's horse, she led the animal to their wickiup.

White Robe emerged from her wickiup a moment later. She hurried to Elk Chaser's side, clucking softly as she helped him out of the saddle and assisted him into the wickiup.

Red Clements slid from the back of his mount. He leaned against his horse's shoulder for a couple of minutes, breathing hard, and then went to sit in the shade.

"You all right?" Mitch asked.

"I will be," Clements replied with a wry grin. "Hell, I been stove up worse than this more times than I care to remember."

"Let me know if you need anything," Mitch said.

"Sure, sure. You go take care of that pretty little gal," Clements said. "Don't pay me no never mind."

With a nod, Mitch went to lift Alisha from the saddle. She smiled at him, laughed softly as he crushed her close for just a moment before releasing her.

Alisha glanced around the village. Was her son here? If not, would these people help her find him?

Until the Comanche had captured her, she had never seen any Indians close up. Now, surrounded by Apaches, she couldn't help feeling a little out of place. It was a large village. Men and women stood outside their lodges in small groups, drawn by the returning war party. Barefoot boys in clouts and little girls in buckskin tunics stared at her, their black eyes wide with curiosity. She felt a flutter of excitement. Could one of those boys be her son?

"Come on," Mitch said, and taking Alisha by the hand, he led her into his mother's lodge.

White Robe looked up as they entered.

"*Shi ma*, this is Alisha Faraday. Alisha, this is my mother, White Robe."

"Your mother!" Alisha exclaimed. "But I thought she was . . ."

Mitch smiled at her. "So did I. I'll explain it to you later."

"Welcome, Alisha," White Robe said, smiling. "Please, sit down."

"Thank you," Alisha said. She sat down on a fur robe, and Mitch sat beside her. Reaching over, he took her hand in his again and gave it a squeeze.

"Will you eat?" White Robe asked.

Alisha glanced at Mitch. She didn't want to be rude, but Mitch had told her the Apache ate mule meat and dog meat, and while she was hungry, she wasn't *that* hungry.

Mitch sniffed the air. "It's venison stew."

Alisha felt her cheeks grow warm. "Yes, I'd love something to eat, thank you."

White Robe finished changing the bandage on Elk Chaser's wound and after making sure he was resting comfortably, she filled two bowls with stew and handed one to Mitch and one to Alisha.

Alisha took a bite, surprised to find it tasted quite good. While eating, she watched Mitch's mother, her mind filling with questions. Mitch had told her his mother was dead, yet here she was, bustling about like any woman anywhere, serving her guests, beaming at her son, tending her wounded husband.

She was a handsome woman, with her thick black braids and dark eyes. She wore a colorful cotton skirt and blouse and moccasins. The ends of her braids were tied with strips of red cloth.

They ate in silence for a time. Alisha noted the way Mitch's mother kept looking at him, the way she touched his shoulder when she passed by. She didn't know why, but she had not expected the Indians to be an affectionate people, but there was no mistaking the love in White Robe's eyes when she looked at her son. No doubt that that love was returned.

"There will be a victory dance tonight," White Robe remarked, "to celebrate your return and your triumph over our enemies, the Comanche."

"Tonight?" Mitch looked at Alisha.

"Yes. The people are anxious to celebrate your victory."

Alisha was wondering if Mitch would say anything about their getting married when the lodge flap was flung aside and a young boy burst inside. He looked to be about four years old and her first impulse was to hope that he might be her son. She had to stop doing this to herself, she thought, or surely she'd go crazy.

"Otter, you have returned!" the boy exclaimed, and hurled himself into Mitch's arms.

"Quiet, *ciye*," White Robe admonished gently. "Your father sleeps." *Father.* As she spoke the word, her heart clutched. She looked at Mitch and knew, beyond any doubt, that he was Rides the Buffalo's true father. And Alisha was his mother. The knowledge seared her heart and soul.

The boy was instantly contrite. His gaze moved to the rear of the lodge, his mouth forming a perfect O when he saw the bandages swathed around his father's middle.

"What happened to my father?" the boy asked.

"He was wounded," Mitch replied. "But he's going to be fine. Don't worry." He smiled at Alisha. "This is my brother, Rides the Buffalo." Mitch ruffled the boy's hair. "This is Alisha."

Alisha's gaze moved from Mitch's face to the boy's and back again. Even without being told, she would have known they were related, the resemblance was so strong. She sighed, thinking they could easily pass for father and son.

Rides the Buffalo sat down beside Mitch, and White Robe handed him a horn spoon and a bowl of stew.

Mitch glanced at Alisha. Rising to his feet, he offered her his hand.

"Where are we going?" Alisha asked as she placed her hand in his.

"For a walk."

"Thank you for bringing my husband home." White Robe smiled at her oldest son fondly. "Do not forget the celebration. It will begin in about an hour."

"Sure, ma," Mitch replied. "We'll be back soon."

White Robe nodded. There was no mistaking the fact that her son had deep feelings for the white woman; just as there was no mistaking the fact that those feelings were returned.

Outside, Mitch headed for the river. There were a lot of secluded places along the riverbank, places where young lovers went to be alone.

At last, he came to a place screened from casual view by a stand of saplings and tall shrubs. Impatient and needy, he drew Alisha into his arms and held her tight. A faint breeze stirred the leaves on the trees, carrying the scent of earth and sage, mingling with the scent of the woman in his arms. Desire stirred within him. He heard her soft laugh as the evidence of his desire pushed gently against her belly.

Drawing back a little, he gazed into her face, and saw his own hunger mirrored in the depths of her eyes.

"Maybe coming down here wasn't such a good idea, after all," he muttered.

"It was a wonderful idea." She nestled against him, as warm and trusting as a kitten.

Lowering his head, he nuzzled her hair, his hands moving restlessly up and down the length of her back, his mind exploding with remembered images of the woman in his arms, of the girl she used to be—Alisha looking up at him the first time they had made love, her eyes wide as she experienced the thrill of desire; Alisha laughing at him the day he fell in the creek; Alisha sobbing in his arms the day her mother passed away; begging him not to go when he told her he was leaving town to find a better life . . . Alisha. She was a part of every good memory he carried with him.

"Lisha."

"I know." She wrapped her arms tight around him, wanting to be closer, wanting to feel the hard length of his body against her own. "Mitch . . ."

"What?" He kissed her, his lips like fire against her skin. "Tell me what you want?"

"You. Just you."

His hand slid up her side, the tips of his fingers brushing along the curve of her breast. Pleasure curled through her belly. So long, she thought, so long since she had felt his hands on her skin. "Mitch . . ."

"Don't look at me like that unless you mean it," he warned.

She waged a silent war within herself . . . her desire battling with her innate sense of morality. She knew it was wrong to be intimate with Mitch before they were married. It had been wrong before; it would be wrong now. This time, she wanted everything between them to be right.

With a sigh, she drew back a little. "I'm sorry."

"Don't be." He traced the curve of her cheek with

his forefinger. "I've waited this long. I can wait another day. Come on," he said, taking her hand in his, "let's walk."

"Tell me about your mother," Alisha said. "I thought she passed away when you were twelve or thirteen."

Mitch grinned into the darkness. "That's what I thought, too. My old man was a real piece of work. To keep me from running away, he told me she was dead. I should never have believed him. Con Garrett never told the truth in his life."

Alisha made a soft sound in her throat. The lie Mitch's father had told him was no worse than the one her own father had perpetuated. "How are we going to find our son?"

"I'll ask my mother tomorrow, see if she knows anything." He shook his head. "Even if we find him, he might not want to come with us."

She had thought of that herself, but it was worse, somehow, hearing him put it in words. She had clung to the fantasy that she would find her son and that all obstacles separating them would miraculously disappear.

"Lisha?"

"What?"

"You must have thought of that."

"Yes, of course, but I refused to dwell on it. I told myself that he'd want to be with me. I'm his mother, but I've just been lying to myself, haven't I?"

"Hey, you don't know that. Maybe he's unhappy where he is."

"No!" She had thought of that, too, of course, imagined that whoever had taken him in had mistreated him. She had wondered if he had decent clothes to wear, enough food to eat, if the people who had adopted him treated him kindly, if his mother tucked him into bed at night and told him stories. In the end, she'd had to believe he was happy and well cared for because to think otherwise was too painful to contemplate.

Mitch swore softly. "We'll find him, I promise."

"Why?" she wailed. "Why did my father have to lie to me?"

"I don't know, darlin'," he said, drawing her into his arms once again.

"I just don't understand how he could have done such a horrible thing."

Mitch took a deep breath. Feeling her need for reassurance, he said, "I'm sure he did what he thought was best for you," and thought he'd choke on the words.

"Oh!" She twisted out of his embrace and began to pace back and forth. "I'm so tired of everyone saying that! How could it possibly have been the best thing for me to give my child away? How could he ever think it was right for my son, our son, to grow up without his mother? How could that be right?"

"I don't know, but I know your old man loved you. He was probably just trying to spare you the shame of raising an illegitimate baby." Mitch took a deep breath, realizing, for the first time, just what Alisha must have gone through, all because of him. She had been the preacher's daughter. If people had learned she was carrying the bastard child of a half-breed, they would have proclaimed her a fallen woman and completely shunned her. She would never have been allowed to teach, never been able to hold her head up in the town again. He suddenly realized that, had he been in her father's place, he would likely have done the same thing to spare his daughter the shame she would have endured.

"I'm sorry," he whispered. "Dammit, Lisha, I would have been here for you if I'd known."

She stopped pacing and took a deep, calming breath. "I know. I'm not blaming you."

"Well, maybe you should. Dammit, I never should have left you."

She looked up at him, smiling through her tears. "No, you shouldn't have, but it's all water under the bridge now," she said, sniffing. "You promised you would never leave me again, and this time I'm holding you to it."

"And you promised you'd marry me," he said quietly.

"I know. Can we really get married tomorrow?"

"Anxious, are you?"

"Yes. Does that surprise you?"

Mitch shook his head. "No. You always were an impulsive girl. Why, I remember the first time I kissed you, I thought you were going to eat me up, you were so hungry for more."

"Oh!" Eyes flashing, she punched him on the arm. "I was not!"

Mitch laughed as he reached out and pulled her up against him. He gazed down at her a minute, and then he kissed her.

Every thought fled Alisha's mind as his mouth covered hers. Warmth and a sense of security washed over her, and with it the deep, inner knowledge that this was right, this was where she was meant to be.

She kissed him back, her tongue dancing with his, her heart pounding with joy. She was in Mitch's arms, and she felt young again, free again. Somehow, everything would work out.

"Lisha, I want to feel you open for me . . . move with me . . . I want to taste you. . . ." He groaned low in his throat. "Feel your heat surround me."

His words caused an ache deep in the core of her being, and she pressed against him, wanting to be closer. A soft moan escaped her lips as his arms tightened around her. She could feel his desire in his kiss, in the tension in his body, the tremor in his arms. Whatever else was wrong in the world, this had always been right between them.

"Lisha." He closed his eyes and took a deep breath. "Dammit, girl, if you keep kissing me like that, I'm not gonna be able to wait until tomorrow."

Happiness welled up inside her and poured forth in a wave of merry laughter.

"Think it's funny, do you?" he growled.

"No, I'm just happy."

She was beautiful when she was happy, with her brown eyes sparkling and her lips slightly parted. She seemed to glow with a radiant inner fire and he knew he'd consider himself a lucky man if he could spend the rest of his life warming himself in her light.

"Come on," he said, taking her by the hand. "I think we'd better go find a crowd before one of us gets in trouble."

Chapter 25

The whole encampment had turned out for the victory dance. Mitch was surprised to see Elk Chaser up and about. He mentioned it to his mother, who just shook her head.

"I told him he should rest," she said in a resigned voice, "but he insisted on being here."

Mitch sat beside Elk Chaser, not certain what to expect.

An air of excitement and anticipation floated amongst the people. A fire burned in the center of the crowd, the low beat of the drum seemed to speak to him, telling him of victories long past, of brave warriors whose blood nourished the earth. The drum. Its voice was like that of the thunder people, speaking to his heart and soul, awakening memories of his childhood, of the things his mother had taught him of the People, of their history and beliefs.

He watched the warriors dancing around the fire, acting out the battle near the cave. When they finished their part of the battle, Fights the Wind began to dance. Clad in clout and moccasins and carrying a bow and a quiver of arrows, he showed how he had fought the

Comanche and been wounded. In an amazing sequence, he showed how the son of White Robe had saved his life. And then, to Mitch's surprise, the warrior walked toward him and offered him the bow and a quiver of arrows.

Mitch nodded as he took the gift, realizing, in that moment, that Fights the Wind had done him a great honor.

Several of the warriors who had been at the battle murmured their approval, making Mitch feel as though he had been accepted as one of them.

The last dance was a dance of thanksgiving to *Usen* for granting the Apache a victory over their enemies.

When the dancing was over, Elk Chaser and Rides the Buffalo returned to their lodge.

After bidding the two of them good night, Mitch took his mother aside. "I need your help."

"What do you need, *ciye*?"

"Alisha and I want to be married tomorrow. Can you arrange it?"

"So soon!" White Robe exclaimed. "And you told me you had no woman. Hah!"

"Ma . . ."

She looked up at him and laughed. "I will see to it." She looked over to where Alisha was standing. "She is lovely, Otter. You have made a wise choice."

"I think so."

"I remember you spoke of her many times when you were a boy. I had often wished that you would bring her home to meet me."

"I wanted to, but I was always afraid he might be there, and I was ashamed of him."

White Robe nodded. "I hope you and Alisha will find the happiness that Elk Chaser and I have found."

"Thanks, Ma."

She smiled at him. "Go, now, and be with your woman. I will take care of everything."

Bending, Mitch pressed a kiss to his mother's cheek, his heart pounding with anticipation. Tomorrow, Alisha would be his.

Mitch stood beside Alisha. It had been a long day. Weddings among the Apache were not elaborate affairs and he had hoped to marry Alisha first thing in the morning. He was anxious to make her his bride, anxious to hold her in his arms again. Anxious to make her his in every sense of the word. He had said as much that morning, and his mother had replied that Rides the Buffalo wanted to go hunting.

"Hunting!" he had replied. "Ma, haven't you been listening? Alisha and I want to get married. Now. Today."

"I hear you, *ciye*. Take your brother hunting. Come back this afternoon, late."

He had started to protest, but she held up her hand. "Go."

So he had taken Rides the Buffalo hunting, but all the while he had been thinking about Alisha, remembering how good she felt in his arms, the eagerness with which she kissed him.

When they returned to White Robe's lodge late that afternoon, they had found Red Clements and Elk Chaser sitting outside, sharing a pipe in the shade.

When Rides the Buffalo started to go inside, Elk Chaser grabbed him by the arm, and shook his head. "The men have been banished from the lodge."

"Why?"

Elk Chaser shook his head. "Only women are allowed in there today. If you are hungry, go see Yellow Flower."

Rides the Buffalo looked up at Mitch, shrugged, and ran off toward Yellow Flower's lodge.

Mitch hunkered down in the shade beside Clements. "What's going on?"

"Why, I hear you're gettin' hitched, boy. Big doin's goin' on in there. Women been comin' and goin' all day."

"Is that right?"

Clements nodded. "They been sewin' and cookin' up a storm in there." He slapped his hand against his thigh. "Gonna be quite a shindig, from the looks of things.

That had been an hour ago. Now, freshly bathed and clad in a new set of buckskins, he stood beside Alisha. Just looking at her took his breath away. She wore a doeskin tunic that had been bleached white, then decorated with delicate, blue glass beads and tiny silver bells. Her long, wavy hair fell loose down her back save for two tiny braids that framed her face. She wore a pair of new moccasins.

It looked like the whole camp had turned out to watch the ceremony.

Mitch took a deep breath as the shaman took his place.

"These two have pledged their hearts to each other," he said. His voice, though low, carried to all those gathered around. "There are no words strong enough to bind a man to a woman, or a woman to a man. With us, the joining of a man and a woman takes place here, in the heart."

The shaman took their hands and joined them together. "Now you will feel no rain, for each will be a shelter to the other. Now you will feel no cold, for each will be warmth to the other. Now you will feel no loneliness, for each will be a friend to the other. You are now two people but there is one life before you. Go now to your dwelling place and enter into your togetherness. And may your days be good and long on this earth."

Slowly, Mitch drew Alisha into his arms and kissed her, sealing the shaman's words upon her heart and soul.

When he released her, he saw his mother beaming at him. Tears glistened in her dark eyes as she came forward to hug him.

"We have prepared a lodge for you near the east bend of the river. Horses await to take you there. You will find wood for a fire, and food to last for three days. Enjoy this, your special time together."

"Thanks, Ma."

"Be happy, *ciye*." White Robe embraced her new daughter-in-law. "Good wishes, my daughter."

"Thank you," Alisha said, pleased that Mitch's mother had so readily accepted her into the family.

Elk Chaser and Red Clements also came forward to offer their congratulations, as did Fights the Wind, who offered Mitch a buffalo robe and a pipe made of white birch.

Rides the Buffalo tugged on Alisha's skirt. "You are my sister now, aren't you?"

"Yes," she said, with a smile. "I guess I am."

Rides the Buffalo grinned shyly. "I always wanted a sister," he confided in a low voice, "but don't tell Little Fox. He would make fun of me if he knew. He does not like girls."

"I won't tell," Alisha promised solemnly.

"Maybe you and my brother will have a baby soon," Rides the Buffalo said candidly.

Alisha looked up at Mitch and smiled. "Maybe."

"I'll do my best," Mitch said.

"Go now," White Robe said abruptly. "Enjoy these days together. Make good memories." She drew Rides the Buffalo to her side and held him tight. Sooner or later, she would have to tell Mitch the truth. She only hoped he wouldn't hate her for it.

Mitch hugged his mother and then, eager to be alone with his bride, he swung Alisha into his arms and carried her to where two white horses were waiting.

At last, after five years, she was his.

The wickiup was located in the shadow of a tall pine. The river ran slow and quiet beside their lodge. Silver bells had been tied to the branches of the tree; their soft tinkling would serenade them in the night breeze.

Mitch lifted Alisha from the back of her horse, letting her body slide slowly against his as he put her on her feet.

"Did I tell you how beautiful you are?" he asked.

"No."

"I'm not sure I can find the words." He grinned at her. "I'm a lawman, you know, not a poet."

She smiled at him. "Try."

"You're beautiful, Lisha. More beautiful than any woman I've ever known." He traced the curve of her cheek with the tip of his finger. "Your skin is softer than dandelion down, prettier than a fresh peach. I want to cover you with kisses, feel you lean into me,

taste your breath on my face when I wake in the morning."

Alisha laughed softly. "Who says you aren't a poet?"

He laughed with her, unable to believe that she was
here, that she was his. "I love you," he said quietly.
"Always have. Always will."

"And I love you."

"Show me," he said, and swinging her into his arms,
he carried her into the wickiup.

The lodge was fragrant with the scent of sage and
sweet grass. Several soft, furry robes had been spread
in the rear of the lodge. Wood was piled in the pit in
the center. There were two willow backrests for their
comfort, food and water, soap to bathe with, a change
of clothes for each of them.

"It's nice," Alisha said, looking around.

Mitch nodded, silently blessing his mother's kind-
ness.

"Lisha?"

She nodded, her dark eyes luminous as she gazed
up at him. She stepped out of her moccasins and then,
slowly, she reached for the ties that fastened her dress
at the shoulders, unfastening first one and then the
other. The soft doeskin tunic slid slowly down her
body to pool at her feet.

Mitch sucked in a deep breath. She had been lovely as
a girl of sixteen; now, more rounded, more voluptuous,
she was a vision. Her skin was smooth, unblemished.
Her golden hair fell over her shoulders, haloing her
face, the perfect accent to her creamy skin.

She smiled as she read the admiration in his eyes,
felt a blush rise in her cheeks as his gaze grew hotter.
"Thank you," she murmured, pleased by his reaction.

His gaze swept over her again. "Thank you," he replied wryly.

She cocked her head at him. "One of us is over-dressed."

"What? Oh." He slipped off his shirt, shucked his leggings and moccasins, removed his clout.

Alisha grinned as she saw the visible evidence of his desire.

"It's your fault I'm in this terrible condition," he said. "What are you going to do about it?"

"What would you like me to do?"

He closed the distance between them and drew her into his arms, his lips brushing the top of her head. "Have you forgotten everything I taught you?"

"Well," she said, nipping his shoulder, "it has been five years."

"It will all come back to you." He ran his fingertips down her spine, cupped her buttocks and drew her hips against his. "Does that remind you of anything?"

"Oh, yes," she said, a little breathlessly. "I'm beginning to remember."

He put his finger under her chin and tilted her face up. "I'll never let you forget again," he promised, and captured her lips with his.

He kissed her until she was mindless, breathless, until her knees went weak and only his arms held her upright. His hands roamed over her body, trailing fingers of fire. His mouth sweetly assaulted hers, branding her as his, awakening memories of summer nights near the creek back home, of winter days spent on a buffalo robe in a dark cave where she had first tasted love.

She moaned and pressed herself against him, wanting to crawl inside his skin, to feel what he felt, to hold him close within her own body and never let him go.

With a low groan, he lifted her into his arms and carried her to the buffalo robes, his mouth never leaving hers as he laid her down, then covered her body with his own.

She clutched at his shoulders, her hips lifting to receive him. She tasted his breath on her face, felt his kisses like gentle rain on her breasts.

It had been five years since she had been with a man, and it was almost like the first time all over again. The wonder of it, the thrill of it, the sheer ecstasy, was beyond description, beyond words, and she gave herself over to his keeping, heart and soul, mind and body. She was his, as she had always been his.

He murmured that he loved her, adored her, taking her as tenderly, as gently, as he had that first time so long ago, losing himself in her warmth, in her sweetness.

The years fell away, all the old hurts healing as their bodies came together with remembered pleasure.

She arched beneath him, her nails raking his back, as they moved with ageless rhythm, seeking, searching, for that one moment when time and memory ceased, when yesterday and today ran together, when two truly became one.

"Mitch . . . my Mitch . . . " She moaned with pleasure as his warmth filled her, his body merging with hers, making her whole, complete . . . .

Like a feather drifting on the wind, she returned slowly to earth, a smile on her face. It had been worth it, she thought, all the tears she had shed, all the pain and heartache she had endured in the last five years, it had all been worth it for this one moment.

She opened her eyes to find Mitch smiling down at her, his dark eyes warm and tender and filled with such love it brought tears to her eyes.

"I didn't hurt you, did I?" he asked.

"Oh, yes, terribly," she teased. "Please, hurt me again."

He laughed softly. "I love you, Lisha."

"Tell me that often, will you?"

"Every day." He kissed the tip of her nose. "And every night."

"And every afternoon?"

"Of course."

"I love you, Mitch. Promise you'll never leave me again. Promise me we'll always be together, as close as we are now."

"I promise."

She flung her arms around his neck. "Oh, I missed you so."

"I know, darlin'. I'm sorry."

She put her finger over his lips. "No more apologies between us. Let's put the past behind us where it belongs."

Mitch nodded. Lowering his head, he rained kissed over her cheeks, her neck, her shoulders, her breasts.

She sighed with pleasure, her hands roaming over his back and thighs, wriggling her hips provocatively, until, with a mock growl, he buried himself deep within her, his heat engulfing her, arousing her, carrying her higher, higher, until waves of pleasure broke over her once more, leaving her weak and drowning in ecstasy. . . .

*   *   *

Later, they bathed in the stream and then, moving upstream to a deep pool, they swam awhile, and then they stretched out on the grassy bank to dry.

Alisha sighed as Mitch drew her up against him. Sated and content, she drew lazy circles over his chest, marveling that he was there, that she was his woman at last.

Lifting up on one elbow, she ran her gaze over him. He was perfect, she thought, from his broad shoulders to his feet. His skin was a dusky brown all over. His arms and legs were well muscled, tempting her touch. His stomach was hard and flat. And that part of him that made him a man . . . she grinned, amused that his desire could be aroused by no more than a glance.

"You laughing at me again?" he drawled.

"No, no, of course not."

"Well, see that you don't." He lifted one brow in wry amusement. "Are you just going to sit there and laugh, or are you gonna put me out of my misery?"

She did laugh, then. She laughed with the pure joy of being alive, of feeling the sun on her bare skin, of being with Mitch, her Mitch. . . .

She was still laughing softly as she covered his body with hers and put him out of his misery.

Chapter 26

They spent the rest of the day near the stream, loving and napping and loving again.

And now they were lying in each other's arms.

"Tell me," she said after awhile. "Tell me what you did while you were away."

He shrugged. "Not much. I told you I was a cowboy for awhile. And a sheriff. When I wasn't wearing a badge, I just drifted." He looked down at her and smiled. "Tried not to think about you being married to another man."

"Did you . . . " She bit down on her lower lip.

"Did I what?"

"Five years is a long time . . . "

He lifted one brow. "Yeah?"

"Women . . . were there other women?"

"Hundreds," he said solemnly.

She felt a rush of jealousy, and then realized he was teasing her again. "How many were there, really?"

"Are you sure you want to know?"

She took a deep breath, prepared herself for the worst, and nodded.

"There weren't any, Lisha, none that meant anything. I danced with 'em at socials and at the Fourth of July picnic, but ... " He shook his head. "How could I think about another woman when I was still in love with you?"

"I'm glad."

He grunted softly. "What about you?" he asked. "What about Smithfield?"

"What about him?"

"You were engaged a long time."

"Nothing ever happened between us."

"Nothing?"

"Nothing much." She smiled. "Just a few kisses."

"How many?"

She laughed softly. "Five," she said. "One a year."

"Uh-huh."

"I never would have married him. I thought I could, but I know now I was just kidding myself. You spoiled me for any other man, you know."

"Keep it that way."

"Yes, master," she replied with a saucy grin. "Whatever you say." She looked at him a moment, still smiling, and then frowned. "You won't take another wife, will you?"

"Another wife? What are you talking about?"

"Mr. Clements told me he has two wives!"

"Is that right?"

Alisha nodded. "He has an Apache wife, and a wife in the East."

"Well, good for him."

Alisha punched him on the shoulder. "He said lots of mountain men have Indian wives. And that lots of Apache men have more than one. So?"

Mitch lifted his hands in a gesture of surrender.

"I'm only half Apache, darlin', and you're woman enough for me."

"Well, I'd better be. I just found you again, and I'm not willing to share you with anyone else, not now, not ever."

"Don't worry, you won't have to." He wrapped his arms around her and hugged her tight.

"You're all the woman I'll ever need," he said fervently. "And I'll never let you go again. Never."

The words, spoken in a low growl, were the sweetest she had ever heard.

At sunset, Mitch stood up. "Come on," he said, offering her his hand, "let's go for a walk." He pulled her to her feet and kissed her. "Ready?"

Her eyes widened. "Aren't we going to get dressed first?"

"Why?" he asked. "There's no one to see you but me. And I want to see all of you."

Her gaze swept over him. "The scenery's not bad from here, either."

Hand in hand, they walked along the bank, pausing to watch the sun as it sank behind the mountains.

"How beautiful," Alisha murmured.

Mitch nodded. "Beautiful, indeed," he agreed. But he wasn't watching the changing colors of the sky. He was looking at Alisha's face.

"Do you think we'll find him?" Alisha asked later that night. They were sitting outside after supper, gazing up at the stars. It was a beautiful evening, warm and clear. Millions of stars twinkled against the indigo night sky; a full moon showered the earth with pale silver light. Crickets and tree frogs serenaded them;

occasionally, the melancholy wail of a coyote drifted on the breeze.

"We'll find him," Mitch said. A son, he thought. I've got a son. It was hard to believe. Every time he thought of it, of what Alisha's father had done, fury rose up inside him, threatening to choke him. "We'll find him," he said again. If the boy was still with the Apache, it shouldn't be too difficult. As soon as they returned to the village, he would ask his mother and Elk Chaser for help. There was a chance that Clements might be of some assistance, as well.

"Do you think he's all right?" Alisha asked. "What if he's being mistreated? Not getting enough to eat?"

"I'm sure he's fine," Mitch said, giving her a squeeze. "Children are prized among the Apache."

Alisha rested her head on Mitch's shoulder. "I don't know how we'll ever find him," she said, and he heard the discouragement in her voice.

"We'll find him," he said again, and hoped he was telling her the truth. The mortality rate among Indian children was high, and there was always a chance, however slim, that whoever had first taken the boy hadn't kept him at all.

Alisha sighed. "Tell me a story, like you used to," she said. "I need to think about something else."

"Later," Mitch said. "I can think of better ways to entertain you."

"Really?" Alisha said with a coy smile. She batted her eyelashes at him. "Do you think I'll like it?"

"I can almost guarantee it."

"Well." She sighed heavily. "If you're sure."

"I've never had any complaints before," Mitch said with a roguish grin.

"Is that right?" she exclaimed.

She started to get up, but Mitch quickly rolled on top of her, neatly pinning her in place. She glared up at him. "No other women, eh?"

"I'm just funnin' with you, sweetheart."

"What if I don't believe you?"

"Lisha," he said in a singsong voice. "Lisha, can you come out to play?"

"No," she said, smothering the urge to laugh.

"Lisha. Lisha."

She laughed in spite of herself, recalling the nights he had called to her from under her window. "Remember the night you threw a rock at my window, and the window broke?"

Mitch grinned down at her. "Your old man came running out of the house with a shotgun. Scared the shit out of me." He laughed. "If he'd been a better shot, I wouldn't be here now."

They smiled at each other a moment, the memory warm between them, and then Alisha cupped Mitch's face and drew his head down toward her. "I'm glad you're here," she whispered. "So glad."

"Lisha . . ."

She writhed beneath him, needing his touch, needing to envelop him, to taste him and touch him. "Now," she pleaded softly. "Now, now, now!"

He needed no further urging, and soon the night was filled with the sweet musk of passion and Alisha's soft cries of delight.

They spent one more day in their special place, laughing and loving, the joy they found in each other erasing all the bad memories of the past. "Will you teach me to speak Apache?" she asked. "I'll need to know it so I can speak to our son."

Our son. Mitch looked at his bride. She could be pregnant now, he mused, and tried to imagine how she would look, her breasts full, her belly swollen with his child. It grieved him that he had not been with her the first time, that he hadn't been there to reassure her, to comfort her, to watch her bloom with new life.

He thrust the thought away. She was right. What was past was past, and there was nothing to be gained by dwelling on it.

"We'll ask my mother to teach you," Mitch said. "I could use some lessons, too. I knew a little of the language when I was a boy, but I've forgotten a lot of it." It was surprising, though, how quickly the words and phrases he had learned were coming back to him, how much he understood. Still, it would be nice to be fluent in his mother's tongue. It was doubtful that their son would speak English.

With regret, they packed their belongings and dismantled the wickiup.

"Thank you," Alisha said as they took a last look around. "Thank you for making our honeymoon wonderful."

"It was my pleasure, darlin'," he drawled. "Believe me."

"Can we come back here again sometime?"

"Sure." He took her in his arms and nuzzled her neck. "But it's not the place, you know. Remember that."

"Hmm, getting a little smug, are we?"

"Who, me?"

"Who, indeed."

"Maybe I need more practice." He kissed her ear,

his tongue sliding over the lobe. "I wouldn't want any complaints."

His breath was warm against her skin, his tongue hot and erotic. "I'm not complaining," she assured him. "Not at all."

"Good. 'Cause I'm willing to practice as much as you think necessary." He grinned impudently. "After all, you're a teacher, and I want to get it right, in case there's a test later."

"Oh, very funny," she said, swatting him playfully on the arm. She looked around again, wanting to imprint this place, this moment, firmly in her mind.

"Ready?" he asked.

"Yes."

He lifted her onto the back of one of the horses, then swung up behind her, his arms sliding around her waist, his hands cupping her breasts.

"Are we riding double?" she asked.

Mitch nodded. "Cozy this way, don't you think?"

"Mmmm, very." She leaned against him, reveling in the touch of his hands on her body. "Hold me tight, so I don't fall off."

"Yes, ma'am," he said.

The other horse followed as they rode away from the stream.

"Mitch, where are we going to stay when we get back to the village?"

"I don't know. With my mother, I guess, until we can build a lodge of our own."

"With your mother?" she exclaimed, horrified at the thought of sharing Mitch's bed with White Robe, Elk Chaser, and Red Clements only a few feet away, not to mention Mitch's little brother.

He laughed as he heard the disappointment in her

voice. "Don't worry, darlin'. We'll find time to be alone."

"Well, I hope so," she grumbled. "After all, you do need lots of practice." She looked over her shoulder and smiled. "In case there's a test."

Chapter 27

◄━◆━►

White Robe listened intently as Mitch and Alisha told her of the last five years, how Mitch had left Canyon Creek to find work, how Alisha had realized she was pregnant, how Russell Faraday had lied to both Mitch and Alisha about the death of their child. So many lies, she thought sadly, so many lives changed.

She hugged Rides the Buffalo to her as Mitch and Alisha left the lodge to go look for Red Clements. The white man had gone off to watch some of the warriors race their ponies across the river. Mitch was hoping that, in his travels, Clements might have heard of a boy who had been adopted by one of the tribes.

White Robe pressed a kiss to the top of her son's head, then sent him outside to play with his friends.

"What will you do?" Elk Chaser asked.

White Robe looked at her husband and slowly shook her head. "I cannot give him up."

"You cannot keep the truth a secret forever. Did you not see the way Alisha looked at the boy? He looks much like his father."

"It is not uncommon for brothers to look alike."

"But they are not brothers. Otter and the woman

need only to ask among the people for a child who was
brought here four summers ago. Rides the Buffalo is
the only one. All who dwell here know he was not
born to us. It is a secret you cannot hope to keep."

Tears rose in White Robe's eyes and dripped, like
silent rain, down her cheeks. "How can I let him go? I
have loved him and nourished him since he was an in-
fant. I have cared for him when he was ill, quieted his
fears in the night. He is as much my son as his father
is."

Elk Chaser gathered her into his arms and held her
close. "You will not lose the boy. Surely Otter would
not take him from you."

"But he will! Alisha will not be content to remain
here. She will want to go back to her own people. They
will take the boy with them. I cannot let him go! I
know it is wrong of me, but I cannot."

"You must tell Otter the truth," Elk Chaser said gently. "If you do not, he will hate you for it. Have there
not been lies enough already?"

With a sigh, White Robe pressed her face to her husband's chest and wept bitter tears. Elk Chaser was
right. There had been lies enough. It was time for
truth.

Rides the Buffalo walked away from his mother's
lodge, his gaze downcast. He didn't answer Little
Fox's call, didn't stop to say hello to his best friend. He
just kept walking. His mother had often told him that
spying was wrong, that one day he would see or hear
something he would regret.

Today was that day.

His mother was not his mother. His father was not
his father.

Otter was not his brother, but his father. His mother was a white woman.

He looked down at his arms, lifted one of his braids. His skin had never been as dark as those of his friends; his hair was not a true black, but a dark brown. It was wavy, not straight.

Now he knew why. He was not a true Apache.

Tears burned his eyes, and he started to run lest someone should see him weeping like a baby.

He ran downstream, his vision blurred by his tears. Why had no one told him the truth?

The white woman was his mother. He had been taken from her at birth. And now she wanted him, but he did not want to go with her.

He ran faster, paying little attention to where he was going. He didn't want to leave this place, didn't want to go live with his white mother. They would be sorry they had lied to him . . . .

Blinded by his tears, he didn't see the chasm until it was too late. He screamed as his left foot went over the edge, and then he was falling, falling, spinning down, down, unable to stop. His right shoulder slammed against the side of the chasm and he cried out as pain splintered through his arm.

"*Shi ma!*" He cried for his mother, and then everything went black.

White Robe took a deep breath as Mitch and Alisha entered the lodge. "Did you talk to the white man?" she asked.

"Yeah, but he didn't know anything." Mitch shook his head as he sat down. Alisha sat down beside Mitch, and he slid his arm around her shoulders and gave her a squeeze. "I guess we'll just have to go from lodge to lodge. Red said he'd ask around when he returns to the Jicarilla."

White Robe looked at her husband. He looked back at her, his eyes kind, and then he nodded.

"That will not be necessary," White Robe said. "I know where he is."

"What?" Mitch exclaimed.

"I know where he is," White Robe repeated.

Alisha leaned forward. "Where?" she asked urgently. "Where is he? How do we find him?"

"He is here."

Mitch stood up, his hands clenched at his sides. He glanced at Alisha. Silent tears tracked her cheeks.

"What do you mean, he's here?"

"Rides the Buffalo is your son."

Mitch stared at his mother. "You let me believe he's my brother. Why? Dammit *shi ma*, why did you lie to me?"

"Otter, you will not raise your voice to my wife."

Mitch ran a hand through his hair. "I'm sorry. Why, Ma? Why didn't you tell me?"

"I was afraid."

"Afraid?"

"Of losing him. I have loved him as if he were my own. I have worried and cared for him when he was sick. He is the son of my heart, as you are the son of my flesh. I love you both."

Alisha took Mitch's hand in hers. He could feel her trembling. "Are you all right?" he asked.

She nodded. "I hoped to find him and now we have, and I can't believe it. He was here all the time." She gave a little shrug. "All I ever thought of was finding him." She glanced at White Robe. The other woman's face was etched with pain. "I never really thought about what would happen after I found him, how it would affect his . . . his other family." Rising, she walked over to White Robe and embraced her. "Thank you for taking such good care of him."

The anger drained out of Mitch as he watched Alisha hug his mother.

"We must think of the boy now," Elk Chaser said. "This will not be easy for him to understand."

Alisha went to stand beside Mitch. "What do you think Rides the Buffalo will say when he finds out?" she asked. "How will he feel, when he learns his parents aren't his parents?"

"I don't know. We'll have to be careful how we approach him."

"It's bound to be a shock."

Mitch nodded. "How do you feel about staying here awhile?"

"I don't know. How long a while?"

Mitch shrugged. "Long enough for Rides the Buffalo to get used to the idea that we're his parents."

"How long do you think that will take?"

"Hell, I don't know. But we can't just say, 'Hi, we're your parents,' and drag him out of here." He glanced over at his mother, now in Elk Chaser's arms. He could tell, by the tremors going through her, that she was crying.

"I'm willing to stay as long as it takes him to get used to the idea." Alisha paused a moment. "As long as it takes for us to get used to the idea. I've thought of nothing but finding my son ever since my father told me the truth, but, deep down, I'm afraid I'm not ready to be the mother of a four-year-old."

"Sure you are, you've had lots of experience, teaching and all."

"Yes, but those are other people's children."

"You'll be a wonderful mother," Mitch said reassuringly. "I just hope I'm a better father than my old man."

"You will be," White Robe said, her voice thick with tears. "You are nothing like him."

"Well, we might as well tell him," Mitch said. "Where is he?"

"He went outside to play."

"I'll go get him," Mitch said. He kissed Alisha on the cheek, then went to embrace his mother. "I'm sorry for losing my temper."

White Robe nodded. "We must think now of what is best for Rides the Buffalo."

Mitch gave his mother's shoulder a squeeze, then left the lodge.

There was no sign of Rides the Buffalo. Mitch asked several boys if they had seen him, and they all said no. One of them remembered seeing Rides the Buffalo running away from the lodge.

Feeling a twinge of alarm, Mitch walked through the village, asking everyone he passed if they had seen Rides the Buffalo. No one had.

Alisha looked up, her gaze filled with anticipation, when Mitch returned to the lodge. "Where is he?"

"I don't know. No one's seen him."

Alisha stood up. "Could he have found out?"

Mitch shrugged. "I don't know how."

White Robe glanced at Elk Chaser. "He listens at the door sometimes. Perhaps he heard us talking."

"Before you came in, I told White Robe she must tell the boy the truth, that it was a secret she could not keep forever."

"So there's a chance he already knows he's my son," Mitch said. He glanced at Alisha. "Our son?"

White Robe nodded. "Perhaps."

"We have to find him," Alisha said.

"Right."

They agreed to split up and search the village one more time.

"Well," Mitch said when they met back at the lodge. "He's not here."

"Where would he go?"

A short, pithy curse escaped Mitch's lips. "I don't know, but I'm going after him."

"I, too, will go," Elk Chaser said.

"Count me in," Clements said. He had followed them back to the lodge.

"I'll take all the help I can get," Mitch said.

"Let us go," Elk Chaser said.

Mitch nodded. "We'll find him, Lisha," he promised.

"Wait, I'm going with you."

"I'd rather you stayed here, with my mother."

"All right. Hurry. Be careful."

Mitch's horse was tethered outside. While Clements and Elk Chaser saddled their horses, Mitch began to cut back and forth, searching the ground for sign. It was nearly impossible to pick out one set of tracks, but he saw a small set of moccasin prints near the door, followed them as they turned away from the lodge.

All too soon, the prints of Rides the Buffalo were lost among dozens of others. But it was a start. The boy was running southwest.

Leading his horse, Mitch followed the tracks until they disappeared. The ground beyond the village was too hard to hold a print.

Mitch glanced over his shoulder as Elk Chaser and

Clements rode up. "I'll ride ahead. You two spread out and see what you can find."

He didn't wait for an answer. Swinging aboard his mount, he put the horse into an easy lope, hollering Rides the Buffalo's name as he went.

There was no sign that the boy had passed this way, nothing but broken ground littered with rocks and brambles and an occasional cottonwood. It was a rough, inhospitable land, avoided by the Apache. Many of their ancestors had been buried here in times past. The Apache believed the spirits of the dead haunted the place.

Mitch reined his horse to a halt. Surely Rides the Buffalo wouldn't have come here.

Filled with worry and apprehension, Mitch headed away from the burial ground, his gaze searching the ground for sign . . . a footprint, a broken branch, an overturned rock, anything that would indicate Rides the Buffalo had passed this way.

Nothing. He reined his horse to a halt and emptied his mind of all thought. Closing his eyes, he tried to imagine that he was Rides the Buffalo, that he'd just heard some very upsetting news. Where would he go?

"Damn!" Lifting the reins, Mitch urged his horse back toward the burial ground. What better place to hide if your whole world had just turned upside down and you didn't want to be found?

Mitch drummed his heels into his horse's flanks, overcome by a sudden need to hurry. As he passed a crumbling burial mound, he drew his horse to a halt. Had he heard a cry, or had it been the wind?

He listened for several minutes. He had just decided he was imagining things when he heard it again, a faint cry, like a cub calling for its mother.

He urged the bay toward the sound. "I'm coming," he hollered.

The bay picked its way over the rocky ground, its ears twitching nervously, only to come to an abrupt halt as a narrow chasm appeared.

Mitch shook his head. There was no way Rides the Buffalo could have crossed the chasm. He pulled back on the reins, cursing himself for thinking the boy would come this way.

"Dammit," he exclaimed. "Rides the Buffalo, where the hell are you?"

"Here! I'm down here."

Dismounting, Mitch went belly down and peered into the depths of the chasm. "Are you hurt?"

"My arm. I think it is broken."

"Damn. Anything else?"

"I can't move. My leg is stuck in a hole." There was a pause, and Mitch heard the boy sob loudly. The sound echoed off the sides of the chasm. "There is a body down here."

Mitch swore under his breath. Had the boy fallen into a grave? "Stay calm, son. The dead can't hurt you. Does the opening get wider at the bottom?"

"No."

Mitch quickly surveyed as much of the chasm as he could see. It was about four feet across. He leaned over the edge as far as he dared. "Can you see me from where you are?"

"Yes."

"All right. Don't move. I'm coming down." He turned at the sound of hoofbeats and saw Elk Chaser and Red Clements riding toward him. "I found him," he called.

Elk Chaser and Clements dismounted. Elk Chaser

glanced around, obviously uneasy at being in this place of the dead.

"He's down there," Mitch said.

Elk Chaser and Clements walked to the edge of the chasm and peered down into the crevasse.

"I'm going down after him," Mitch said.

"How'n hell you gonna bring him up?" Clements asked. "We ain't got no rope, and you can't carry him."

"I'll need you to go back to camp and get one," Mitch said. "In the meantime, I'm gonna climb down there. He says he'd got a broken arm, and that his leg is stuck in a hole."

Red Clements listened carefully, nodding all the while. "All righty," he said. "I'll be back 'fore ya know I'm gone."

"Red, give me your neckerchief and your belt, will you?"

Clements untied his kerchief and removed his belt and handed them to Mitch with a grin. "Anything else ya need?"

"No. Thanks."

"All righty then, I'll be goin'."

"Be sure to let his mother know we have found him," Elk Chaser said. He paused, then added, "Both of them."

"Will do." Clements climbed into the saddle and headed back to the village at a gallop.

Mitch tied the kerchief around his own neck, fastened the belt around his waist, then rubbed his hands together. "I'm goin' down. See if you can put a travois together."

"It will be ready when you return," Elk Chaser replied.

With a nod, Mitch sat down on the edge of the

chasm, then turned and with his back braced on one wall and his feet against the other, he began to work his way down. The rough surface quickly shredded his shirt, but he gave no heed to the damage being done to his clothing, or his back. His only thought was for the boy trapped at the bottom of the chasm. Rides the Buffalo. His son.

It seemed to take hours for him to reach the bottom. Rides the Buffalo was hunched against a bunch of rocks. His face was pale. There was dried blood on one cheek, his shirt and clout were torn, there were long scrapes on his arms and legs. He held his right arm close to his chest. His right leg was angled to one side, his foot jammed beneath a large rock and the side of the crevasse.

"Hey," Mitch said. "How you doin'?"

"I am all right," Rides the Buffalo said bravely.

"Sure you are. I'm gonna get you out of here just as soon as I can."

Rides the Buffalo nodded.

"I'm gonna try to lift that boulder off your foot," Mitch said. "When I do, I need you to pull your leg out as quick as you can, all right?"

Rides the Buffalo nodded.

"All right, here we go," Mitch said. It was a large rock. He put his hands under a gap beneath the rock and the ground, bent his legs to get some leverage, took a deep breath, and lifted. "Now!"

Rides the Buffalo groaned as he jerked his foot from under the rock.

With an oath, Mitch let the rock settle to the ground again. "You all right?"

Rides the Buffalo nodded, and Mitch knew the boy was trying not to cry.

Mitch turned his back to the boy while he examined his foot, giving Rides the Buffalo as much privacy as he could. The boy's ankle was badly swollen, but Mitch didn't think it was broken.

"All right," Mitch said. "I'm gonna strap your arm close to your chest to keep it immobile while we climb out of here." He took a deep breath. "I'm afraid it's gonna hurt like hell."

Rides the Buffalo swallowed hard, then nodded. He closed his eyes, his jaw tightly clenched, as Mitch used Clements's belt to strap Rides the Buffalo's arm to his chest.

He was just finishing up when Clements called his name.

"Yeah?" Mitch hollered back.

"Here comes the rope."

Mitch stood against the side of the crevasse, shielding Rides the Buffalo with his body, as the free end of the rope dropped over the side. He gave the rope a sharp tug. "You sure you've got the other end tied off good?"

"Yeah. Ready when you are."

Mitch deftly tied the end around his chest, then turned to the boy. "You ready to get out of here?"

"Are you really my father?"

"Yes."

"And the white woman is my mother?"

"Yes. We'll talk about it later. Right now we need to get you out of here."

Rides the Buffalo nodded.

"Here we go. I'll need you to hold on to me as tight as you can with your left arm, all right? I know this is gonna hurt, but it's the only way out."

Rides the Buffalo nodded, his dark eyes filled with trust as Mitch bent down and lifted him into his arms.

"All right," Mitch hollered. "We're ready."

It was a slow, torturous climb, holding the boy, trying to keep them both from being scraped against the rocks as they were slowly pulled up out of the crevasse. Once, the rope slipped and they fell several feet. Mitch felt his heart leap into his throat at the thought of plummeting earthward and landing on the rocks below, but then their descent stopped and they were again being reeled up, like a fish on a line.

When they neared the top, Mitch saw that there were three warriors on the rope. His mother and Alisha hovered nearby, flanked by dozens of men, women, and children.

Spirit Walking came forward to lift Rides the Buffalo from Mitch's arms; a warrior unknown to Mitch came to help him up over the edge of the crevasse.

White Robe ran forward, her face lined with concern as she knelt beside the travois where Rides the Buffalo lay, his eyes closed, his face pinched with pain.

They didn't waste any time getting back to the camp. Mitch carried Rides the Buffalo into White Robe's lodge. His mother entered close behind him.

Red Shield, the shaman, had been summoned and was already there, waiting for them.

The inside of the lodge was redolent with the scent of sage and sweet grass. Mitch placed Rides the Buffalo on a robe, then went to stand near the door, out of the way. Alisha came in to stand beside him. Elk Chaser stood on the other side of the doorway. Red Clements waited outside.

White Robe knelt beside Rides the Buffalo, brushing a lock of hair from his brow, crooning softly as the shaman examined the boy's wounds. Rides the Buffalo cried out as the medicine man explored the break in his arm.

Red Shield sprinkled hoddentin into the fire, rubbed some on Rides the Buffalo's forehead, and then offered the boy a piece of yarrow root, which would numb the pain and make him drowsy.

Mitch put his arm around Alisha as the medicine man spread a layer of moss over the break in the boy's arm, then wrapped it in a piece of wet hide. As it dried, the hide would harden, molding itself to the boy's arm, keeping it immobile. Red Shield treated the boy's ankle in the same manner.

As the medicine man stood up, Mitch released a breath he hadn't realized he'd been holding. He didn't think he'd ever experienced anything more heart wrenching than seeing his son in pain and being unable to help. His son. Damn, but that sounded good.

Red Shield was gathering his belongings when Alisha tapped him on the shoulder. "Sir, would you please look at Mitch's back?"

The old shaman grinned, amused at her use of the word "sir."

"I'm fine," Mitch said.

"No, you're not," Alisha insisted. "Sit down."

White Robe stood up and walked behind Mitch, gasping when she saw the abrasions on his back. In their concern for Rides the Buffalo, they had forgotten that Mitch had also sustained some injuries.

"Look at his left hand, too, please," Alisha said.

Mitch was muttering under his breath as he sat down. Alisha removed what was left of his shirt, shook her head, and tossed it in the fire pit.

Red Shield opened his packets of herbs and salves.

After washing away the blood, he applied a thin layer of bear grease over the cuts and abrasions on Mitch's back, then wrapped a length of soft cloth around Mitch's chest.

"My hand's fine," Mitch said as the shaman began to examine it.

Red Shield grunted softly, and after washing away the blood, he applied a coat of bear grease over Mitch's palm and wrapped it in a strip of cloth.

"Keep dry," the shaman said in his reedy voice.

"Thank you," Alisha said.

Red Shield nodded, then took his leave.

Tomorrow, Elk Chaser would leave one of his best horses and a haunch of venison at the medicine man's lodge in payment.

Later, when Rides the Buffalo was sleeping soundly, Alisha, Mitch, his mother, and Elk Chaser sat beside the fire, a strained silence between them.

Alisha slipped her hand into Mitch's, needing his strength.

Mitch looked at his mother. "Why didn't you tell me?"

"I didn't know," she said quietly. "I took the child from a trader. He knew nothing of the baby's birth. . . ." She paused to glance at Alisha. "Save that the mother did not want it because it was of mixed blood."

"That's not true!" Alisha exclaimed. "My father told me the baby was dead."

"More lies," White Robe remarked. "I did not realize the child was yours until Otter said you had come here looking for your son. I knew then that he was the father of Rides the Buffalo." She smiled sadly. "Rides the Buffalo is very like his father. I noticed it often as he was growing up. I did not know then that Otter was his father, and I thought it was only my imagination, that I was only seeing the similarities between them because I missed my own son."

White Robe looked at Mitch, her dark eyes filled with love and pain. "I love your son. I could not love him more if I had carried him in my womb."

"*Shi ma . . .*"

"Please do not take him from me." White Robe looked at Alisha. "I know he is your son, but he is also my son."

"I understand," Alisha said. "I know this must be very difficult for you, but I love him, too. My arms have been empty of him all these years."

White Robe nodded. "But you will not take him now. He needs time to heal." She took a deep breath, fighting the urge to cry. "He needs time to . . . to get used to the idea that I . . . I am not his true mother."

"We're not taking him anywhere, Ma," Mitch said. "At least not right away. Isn't that right, Lisha?"

"Yes. We have to think of Rides the Buffalo's feelings. We must make him understand that we all love him, that he hasn't lost those he loves."

Relief was visible in White Robe's face. "Thank you, my daughter."

Alisha smiled as she looked at White Robe and Elk Chaser. "We're all family now," she said, squeezing Mitch's hand. "And we have to do what's best for our son."

Chapter 28

There was an air of tension in the lodge the following day. White Robe hovered near Rides the Buffalo, offering him broth and drinks of water. Alisha caught the older woman looking at her from time to time, her eyes troubled.

Elk Chaser had left the lodge early to go hunting, and Mitch had decided to go with him. Alisha wished Mitch had stayed. She tried to make small talk, but she couldn't think of anything to say, couldn't think of anything, save the fact that she had found her son. She wanted to sweep him into her arms and hold him tight, but his injuries prevented that. In any event, she wasn't sure what his reaction would be, or how he felt about learning that White Robe wasn't his mother.

Late in the afternoon, Rides the Buffalo fell asleep. White Robe left the lodge, saying she needed to go gather some wood. Alisha nodded, wondering if White Robe had purposefully waited until the boy was asleep, thus assuring that Alisha would not have a chance to talk to him alone. Such tactics should have made her angry, but it didn't. She understood White Robe's feelings only too well.

Alisha went to sit beside her son. Her son. Tears stung her eyes as she brushed a lock of hair from his brow. Her son. She had missed so much of his life. How would she ever make it up to him? She had so much to tell him, so much to learn. She didn't know anything about him, what he liked to eat, what games he liked to play. Doubts plagued her. What if he didn't like her? What if he refused to leave White Robe and Elk Chaser? She couldn't very well drag him kicking and screaming out of the village.

"Stop it," she muttered. She took a deep breath. One step at a time. That was what she always told her students when they were learning to solve a new problem. One step at a time. She had found her son. Everything else would take care of itself.

She smiled when she realized Rides the Buffalo was awake. "How do you feel?"

"My arm hurts."

"Is there anything I can do?"

He shook his head, his expression thoughtful. "Are you truly my mother?"

"Yes."

He glanced around the lodge. "Where is . . . ?" He hesitated.

"White Robe has gone to gather wood. She'll be back soon. Can I get you anything? Something to eat? A drink of water?"

"No." He looked past her, a smile lighting his features as White Robe stepped into the lodge.

Alisha nodded at White Robe, then went outside, wondering if her son would ever smile at her like that.

The next day passed uneventfully. White Robe spent the morning scraping the hair from the hide of the deer Elk Chaser had killed the day before.

Alisha sat with Rides the Buffalo, telling him fairy tales. Her stories were quite different from the Coyote stories he was familiar with and he listened intently. She caught him staring at her from time to time, knew he had questions about her and Mitch, about what the future held. She was eager to tell him the truth, but she bit back the words. Hard as it might be, she would wait until he was ready to ask.

Alisha snuggled closer to Mitch. A glance at the smoke hole showed that the sky was growing light. It would be morning soon. She wondered what she would say when Rides the Buffalo asked about the past. Sooner or later he was bound to wonder why he lived with the Apache instead of with his mother. She tried to imagine what he must be feeling, thinking. No doubt it had been a terrible shock, learning that White Robe was not his true mother. She only hoped that he would give her a chance to explain, that, after she had told him everything, he would understand, that he would accept her.

She looked at Mitch, sleeping peacefully beside her and envied him. She had hardly been able to sleep at all. Rides the Buffalo had cried twice in his sleep. She had awakened instantly, every instinct urging her to go to him, but White Robe had always been there, crooning softly to the boy, offering him a drink of water, soothing him with her touch and her soft words. It had pained her to hear her son call another woman *shi ma* . . . mother.

With a sigh, she closed her eyes, praying that somehow everything would work out. . . .

* * *

Alisha woke with a start, the last vestiges of her dream vanishing in the low rumble that met her ears. Thunder? She rolled over to look at Mitch, saw that he was on his feet, hastily pulling on a shirt, grabbing his rifle.

"Stay with my mother!" He gave her a quick, hard kiss that felt strangely like good-bye, then ran out of the lodge.

Elk Chaser and Red Clements streamed out behind him.

Alisha sat up. "What is it?" she asked White Robe. "What's wrong?"

"Soldiers."

There was a wealth of meaning in that single word.

White Robe threw a blanket around Rides the Buffalo's shoulders, then glanced at Alisha. "Hurry."

Alisha stood up, the tension in the lodge a palpable thing. She heard another rumble, and realized it wasn't thunder. It was gunfire.

She pulled her tunic over her head, took the sheathed hunting knife that White Robe thrust at her. Following White Robe's lead, she tucked the sheath into her belt, then followed the older woman out of the lodge.

Outside, women and children and men were running in a dozen directions. Carrying Rides the Buffalo in her arms, White Robe fell in behind a group of women who were hurrying toward the broken ground where Rides the Buffalo had fallen.

Alisha glanced over her shoulder. Warriors, some on foot and some on horseback and some barely old enough to be warriors, were moving toward the entrance to the stronghold. In the distance, she caught sight of Mitch.

She stared after him, torn between her need to be with him and the need to go with her son, to protect him.

"Alisha!"

She turned at the sound of her name, saw that White Robe had stopped and was waiting for her.

"Hurry, Alisha. We must hide. You cannot help Otter now."

White Robe was right, of course. There was nothing she could do. With a prayer in her heart, she hurried after White Robe and the other women and children.

Mitch stood near the rancheria's entrance alongside Elk Chaser and Red Clements.

"Look!" Elk Chaser pointed down the narrow entrance, gesturing at the four Indian scouts riding ahead of the soldiers. *"Gusanos!"*

Mitch wasn't sure what the word meant, but a cussword sounded pretty much the same in any language. He remembered thinking that a few good warriors could hole up here and hold off an army, and that might have been true if the army didn't have Apache scouts riding with them. He swore under his breath. There was a second entrance to the rancheria; no doubt the scouts knew where it was.

The first clue they had that the back entrance had been breached was the high-pitched scream of a woman, followed by several gunshots.

Half the warriors gathered at the front immediately struck out for the back entrance.

And then all hell broke loose as the narrow entrance to the rancheria exploded, sending dirt and chunks of rock flying in every direction.

It didn't take a genius to figure out that the Indian

scouts had made their way to the entrance sometime in the night and planted a few sticks of dynamite.

The explosion was deafening.

Soldiers poured through the defile, shooting at anything that wasn't wearing sweat-stained cavalry blue.

The shrill war cry of the Apache rose in the air as the warriors fought to defend their wives and children. Dust and grit filled the air, along with the roar of rifle fire and the acrid stench of gunpowder. And over all, the cloying scent of blood, the sharp stink of fear.

Mitch took cover behind a tree trunk, methodically picking off every soldier that came into range. All around him, men were engaged in combat.

Adrenaline surged through him, backed by a powerful rage against the soldiers who had attacked his mother's people without provocation.

Elk Chaser and Red Clements fought close by, their earlier wounds forgotten as they fought for their own lives and the lives of the women and children.

It didn't take long to realize that the Indians were outnumbered. More and more soldiers poured into the Apache stronghold. The warriors began to fall back, disappearing into the rocks and crevices, leaving no more trace than smoke drifting on the wind.

"Come!" Elk Chaser shouted.

Mitch turned to follow, with Red close behind him, only to run into a fresh wave of soldiers. Mitch raised his rifle, sighting down the barrel at the nearest one. He squeezed the trigger, only to hear the hammer click on an empty chamber.

A slow smile spread over the soldier's face as he fired his rifle.

Mitch reeled backward as the bullet plowed into his right shoulder near his collarbone. There was no pain, but his arm and hand went numb and he dropped the rifle.

He was reaching for his knife with his left hand when pain exploded through the back of his head.

As from far away, he heard Elk Chaser shouting his name. He tried to answer, tried to move, but to no avail. And then he was spiraling down, down, into a turbulent sea of pain and darkness . . . .

He regained consciousness slowly, aware of a burning ache in his shoulder, a dull pounding in his head. Noise hovered around him—the whinny of a horse, the muffled cry of a child, the harsh rattle of death, and over all the high-pitched keening of women grieving for their dead.

Opening his eyes, Mitch turned his head slowly to the right, and then the left. He was lying on a blanket on the ground. Someone had slapped a bandage over the bullet hole in his shoulder. Lifting his left hand, he felt a bandage swathed around his head. An army surgeon stood a few yards across the way, dispensing medical aid and orders. A private stood at the doctor's elbow to assist him.

Feeling unutterably weary, Mitch closed his eyes again, wondering where Alisha was . . . .

Alisha! Ignoring the pain that lanced through him with every movement, Mitch struggled to sit up. He had to find Alisha, had to find his mother and his son.

"Here now," the doctor exclaimed, hurrying toward him. "Lie down, you damn fool!"

"I'm all right," Mitch growled.

"Like hell. Anyway," the doctor went on, gesturing at Mitch's ankles, "you're not going anywhere."

Frowning, Mitch followed the doctor's gaze, a foul

oath rising to his lips when he saw the shackles hob-
bling his feet. "What's going on?"

"I reckon you'll find out soon enough. Now, just lay
back there and rest. We'll be pulling out as soon as I
finish up here."

Ignoring the doctor's orders, Mitch sat up and took
a good look around. There were two rows of
wounded. He was with the Apache injured. Wounded
soldiers were spread out a few yards away, shaded by
a tarp someone had fashioned from a couple of deer
hides.

Five bodies, shrouded in blankets, awaited burial.

The bodies of the Indian dead—men, women, and
children—had been piled in the center of the village
like so much refuse waiting to be burned.

A small group of women and children were huddled
to one side; about two dozen warriors, their hands
bound behind their backs, were hunkered down a
short distance away. He recognized Elk Chaser among
them. Standing a little apart, also shackled, was Red
Clements. Four, armed troopers guarded the prisoners.

Damn. Where was Alisha?

Soldiers moved among the lodges. Mitch felt his
anger rise when he saw they were looting the wickiups, taking bows, arrows, robes, lances, and whatever
else caught their eye, for souvenirs, then torching the
lodges. Soon, the crackle of flames and the scent of
smoke filled the air.

Other Blue Coats were rounding up the horses,
herding them toward the entrance of the stronghold.

Two hours later, the village had been destroyed. The
wounded who were well enough to ride were
mounted. The others had been loaded on travois.

The captives were on horseback, hands lashed behind their backs, their feet secured to the stirrups.

Mitch was at the rear of the line of prisoners. He was beginning to hope Alisha had escaped when he saw her being escorted to her horse by a tall, good-looking soldier who helped her mount, then adjusted her stirrups, smiling all the while. Mitch was overcome by the sudden urge to smash his fist into the soldier's smiling face.

Alisha settled herself in the saddle, her gaze roaming over the captives, coming to rest on Mitch's face. "Are you all right?" She mouthed the words.

Mitch nodded. "You?"

Alisha nodded, her expression worried.

"Have you seen my mother? Rides the Buffalo?"

Alisha shook her head, then turned as the soldier spoke to her. She looked at Mitch, her heart in her eyes, as the soldier led her horse to the front of the column.

A bugle sounded. The soldiers mounted and fell in.

Mitch took a last glance over his shoulder, hatred filling his heart as he looked at the devastation the soldiers had left behind. He stared at the bodies in the center of the village, wondering if his mother and son were among them.

Chapter 29

The ride down the mountainside was hell. His arm ached, his head throbbed unmercifully. But worse than the physical pain, was the agony of not knowing if his mother and son were dead or alive. He clung to the hope that they had escaped, that they had found a place to hide. If they were alive, they would seek shelter with one of the other Apache bands.

They had to be alive. He couldn't have found his mother again after so many years only to lose her now. And his son . . .

Mitch closed his eyes, remembering his initial shock when Alisha had told him he was a father, remembering his fear when he looked over the edge of the crevasse and knew Rides the Buffalo was down there, the wondrous sense of awe that had swelled within his heart when he held his son in his arms. His son. He had been unprepared for the protective feelings that had risen within him as he held the boy, the sudden, overpowering realization that he would do anything necessary to ensure his son's survival. And later, watching the medicine man treat the boy's wounds, he knew he would gladly have endured the pain in his son's place. The thought of losing Rides the Buffalo now, of never seeing him again, was like a knife in his heart.

Please, God, please let them be alive.

He rose up in his stirrups a little, trying to see Alisha, but she was too far ahead.

Settling into the saddle, he closed his eyes again. There was nothing he could do now but rest and wait.

Alisha breathed a sigh of relief when they reached the bottom of the narrow mountain trail. Turning her horse around, she lifted one hand to shade her face from the sun as she watched the rest of the column make its way down the trail.

Soldiers first, then the captive Apache, then more soldiers followed by the Indian scouts. Traitors, she thought. She scanned the riders for Mitch, wondering how badly he had been hurt. She saw Elk Chaser and Red Clements among the captives. She had been surprised when one of the soldiers took Red captive. Later, she had heard two of the soldiers talking about him, calling him a squaw man and a renegade because he sided with the Indians.

She wondered if White Robe and Rides the Buffalo were all right. The last she had seen of them, they had been scrambling up a rocky incline. She had been behind them when her foot slipped on a rock and she had tumbled back to the bottom.

Several soldiers had been chasing them. Alisha's heart had jumped into her throat when she saw one of the troopers lift his rifle, aiming at White Robe's back. With a cry, she had grabbed the man's arm, begging him to help her. He had started to push her away until he saw she wasn't an Indian and then he had quickly stooped to help her to her feet. When she looked back up the hill, White Robe and her son were gone.

It took over an hour for the entire column to reach the bottom of the trail. She had asked one of the soldiers where they were going, and he had told her they were headed for Fort Apache. The soldier had assumed she was an Apache prisoner and had assured her that she would be well cared for, that they would notify her family that she had been found. Alisha had played along, thinking that she might be of more help to Mitch and the others if the soldiers thought she had been captured by the Apache. Alisha had asked what was going to happen to the Indians. In an effort to assure her, perhaps, that she was safe, he had told her that the warriors would be imprisoned, or perhaps sent to Oklahoma. The women would be kept on the reservation.

They rode for several hours before the captain called a halt. Two tents were set up, one for the captain, and one for the wounded soldiers.

The prisoners, Mitch and Red Clements among them, were herded into a group. Two guards stood nearby. Mitch turned his head, and she saw that the bandage around his head was stained with dried blood.

Several other troopers guarded the Indian ponies.

The Indian scouts were gathered into a small group, off by themselves. Alisha wondered if they were Apache, and if so, why they were acting as scouts for the cavalry against their own people.

Shortly after the captain called a halt, Alisha was given a seat in the scant shade offered by one of the tents. A tall, lanky trooper who looked to be no more than seventeen or eighteen brought her a canteen of water and some beef jerky. He blushed hotly when she thanked him.

It was, she thought, going to be a long, long day.

Mitch sat on the ground between Elk Chaser and Red Clements.

"Well," Clements muttered, staring at his bound hands, "ain't this a hell of a mess."

Elk Chaser grunted in agreement. He looked over at the Indian scouts, his eyes dark with hatred.

Mitch glanced at Elk Chaser. "Do you know if they got away?"

Elk Chaser shook his head.

"Why did they attack the village?" Clements wondered aloud. "That's what I'd like to know." He looked at Elk Chaser. "Any of your people been making war lately?"

"The Blue Coats do not need a reason," Elk Chaser said with a sneer.

"One of their forts was attacked," Mitch said. "I overheard two of the troopers talking about it."

Elk Chaser grunted. "The Blue Coast cannot tell one tribe from another. They will not rest until they have wiped our people from the earth."

Mitch swore softly. At least Alisha was alive and well. One of the cavalry officers would look after her, see that she made it home. He closed his eyes. His head hurt, his shoulder hurt. He was hot and thirsty and tired. "Anybody got any ideas about how to get out of this?"

"I don't have an idea in hell," Clements said, "but we'd better think of one afore we get to the fort. I ain't lookin' forward to no jail time. I got people waitin' on me, dependin' on me."

A faint smile curved Elk Chaser's lips. "Rest, my brothers," he said quietly.

"You know somethin' you ain't tellin' us?" Clements asked.

"I know that many of our warriors escaped. They will send the women and children to our brothers in the south, and then they will seek vengeance for our dead."

Red Clements looked at Mitch and grinned. "Sounds like there might be another battle."

Mitch nodded. "I reckon."

By nightfall, the camp was well established. Guards walked the perimeter, the horses were contained in a rope corral, the prisoners had been fed and were bedded down for the night.

Alisha had been offered the captain's tent, but she had refused it. She wanted to be outside, wanted to be able to see Mitch.

The Apaches had been very quiet. There was no conversation among them. Even the children were silent, their dark eyes wide and watchful, as if they were waiting for something to happen.

Wrapped up in her blanket, her head pillowed on her arm, Alisha gazed toward the group of captive men. She couldn't see Mitch in the dark, but it comforted her to know he was nearby.

She looked up at the vast indigo vault of the sky, picking out the constellations. It reminded her of the summer nights she had snuck out of the house to meet Mitch down by the creek. They had often stretched out on a blanket, her head pillowed on his shoulder as they watched the stars. She had always been at ease with Mitch. Even back then, she had known she could rely on him, that he would protect her, that she could tell him anything and he would listen. He had been her best friend in all the world. When he left town, he had left a huge hole in her life and in her heart that no one had ever been able to fill.

And now, at long last, she was his wife.

She fell asleep, clinging to the hope that her son was still alive, that, somehow, they would all be together again.

Mitch came awake with a start, not knowing what had roused him. And then he heard it again. A faint cry, like that of a nightbird. He turned to look at Elk Chaser and saw that the warrior was awake and staring into the distance.

"What's up?" Red Clements whispered.

Mitch shook his head. "I'm not sure." His eyes narrowed as he heard the same cry again. He grinned as he glanced over at Clements. "Jail break, maybe."

Alisha woke suddenly, glad to escape the nightmare she had been having. It was still dark, and the camp was quiet save for the intermittent snores coming from the soldiers sleeping nearby.

Rising, she crept away from the encampment, seeking a place where she could relieve herself. A clump of mesquite a good distance from the camp was the only cover and she ducked behind it, thinking she would never complain about the outhouse back home again.

She was about to return to her blankets when an arm curled around her neck and a large, callused hand covered her mouth, trapping her cry of terror in her throat.

*   *   *

Mitch felt a quick sense of fear as a hand holding a knife reached out of the darkness. That fear was quickly replaced by a sense of relief as his bonds were cut.

Impossible as it seemed, two Apache warriors moved among the captive warriors, cutting them free. Like shadows fleeing the sun, the freed warriors silently scattered and disappeared into the darkness as if they had never been there.

Mitch followed Elk Chaser, his heart pounding as he waited for a sentry to raise the alarm, but all remained quiet.

When they were out of sight of the camp, a warrior appeared leading two horses. Elk Chaser swung aboard the near one, then looked down at Mitch.

"We will separate and meet at the place of the talking trees."

Mitch nodded, then glanced back toward the camp. "Alisha . . ."

Elk Chaser looked past Mitch and smiled.

Turning, Mitch saw two riders coming toward him. Alisha was one of them.

"At the talking trees," Elk Chaser said.

"What of my mother?"

"She will be there," Elk Chaser replied. The words *if she can* hovered, unspoken, between them.

With a wave of his hand, Elk Chaser disappeared into the darkness, along with the warrior who had been holding the horses.

Mitch swung onto his horse's back, then rode over to Alisha. "Are you all right?"

"I'm fine," she said tremulously. "Are you?"

A gunshot from the camp was the first indication that their escape had been detected. It was followed by

a shrill war cry, and more gunfire. In the flash of gunfire, Mitch saw several warriors fleeing in the direction
Elk Chaser had gone.

"Let's get the hell out of here," Mitch said.

She didn't argue. With one hand wrapped around
the reins, and the other clinging to the saddle horn, she
followed Mitch into the darkness.

They hadn't gone far when another horse and rider
came into view. Mitch swore, thinking the cavalry had
found them, then grinned as he recognized Red
Clements.

"This way!" Red hollered. "I know a place where we
can hole up till the shooting stops."

With a nod, Mitch and Alisha fell in behind him.

They rode for an hour, alternating between a gallop
and a trot. The sun was clearing the horizon when
Clements pulled his horse to a halt. Dismounting, he
waited for Mitch and Alisha.

"We walk from here," Red said.

Alisha slid gratefully out of the saddle, watched, in
openmouthed astonishment, as Red took a step toward what looked like solid rock and disappeared
from sight.

Mitch grunted softly as he stepped forward, only
then realizing that there were actually two huge boulders side by side that appeared to be one solid object.
The opening was just wide enough for a horse to pass
through.

Turning, he smiled at Alisha. "Come on."

The narrow defile, which was about ten feet long,
opened into a small, grassy space ringed by boulders.
Alisha thought it looked like a fairyland, with a carpet
of green grass and a tiny pool fed by an underground

spring. A few shrubs grew near the water. A bush seemed to grow out of one of the rocks.

"We'll rest here a mite," Clements said.

"How did you find this place?" Alisha asked.

"My wife's people use it for a hideout from time to time." Clements patted his horse on the shoulder, then removed the bridle and gave the animal a swat on the rump. Alisha grinned as she recognized Sophie.

Mitch removed the bridle from his mount, too, then turned and helped her remove her horse's bridle and saddle. She realized her horse was the only one wearing a saddle. Mitch turned her horse loose to graze with the other two.

"Do you think the others got away safely?" Alisha asked.

Clements nodded. "Sure. Them 'Paches know their way around this desert the way a woman knows her way around her kitchen."

"What about the women?"

Clements chuckled. "They'll be all right. I reckon their men will go after them soon as they regroup." Clements looked at Mitch and frowned. "You look all done in."

"Yeah, that's how I feel, too."

Clements removed a small pile of rocks, dug down a foot or so, and pulled out a bundle, which turned out to be a buffalo robe. Inside the robe were several small buckskin pouches. He opened one and pulled out several hunks of dried venison. He handed one to Alisha and one to Mitch, then spread the buffalo robe on a flat stretch of ground and sat down.

Alisha murmured her thanks. The jerky was old and tough but it was better than nothing, and she ate it without complaint.

"Well," Red remarked with a lopsided grin, "I'm all tuckered out."

Mitch grunted softly. He hated to admit it, but a nap sounded damn good. Lowering himself onto the robe, he held out his hand for Alisha. She sank down beside him, her head on his shoulder, one arm draped across his chest.

Clements stretched out on the other side of the robe and was instantly asleep.

Alisha ran her fingers over Mitch's cheek. "Are you sure you're all right?"

"Yeah." It was almost the truth. His arm hurt like the devil, his head ached, but he'd been hurt worse a time or two in the past.

"Do you think Rides the Buffalo is all right?"

"Sure, darlin'."

"Are you just saying that to make me feel better?"

Mitch chuckled. "I'm trying to make us both feel better."

"I can't lose him again, Mitch. I just can't."

"I know." He kissed her cheek. "Let's hope for the best. That's all we can do."

With a sigh, she closed her eyes and snuggled closer. He was right, there was nothing to do but wait, and hope.

And pray.

Chapter 30

When she woke, the sun was high in the sky and she was alone on the buffalo robe.

Scrambling to her feet, she felt a momentary sense of panic, but then she saw the horses grazing peacefully near the seep and knew that everything was all right.

Combing her fingers through the tangles in her hair, Alisha walked toward the water.

Sophie whickered softly at her approach.

"Hi, girl," Alisha murmured. She stroked the horse's neck for a few moments, then knelt down and drank from the cool, clear water, wondering where the men had gone.

Rising, Alisha leaned against Sophie's shoulder, idly scratching the mare's ears, her thoughts turning toward the battle. It had been like a scene out of hell . . . the sudden appearance of the soldiers, the noise and confusion, the stink of gun smoke and death.

The warriors had burst out of their lodges to defend their homes and loved ones, trusting that the women would get the children to safety. And the children . . . though they were wide-eyed with fear, they hadn't made a sound.

A prayer for the safety of her son and her mother-in-law rose from her heart. Rides the Buffalo had to be all right, she thought. Surely she would sense it if something had happened to him.

Feeling suddenly restless, she started walking toward the far side of the enclosure. Sophie trailed at her heels like a puppy.

There were berry bushes on the far side of the spring. Alisha picked a handful, eating them as she walked along. It was remarkable that this tiny spot of greenery could exist in the middle of this huge pile of rocks in the midst of the desert.

Walking on, she found an arrowhead made of obsidian. Bending, she picked it up. It was smooth and warm in her hand.

She walked on, with Sophie following her. It was peaceful here, she thought, a tiny oasis of solitude. She wondered how many men and women had sought refuge in this place in years gone by, wondered what it would be like to make love to Mitch here, in this place, under the stars. There was no chance of that, she thought, not as long as Red Clements was with them.

She smiled as she thought of Clements. For all his rough speech and ways, she had grown very fond of him. She wondered what his wife in the East was like. Try as she might, she couldn't imagine Clements walking down a city street, or wearing city clothes. Far easier to picture him in buckskins, hunkered down around a campfire.

Two wives. Alisha shook her head. It was beyond comprehension.

With a sigh, she turned back toward the buffalo robe, her heart skipping a beat as she saw Mitch striding toward her.

Smiling, she ran into his arms.

"Hey." He wrapped his left arm around her and hugged her tight.

"Hey yourself," she retorted. "Where have you been?"

He kissed her soundly. "Hunting."

"Hunting?"

Mitch nodded. "We managed to trap a couple of rabbits. And Clements found some skunk cabbage."

"How are we going to cook the rabbits?"

Mitch grinned at her. "Thought we'd eat 'em raw."

"Mitchy!"

He laughed at her. "Don't worry. Clements has a flint."

"Well, thank goodness."

"Hey, if you're hungry enough, you'll eat just about anything."

"I guess so."

"I know so."

"I found some berries over there," she said, gesturing over her shoulder.

"I know," Mitch said with a roguish grin. "I tasted 'em when I kissed you." He drew her into his arms, one hand sliding down over her buttocks to draw her up against him. "Give me another taste."

"Mitch!"

"What?"

"We're not alone."

Mitch glanced over his shoulder. "Pay no attention to Red. He's busy skinning our dinner."

He drew her up against him once more, showering her with kisses, driving every other thought from her mind. Like a flower unfolding in the heat of the sun, she opened for him, wanting more, more.

Alisha moaned softly, her need blossoming, surging within her. Her body responded instantly to the touch of his hands and lips. Her breasts felt full, heavy. Warmth rose up within her, spreading outward.

She ran her hands up and down his back, over his bare chest, loving the feel of his skin beneath her fingertips—the hardness of him, the heat of him.

"Mitch . . . "

"What do you want, darlin'?" he murmured.

"You. Just you."

"Now?"

She blinked up at him, breathless and aching. "Isn't there somewhere we can be alone?"

Mitch glanced around, searching for someplace where they could be alone, and finding none.

"Guess we'll have to wait awhile," he murmured.

Alisha nodded, though waiting was the last thing she wanted.

"Tarnation," growled a voice. "You two ever gonna come up for air?"

Startled, Alisha peered around Mitch to see Red Clements smirking at them.

"Go away, Red," Mitch growled.

"I reckon I could go out and have a look around," Clements offered, "even though we just come from outside and there weren't nothin' there."

"Thanks, Red."

"Yeah, yeah," Clements muttered irritably, but there was a humorous glint in his eyes when he said it. "I'll be back in an hour or so."

"Be careful out there," Mitch warned.

Clements grunted. "You two be careful in here."

Feeling her cheeks grow hot, Alisha buried her face

against Mitch's chest, certain she would never be able to look Clements in the face again.

Mitch put his finger beneath Alisha's chin and tilted her face up. "Change your mind?"

Alisha shook her head. "No." She touched the bandages on his arm and head. "But maybe we should wait. I don't want to hurt you."

"I'm already hurting," he said, nuzzling her ear. "But I know how you can make it better."

"Hmmm, I'll just bet you do."

"I'd pick you up and carry you to my lair like a proper savage," Mitch growled, "but I'm afraid this time you'll have to walk."

"That's all right," she said, laughing. "You'd better save your strength."

"Gonna wear me out, are you?"

"Maybe," she replied with a saucy grin.

Taking her by the hand, Mitch led Alisha to the buffalo robe and drew her down beside him. Wrapping his good arm around her, he kissed her.

She melted against him, her body molding to his, hardly aware that he was removing her tunic, removing his clout, until she felt his skin against hers. It was a feast for the senses, with the buffalo robe soft and warm beneath her and Mitch's hard, muscled body at her side. A soft breeze ruffled her hair, she felt the sun on her face, felt a wild stirring deep in her loins. For the first time in her life, she felt free, uninhibited by convention, by what was right or wrong. She wasn't the preacher's daughter here, didn't have to worry about town gossip, or what the school board would think. She could say and do whatever she wished without fear of approbation.

It was a heady feeling, to be free, to be in Mitch's arms, to know he loved her. Ah, what heaven to be able to taste him and touch him to her heart's delight, to hear him whisper her name, his voice filled with love and desire.

To whisper his name in return. "Mitch . . . Mitch . . . " Nothing but his name, the very sound of it, the very word itself making her heart swell with love.

"I'm here, darlin'."

"Kiss me."

He smiled down at her. "Here?" he asked, kissing her forehead.

"Lower."

"Here?" He kissed her nose this time.

"Lower."

"Here?" He dropped a kiss on her left cheek, and then her right. "Or here?" His lips slid to her mouth, lingering there as his tongue slid inside for a quick taste. She tasted of berries warmed by the sun.

Alisha made a soft purring sound of pleasure as his tongue slid over hers. She moved restlessly beneath him, wanting to be closer, to feel him surround her, envelop her. Only when he was a part of her did she feel complete. She welcomed his weight on top of her, loved the feel of his skin, hot and moist against her own.

She lifted her hips to receive him, sighing with pleasure as their bodies merged. His mouth burned a path from her lips to her breasts and back up again, his voice a husky whisper as he told her he loved her. She ran her hands over his back, shoulders, his chest, clung to him as his movements quickened, as the heat built between the two of them, until there was no time for thought, until she trembled beneath him, caught up in a maelstrom of emotion and liquid heat that spread through her, hotter and hotter, until, together, they plunged over the edge into ecstasy.

Chapter 31

Warmed by the sun, drifting in the hazy afterglow of lovemaking, Alisha rested her head on Mitch's shoulder and watched the fluffy white clouds drifting across the sky.

"Look," she said, "that one looks like a buffalo."

Mitch made a soft sound of assent. Finding shapes in the clouds had been something they had done often as children.

"And that one," she said, pointing. "It looks like a mother holding a baby."

"And that one," Mitch said, kissing the top of her head, "looks like us."

"Us?" She stared in the direction he pointed and saw two clouds that did, indeed, look like a man and woman lying side by side.

She sighed and snuggled closer, her fingers making lazy circles on his chest. What a wanton she had become, she mused. Even in her wildest dreams, she had never imagined she would be lying naked on a buffalo robe, with Mitch beside her. It was a wondrous feeling, the sun warm on her skin, the furry robe beneath her,

272 *Madeline Baker*

the breeze ruffling her hair. And Mitch's arm around her, making her feel warm, secure. Loved.

"We'd better be getting dressed," Mitch remarked, a note of regret in his voice. "Red'll be back soon."

"Oh!" Alisha bolted upright and reached for her tunic, horrified by the thought of Red coming back and finding her and Mitch lying naked on the buffalo robe. It was bad enough that Red knew why they had wanted to be alone.

"Hey!" Mitch grabbed her arm and pulled her back down beside him. "Not so fast."

"But you said . . ."

"Never mind what I said." Mitch rolled on top of her, resting his weight on one elbow. "I don't want to let you go."

"But Red . . . he'll be . . . soon . . . oh, uh-oh . . ." With a sigh, she slid her arms around his neck and kissed him back. It wasn't fair, she thought, that he had such power over her. One kiss and she melted like dew beneath the sun.

He deepened the kiss, kindling the flame already burning inside her. That quickly, she wanted him again.

"Mitch . . ."

"I'm here, darlin'."

"I love you."

"I love you, too." He kissed her again, intent on showing her just how much, and then Sophie whinnied. Muttering an oath, Mitch rolled to his feet and draped a corner of the buffalo robe over Alisha. "Red's back."

"Oh!" Grabbing her tunic, Alisha ducked under the buffalo robe and shimmied into her dress.

By the time Red reached them, she was dressed.

Red took one look at Alisha's tangled hair and
flushed face, and grinned. "Guess I should have made
it two hours." He dropped a couple of birds near the
fire pit, then grinned at Mitch. "You told me you didn't
like rabbit."

"Thanks," Mitch said dryly. "See anything out
there?"

"Nah. It's all clear."

Mitch nodded. "We'll leave for the talking trees
tonight then."

"Suits me."

"Talking trees? What's that?" Alisha asked.

"It's a rendevous point. Elk Chaser said to meet him
there."

"How far is it?"

"About two hours from here. Elk Chaser took me
there shortly after I arrived."

Alisha nodded. If their son was still alive, he would
be there.

They left the canyon at nightfall. Alisha rode between Mitch and Red, wondering if Rides the Buffalo
and White Robe had made it to the talking trees place
safely, wondering what the future held for all of them.
It was hard to believe her life had once been dull, she
mused, as they crossed a shallow ravine. In the last
few weeks she had been captured by Indians, hidden
in a cave tending a wounded man, met her son, married her childhood sweetheart in an Apache ceremony,
and been in the midst of a battle. Surely that was
enough excitement for anyone. All she wanted now
was to settle down with her husband and son. She
wondered if Mitch would want to stay in Canyon
Creek. She knew he had always hated it there—but it

was a nice town. She had never lived anywhere else; but if Mitch wanted to sell his father's ranch and leave town, she would go wherever he asked. It didn't matter where they lived, so long as the three of them were together.

She placed her hand over her belly, wondering if she might be carrying a baby even now. She remembered being in the family way before, the wonder of it, the awe that had come with the realization that she carried a new life within her. She remembered how her arms had ached to hold her baby, how her breasts had ached as they filled with milk. It would be different this time, she thought. Mitch would be there beside her. She imagined how it would be, watching their child grow, watching it do all the things she had missed before.

A coyote howled in the distance, putting an end to her reverie.

A short time later, a warrior materialized out of the darkness. He spoke to Mitch, and then disappeared back into the shadows.

They rode on for another few yards, and then Alisha saw a few hastily constructed wickiups silhouetted in the faint glow of a campfire. The "talking trees" were cottonwoods. She could hear them whispering to each other as the wind stirred the leaves.

Mitch reined his horse to a stop. Dismounting, he came to help Alisha down.

She glanced around the village, looking for some sign of Rides the Buffalo, realizing as she did so that if he was here, he would probably be asleep.

She followed Mitch toward the campfire, where a dozen or so warriors were sitting, talking quietly.

"*Yah a teh*," he said.

"*Yah a teh*," replied Fights the Wind.

"Is my mother here?"

Fights the Wind gestured toward the nearest wickiup. "She was wounded in the battle. My woman is looking after her."

"Is she badly hurt?" Mitch asked anxiously.

"She will recover."

Mitch nodded. "Is Rides the Buffalo with her?"

"No."

"Mitch!" Alisha's hand clutched his arm and he drew her up against him, afraid to ask the next question.

He swallowed hard, steeling himself for the worst. "Is the boy dead?"

"I do not know. Red Eagle found your mother unconscious and brought her here. When she awoke, she had no memory of what happened." Fights the Wind looked at Alisha, his gaze sympathetic. "There is room for you in my wickiup," he said. He looked at Red Clements. "You are also welcome."

"Obliged," Red replied.

"What of Elk Chaser?" Mitch asked.

"We have not seen him." Fights the Wind held a stick in his hand. He broke it in half and tossed the pieces into the fire. "We have sent runners to our brothers in the north and the south," he said. "Soon, our young men will have new songs to sing." He looked up at Mitch, his face hard. "Our people will be avenged."

Mitch nodded. Taking Alisha by the hand, Mitch headed for Fights the Wind's lodge. Clements trailed behind.

The glowing embers of a fire offered the only light inside the lodge. Glancing around, Mitch counted three women, two men, and four children wrapped up in blankets.

"I think I'll bed down outside," Clements whispered. "There ain't enough room in here to skin a cat."

"Yeah, I think you're right." He looked at Alisha. "Do you mind sleeping outside?"

"No."

Moving into the center of the wickiup, Mitch looked for his mother, his anxiety easing a little when he saw her sleeping peacefully between the daughters of Fights the Wind.

Taking Alisha by the hand, he followed Clements out of the lodge. Pulling a blanket from the back of his horse, he handed it to Alisha. "Find us a place to bed down. I'll be along as soon as I take care of the horses."

"Mitch . . . "

The pain in her voice tore at his heart. "I know, darlin'."

She looked up at him, and even in the dim light, he saw the tears in her eyes. "He can't be dead. He can't be! I'd know if he was."

"I'll go back to the rancheria tomorrow," Mitch said.

"I'm going with you."

"All right. Get some rest now."

She nodded. Wrapped up in her grief, she found a place to spread the blanket. She huddled there, her hand over her mouth to stifle her sobs.

"Your gal all right?"

Mitch glanced over his shoulder at Clements. "As well as can be expected, I guess."

"I'm sorry about the boy."

"We're going back to the rancheria tomorrow."

"Back? You reckon that's a good idea?"

"Probably not, but she won't rest until she knows. And neither will I."

Clements nodded. "What do you reckon happened to Elk Chaser? He should have made it here before us."

"I don't know." Mitch stripped the rigging from Alisha's horse. The movement set his wounded arm to throbbing and he swore as he dropped the saddle to the ground, then tethered the animal to a tree.

Wordlessly, Clements picked up a handful of grass and began rubbing his horse down with it. Life was hard sometimes, he mused. Damn hard. "I'm heading out tomorrow myself," he remarked. "My wife back in St. Louis probably thinks I've been kilt. Course, I've got to stop by and visit Mountain Sage afore I head east." Clements looked over at Mitch and grinned. "Ain't easy, keepin' two women happy."

"Yeah," Mitch replied dryly. "You look real upset about it."

"Well, I do my best. Iffen you want, I'll ride on back to the rancheria with ya."

"Obliged for your offer, but I think your women probably need you more." Mitch stared into the distance, thinking about his son. Rides the Buffalo had been well-taught in the ways of survival. He was a capable hunter. He knew how to find food and water and shelter. But, dammit, he was still just a four-year-old boy. A boy with a broken arm and a bum ankle.

Clements nodded. "I hope you find him."

"Thanks, Red."

"Iffen ya ever need me, send word to the Jicarilla, or leave a message for me at the hotel in Canyon Creek."

*   *   *

"I don't remember what happened," White Robe said. "One minute we were running up the hillside, looking for a place to hide, and the next, I woke up here." She clutched Mitch's hand. "Please find him for me, *ciye*. I must know if he's . . . I must know."

"I'll find him, Ma," Mitch promised. "I'll bring him back to you." The words *dead or alive*, though unsaid, echoed in his mind.

"What of Elk Chaser?" White Robe asked.

"I don't know. No one has seen him."

White Robe closed her eyes. "I fear he is gone."

"Ma?"

A single tear slipped down her cheek. "He would have been here by now, if he could."

"He saved my life, you know?"

White Robe shook her head. "How?"

"During the battle, a Blue Coat had me in his sights. Elk Chaser killed him."

White Robe smiled faintly. "He told me of a vision he had, in the cave after he was wounded. He said he wanted to join with his ancestors but he was told he could not, that if he did, one who was alive would die. And now . . . "

"Ma." Mitch squeezed his mother's hand. She looked frail lying there, older. A bullet had grazed her left temple during the battle, and he found himself staring at the cloth wrapped around her head, thinking how close he had come to losing her.

"He is gone," she said. A high-pitched keening, like that of a wounded animal, rose in her throat as she turned her back to him.

Mitch felt a swift surge of hatred for the U.S. Cavalry, for the misery they had caused his wife and his mother. He rubbed his shoulder. He had a score to settle, too, he thought. Runners had already been sent to advise the other clans of the treachery of the Blue Coats. Soon the warriors would gather together to seek vengeance for their dead.

Mitch blew out a deep breath, knowing he would ride the war trail alongside his mother's people to avenge the lives of Elk Chaser, and his son.

They left the canyon at first light. Alisha knew that Mitch could have made the journey faster alone, but she refused to be left behind to wait and wonder. If Rides the Buffalo was alive, she wanted to be there when he was found and if he wasn't . . . she wanted to be there for Mitch. Spirit Walking had also insisted on riding along.

She looked over at Mitch. He wore a clout, leggings, and moccasins. His buckskin shirt was stained with blood. She stared at the hole near his shoulder, shuddered to think how close she had come to losing him.

She studied his profile. He had changed somehow. There was a new hardness about him that hadn't been there before, an anger that she sensed simmering just beneath the surface.

He had always kept his feelings to himself. Even as a boy, he had never willingly shared his pain with her. He was hurting now, she thought, both physically and emotionally. Growing up, he had always hidden away in his cave to nurse his wounds. She had often followed him there, refusing to leave even when he told her to. Sometimes she had just sat there quietly so he wouldn't be alone; sometimes she had ignored his harsh words and wrapped her arms around him, holding him tight until she felt the hurt and anger seep away.

That morning, before they left the canyon, she had asked him if his head hurt, if his arm hurt, and he had shrugged and told her not to worry, he was fine.

But he wasn't fine. She had seen his face when he told his mother good-bye that morning, seen the pain in his eyes, heard it in his voice.

They rode steadily all that day, stopping only briefly to eat, and rest the horses. Spirit Walking rode quietly behind them, keeping an eye on their back trail.

Once, far off in the distance, they saw a cloud of dust.

"Soldiers," Mitch muttered. It was the first word he'd said in hours.

She felt her own tension mount as the hours passed. Mitch had said they would reach the rancheria by nightfall, and with every passing minute she grew more and more aware that the waiting would soon be over. She tried to prepare herself for the worst even as she hoped for the best.

Rides the Buffalo couldn't be dead, not when she had just found him. She'd hardly had any time to talk to him, to get to know him. She didn't know what his favorite color was, if he was ticklish, if he liked sweets, if he shared her allergy to strawberries.

It was near dusk when they reached what was left of the village. Alisha was bone-weary by the time they reached the entrance to the rancheria.

Alisha felt the sting of tears as she glanced at the carnage the soldiers had left behind, at the blackened lodgepoles, at the burned remains of the Indian dead. A small breeze stirred the ashes from a cold cookfire. And over all hung the acrid smell of death.

"Lisha?"

"Oh, Mitch, I hope he hasn't seen this."

"Yeah." Mitch glanced around. They couldn't stay here.

Reining his horse toward the river, he found a smooth stretch of ground. Brush and trees screened the village from sight.

Dismounting, Mitch offered Alisha his hand and she slid out of the saddle. He wrapped his arm around her and held her close for a moment.

She could feel the tension in him, see it in the clenched muscles of his jaw.

He held her for a moment more, then led her horse to a tree and began to unfasten the cinch.

"Here," she said, "let me do that."

"I can do it."

"Your arm . . . "

"I said I can do it."

She bit down on her lip to keep from arguing, watching while he stripped the rigging from her mount, then tethered the horse to a tree.

"Why don't you two set up camp?" Mitch suggested.

"What are you going to do?"

He swung onto the back of his horse. "I'm gonna go have a look around."

"Mitch . . . "

"I won't be gone long."

"I will go with you," Spirit Walking said, reaching for his mount's reins.

"No, you stay here with Alisha."

Spirit Walking nodded.

Mitch rode through the burned-out village, heading for the broken land where Rides the Buffalo had been found when he ran away. The boy had told him that he liked to go there to be alone, even though his mother had told him time and again that he shouldn't.

He felt his anger rising, growing stronger, as he passed lodge after lodge that had been looted and burned. The unfairness of it, the waste of lives and property, the incalculable suffering . . . he shook his head. Living in the West, he was aware of the constant warfare between the Indians and the whites. He knew there had been atrocities on both sides. He had heard of ranches being attacked, horses and cattle stolen, families killed, homes burned. Several years ago, the Mimbreno chief, Mangus Coloradas had entered an enemy camp alone, intent on making peace. Two armed guards had been placed in charge of the chief. One of them had heated a bayonet in the campfire and stabbed Mangus Coloradas in the leg. When the warrior sprang up, the guards both fired their rifles at him. There had been bloodshed and violence on both sides. Being somewhat caught in the middle of both worlds, Mitch had never taken sides, knowing that both Indians and whites had legitimate grievances, but this attack was personal. His son was missing, and most likely dead. His mother was wounded. Her husband was missing.

He scoured the ground for sign, but it was impossible to distinguish one small set of prints from the dozens and dozens of footprints and hoofprints.

"Rides the Buffalo, can you hear me?"

Mitch reined his horse to a halt, listening as his voice echoed off the canyon walls . . . *Hear me . . . hear me. . . .* Please, Mitch thought, please hear me.

He rode onward, nearing the crevasse where Rides the Buffalo had fallen, the only sound that of his horse's hooves on the hard-packed ground. Every movement jarred his wounded shoulder, and he cursed the Blue Coat who had shot him.

He swore again, recalling the battle, the odd sense that he was fighting himself as he took aim against one of the troopers. As a lawman, he had killed white men before. It had been part of the job. But fighting against the U.S. Cavalry . . . he shook his head. There was no way to explain it. He didn't understand it himself.

"Rides the Buffalo! Can you hear me?"

He listened for several moments, but heard only silence. If the boy hadn't come here, then where the devil was he?

Reining his horse around, he made a wide sweep of the area, conscious of the fact that it would be dark soon, that scavengers would be out searching for food. There were mountain lions in the hills. A small boy would be easy prey.

He rode to the far end of the rancheria, growing more and more discouraged, more and more afraid of what he might find. He couldn't go back without Rides the Buffalo, couldn't bear to see the worry in Alisha's eyes.

He called the boy's name again, and then again.

"Here."

Mitch jerked his horse to a stop, his gaze sweeping the area. Had he really heard a voice? "Rides the Buffalo, answer me."

"Here. I am over here." Relief washed through Mitch like a tidal wave. Swinging out of the saddle, he ran toward a jumbled pile of rocks and boulders. As he drew closer, he saw a small hand emerge through a child-sized gap in the rocks.

Dropping to his knees, Mitch peered into the pile of rocks. "You all right in there?"

"I am hungry."

Ignoring the pain in his shoulder, Mitch reached into the narrow opening and lifted Rides the Buffalo out. The boy moaned softly as Mitch gathered him into his arms.

"Sorry," Mitch said, quickly loosening his hold on the boy. Setting Rides the Buffalo on his feet, Mitch quickly checked him over. His broken arm was still wrapped in deer hide. The wrap around his foot had worked its way loose and Mitch saw that his ankle looked more swollen than before. Mitch noticed he wasn't putting any weight on it. His arms and legs were scratched, there was a cut on his cheek.

Carefully, he lifted Rides the Buffalo into his arms and placed the boy on the back of his horse, then vaulted up behind him and clucked to the horse, eager to get back to Alisha, to see the look on her face when he rode up with their son.

It hadn't taken much time to set up camp. Alisha spread their blankets on a smooth stretch of ground, used a piece of wood to dig a pit for a fire, put their foodstuffs within easy reach. Spirit Walking had gone off to see if he could find some fresh meat.

She paced a small area for several minutes and then, as if drawn by some invisible cord, she ventured up the path toward the village.

She picked her way through the wreckage, remembering her trepidation when she first arrived, remembering how Mitch's mother had made her feel welcome.

A few items remained miraculously intact: a doll made of cornhusks, a single moccasin, a clay pot. She picked up the pot, recognizing it as one that belonged to White Robe. A terrible sadness engulfed her as she looked around, remembering how the village had looked only days ago, filled with men and women she was just beginning to know. In the short time she had been with the Apache, she had found them to be a warm, friendly people, nothing like the savages the people in town claimed they were.

With a sigh, she turned away from the ruined village and made her way back to the river. She shivered as darkness spread a cloak over the land.

Where was Mitch? And where, oh where, was their son?

Chapter 32

"Where is my mother . . . ?" Rides the Buffalo asked, his tone uncertain.

"She's waiting for you at the place of the talking trees," Mitch said, letting *she* remain ambiguous. He pulled back on the reins a little, slowing his horse's pace to avoid jarring the boy any more than necessary.

"And my . . . where is Elk Chaser?"

Mitch considered a lie, but there had already been too many lies told. "I don't know, son."

Rides the Buffalo turned in the saddle so he could see Mitch's face. "Are you really my father?"

" 'Fraid so. Is it such a terrible thing?"

Rides the Buffalo regarded him through somber black eyes. "Are you going to take me away from my . . . from White Robe?"

"Not if you don't want to go."

"Why did I not grow up with you and the white woman?"

"It's a long story, son."

"I want to know."

Mitch sighed. If the boy was old enough to ask, he was old enough for the answer. "Your mother and I were in love. Our parents didn't approve, so I left home to find a place where your mother and I could be together. Her father found out and sent me a letter, a message, saying that she had married another man. I believed him. I didn't know your mother was pregnant with you at the time. When you were born, her father sent you away, and told your mother that you had died." Mitch paused. "Do you understand?"

Rides the Buffalo nodded.

"Your mother would never have given you away, son, you've got to believe that." Mitch took a deep breath. "She's waiting for us."

"She is here?"

"Yeah."

"Do I have to call her mother?"

"Not if you don't want to. I'm sure she'd like it though. She loves you."

Rides the Buffalo's eyes widened. "She does not even know me."

"She's still your mother. I expect you to treat her with the same respect you give White Robe, who is your grandmother. The same respect due all women."

Rides the Buffalo nodded. Like all Apache children, he had been taught from birth to treat his elders with respect.

"We'll be there soon," Mitch said. He felt a shudder go through the boy. Was it pain, or fear?

Alisha looked up from the meal she was preparing at the sound of hoofbeats, felt her heart begin to beat wildly as she saw the burden in Mitch's arms.

Leaping to her feet, she ran to meet them.

"Is he all right?" she asked anxiously, and then, seeing that Rides the Buffalo was asleep, she lowered her voice. "Where did you find him?"

"He was hiding in a pile of boulders at the far end of the rancheria," Mitch said. "Near as I can tell, he's none the worse for wear."

Reaching up, Alisha took Rides the Buffalo from Mitch and cradled him in her arms. Love welled up inside her as she held her son to her breast at last.

She gazed up at Mitch, her eyes bright with tears. "Thank you," she murmured tremulously. "Thank you."

Mitch nodded, thinking he had never seen a more wondrous sight in all his life than Alisha holding their son in her arms.

Mindful of his injured shoulder, he slid carefully to the ground and tethered his horse near Alisha's.

"He's heavy," Mitch remarked. "Do you want me to take him?"

Alisha shook her head. "He is heavy," she said, smiling as she hugged her son closer, "but it's a welcome weight."

Moving closer, Mitch draped his good arm around Alisha's shoulder, then brushed a kiss across her cheek.

"We're together," Alisha said. "A family, at last."

"He looks like you," Mitch remarked.

"Like me? No." She shook her head. "He looks like you, every inch."

"Be that as it may, I see you in him as well."

"Do you think he'll ever love me, the way he loves White Robe?"

Mitch nodded. "In time. Where's Spirit Walking?"

"I'm not sure." She gestured at the hare cooking on a spit over the fire. "He brought that and then left again."

Rides the Buffalo woke up long enough to eat, then quickly fell asleep again.

Alisha gathered him into her arms once more and held him all through the night, reluctant to put him down. She stroked his hair, his cheek, counted each finger and toe. Her son, in her arms at last.

Her heart swelled with love as she gazed down at him. Her son. Tears filled her eyes and dripped onto his cheek and she kissed them away.

Looking up, she saw Mitch watching her and she knew everything she had ever wanted, would ever want, was there, within reach at last.

She had thought Mitch would want to go back to the place of the talking trees in the morning, but he seemed to be in no hurry to leave and when she remarked on it, he told her he thought Rides the Buffalo needed a few days of rest before they made the journey. Knowing that his mother would be worrying, Mitch asked Spirit Walking to go back and tell White Robe they had found Rides the Buffalo.

Alisha suspected Rides the Buffalo was well enough to travel, but that Mitch was using it as an excuse to give her time to spend alone with their son. Giving them both time to get to know their son better.

She was glad to see that the tension had drained out of Mitch, that some of the anger had faded from his eyes.

Rides the Buffalo woke just after dawn, his stomach growling loudly. Alisha offered him something to eat and drink. He was asleep again almost immediately.

He slept most of that day. Alisha sat beside him, reaching out now and then to touch him, to reassure herself that he was really there. He was a handsome child, with his wavy brown hair and copper-hued skin, so like his father.

Mitch went hunting in the morning and returned with a rabbit and a couple of quail. The fresh meat was a welcome addition to the larder.

Rides the Buffalo woke late in the afternoon. Mitch took him downstream to bathe and relieve himself while Alisha washed the boy's vest and leggings.

When they returned, the air was fragrant with the scent of roasting rabbit.

Mitch ruffled Rides the Buffalo's hair. "Let's see what kind of cook she is, shall we?" Mitch grinned as the boy's stomach rumbled loudly. "Good thing she skinned that rabbit. I think you'd eat it, fur and all."

Rides the Buffalo looked up at Mitch and laughed, and somehow that broke the tension between them.

Mitch and Alisha spoke of trivial things while they ate. Rides the Buffalo said little, his gaze constantly moving between them.

Alisha smiled at him, hoping he would soon be comfortable in her presence. It was all she could do to keep from sweeping him into her arms, but she knew the first move had to be his.

"How's your arm feeling?" she asked. "Does it hurt much?"

Rides the Buffalo shrugged. "A little."

"And your ankle?"

"It hurts, but . . ."

"Only a little," Alisha said with a smile.

Rides the Buffalo grinned at her.

"This must be difficult for you," Alisha said, gesturing from herself to Mitch. "Learning that we're your parents."

Rides the Buffalo nodded, his expression solemn.

"Do you have any questions we can answer for you?"

"Do I have to stay with you?"

Alisha looked at Mitch, not knowing what she should say.

"We'd like for you to come and live with us for a while," Mitch said.

"Where do you live?"

"In a place called Canyon Creek. I have a ranch there."

"Is it far away?"

"Not too far," Mitch said.

"Does my mother . . . does White Robe no longer want me for her son?"

"Of course not," Mitch said quickly. "She loves you as much as ever. She's your grandmother, and more than welcome to come with us. I should like that very much."

A look of astonishment passed over Rides the Buffalo's face, and Mitch knew the boy had not considered that he might be able to stay with his mother and grandmother.

"So, you see," Mitch said, "she will still be part of your family. Our family."

"What if I do not want to go with you?"

Mitch glanced at Alisha, then shook his head. "We won't force you to go with us," he said. "Your mother and I want you to be happy."

Rides the Buffalo looked at Alisha. "*Shi ma.*"

Alisha nodded. She blinked rapidly, but couldn't keep the tears from welling in her eyes. "Yes," she said. "Oh yes."

"Did you believe your father when he said I was dead?"

"Yes, but I came looking for you as soon as I learned you were still alive."

"You didn't give me away?"

"No, of course not! Why would I have done that?"

"Because I am Apache. The whites hate us."

"Oh, no," Alisha said. She laid her hand on his arm. "That's not true. Your father is Apache, and I love him. Just as I love you."

"How can you love me? You do not know me."

Mitch sighed. Rides the Buffalo had asked him the same question.

"You're my son," Alisha said. "I loved you before you were born, when you were in here." She placed her hand over her womb and smiled.

"Were you glad you were going to have a baby?"

"Oh, yes. Very glad."

Rides the Buffalo considered that for several moments. And then, with a weary sigh, he scooted closer to Alisha, curled up beside her, his head in her lap, and closed his eyes.

Alisha glanced at Mitch, pleasure and astonishment evident in her expression.

"I guess he likes you," Mitch remarked with a smile. "But then, so do I."

Later, after Rides the Buffalo had been tucked into bed for the night, Mitch and Alisha went for a walk along the river. A full moon played among a handful of wispy clouds. A warm breeze whispered ancient stories to the cottonwoods. Frogs and crickets played a lively serenade.

"Beautiful night," Alisha mused. "Kind of reminds me of summers back home, when we walked by the creek."

Mitch laughed softly. "Bet I know what day you're remembering." He gave her hand a squeeze. "I never did get even for that day you pushed me in the river."

Alisha looked up at him and laughed, and then, seeing the look in his eyes, she shook her head. "You wouldn't!"

"It'll cost you."

"Cost me? How much?"

His gaze moved over her, hot as a summer's day. "Make me an offer."

"One kiss."

"Not good enough."

"Two?"

"Miser."

"Three?"

He shook his head. "You've got to do better than that."

"Well, what do you want?"

"The same thing I've always wanted. You. All of you. Every inch. Every touch."

"Oh, Mitch . . . " She loved him with her whole heart and soul. Loved him as she had never loved another.

"You look like you swallowed a piece of the sun."

"That's how I feel, too. I'm so happy." She stood on tiptoe. "Kiss me, please."

"Anytime, darlin'," he drawled. "Anytime."

She closed her eyes as his lips found hers. Magic, she thought, it was magic, the desire that sparked so quickly to life, the way his touch made her heart race, made every fiber, every inch of her flesh come achingly alive, achingly aware. His clever hands moved knowingly over her body. His kisses fell like warm rain on her face, her neck, her breasts.

Bending down, he took hold of the hem of her tunic and lifted it over her head, and then, ever so slowly, he kissed his way back up to her lips. She was quivering with desire, burning with need, when his mouth covered hers again.

Her hands trembled as she divested him of his clothing, pulled him down on the cool grass beside the river. Straddling his hips, she began to kiss him, gasping with pleasure as his flesh melded with hers.

He urged her on until he felt her shudder with pleasure, and then he rolled her over and found his own fulfillment in her sweet flesh.

They stayed in the valley for three days. Alisha would have liked to stay longer, but Mitch was suddenly anxious to get back to the place of the talking trees and let his mother see that Rides the Buffalo was alive and well. She felt guilty then, for wanting to wait longer.

Rides the Buffalo seemed in good spirits. The swelling in his ankle had gone down. His arm did not pain him overmuch, though it would be weeks before the break mended completely.

Mitch lifted Alisha onto the back of her horse, then settled Rides the Buffalo behind her. Knowing, somehow, that he would never see this place again, he took a last look around, wanting to imprint it in his memory. And then he swung onto the back of his own horse and led the way down the narrow mountain trail that led out of Apache Pass.

Chapter 33

It was close to midnight when they reached the place of the talking trees. Two warriors stepped out of the shadows as they neared the entrance. One of them lifted a hand in recognition, and then the two men faded back into the shadows, disappearing so completely Alisha wondered if they had actually been there.

The canyon was dark save for the last faint embers of a fire near the center of the camp. Rides the Buffalo was asleep. Dismounting, Mitch lifted him from the back of the horse and ducked inside Fights the Wind's lodge.

The warrior sat up as Mitch stepped inside.

"It's all right," Mitch said. "It's me."

Fights the Wind grunted softly. "I see you found the boy."

"Yes."

"Otter, is that you?"

"Yes, *shi ma.*"

White Robe sat up, her arms outstretched. "My son. Give me my son."

Picking his way through the half-dozen or so people

sleeping in the lodge, Mitch knelt beside his mother and placed Rides the Buffalo in her arms.

Rides the Buffalo's eyelids fluttered open. He smiled when he saw White Robe. Snuggling against her, he closed his eyes and went back to sleep.

"He is well?" she asked. Her gaze moved over Rides the Buffalo's face. "His arm . . . ?"

"He's fine. Just tired is all."

White Robe held the boy close a moment, then, settling him on the blanket beside her, she laid back down, one hand stroking his hair.

Mitch turned to find Alisha standing in the doorway. He glanced around, quickly realizing there was no place for them to sleep. Making his way toward her, he took her hand and left the wickiup.

Outside, he unsaddled her horse, then, grabbing the buffalo robe draped over his horse's withers, he took Alisha's hand and led her away from the wickiups. Finding a flat stretch of ground, he spread the robe, then drew her down beside him.

Alisha rested her head on his shoulder. "She's not going to let him go, is she?"

"Lisha . . . "

"What are we going to do?"

"We must be patient. It'll be fine."

"I know we said we wouldn't take him from her, but I don't want to stay here forever. I want to go home."

"I know." For a time he had entertained the notion that they would stay here and make their home with the Apache, but he had given up that idea when the cavalry attacked the village. On his own, he might have stayed to fight, but he couldn't risk Alisha's life, or the life of his son. The war between the Apache and the whites wouldn't end until the Apaches had been killed or they were all confined to reservations. In the meantime, there would be more battles, more lives lost.

He brushed a kiss across her cheek. "Get some sleep, darlin'."

"Mitch . . ."

"We'll talk about it in the morning."

With a sigh, she snuggled against him and closed her eyes. He was right. There was nothing they could do tonight.

Mitch woke abruptly, wondering what had awakened him. Sitting up, he saw a large group of warriors gathered near the lodge of Fights the Wind.

He glanced at Alisha, sleeping soundly beside him. Being careful not to disturb her, he slipped out from under the buffalo robe and went to see what was going on.

A warrior he didn't recognize stood in the middle of the group, speaking rapidly. The Apache warriors gathered around him nodded, exclaiming, "*Ai, ai.*"

Mitch moved around the circle until he found Fights the Wind. "What's going on?"

"Many Horses just arrived. He has come from our brothers, the Jicarilla. They want us to join them to fight the Blue Coats."

Mitch glanced at the faces of the men gathered nearby. It was easy to see they were anxious to fight, anxious to strike back at the Blue Coats for the unwarranted attack at Apache Pass.

He couldn't blame them. "How soon will you be leaving?"

"As soon as our women can be ready to go. Will you join us?"

Mitch turned as Alisha came up beside him.

"Go?" she asked. "Go where?"

Mitch gestured at the Jicarilla warrior. "He's come to ask for our help in fighting the soldiers."

"Another fight?" Alisha asked anxiously. "When? Where? Not here?"

"No, not here."

"Mitch, you're not going with them?"

He hesitated. "No."

"Thank God."

"We will miss you," Fights the Wind said. "You fight like one of us."

It was, Mitch thought, the finest compliment he had ever received. He felt a keen sense of regret as he turned away from the warriors. He had come to love and respect these people and couldn't help feeling that he was turning his back on them, that he owed it to them to stay and fight.

But then he looked down into Alisha's face, saw the worry and the fear in her eyes, and knew he couldn't ask her to stay. She wanted to go home, and he couldn't blame her for that.

"Mitch?" She gazed up at him, her expression troubled. "You want to stay, don't you? You want to fight with them."

He nodded. He had never lied to her before; he wouldn't start now.

"How can you? The soldiers are your people as much as the Apache."

"Are they?" He shook his head. During the fight in the rancheria, the soldiers had been the enemy, nothing more. "It doesn't matter. I'll take you home."

She looked up at him for several minutes, and then shook her head. "No, we'll stay."

"Lisha . . . "

"I don't want you feeling guilty later, and blaming me."

"And I don't want to risk having you or Rides the Buffalo get hurt."

"We're staying," she said firmly. And with a toss of her head, she pushed her way through the warriors.

Frowning, Mitch watched Alisha make her way toward Fights the Wind's wickiup.

"She is a wise woman," Fights the Wind remarked.

"Yeah," Mitch drawled. "Pretty, too."

Fights the Wind slapped Mitch on the back. "Come, there is much to do."

In a remarkably short time, the camp was dismantled and the people were ready to go.

Mitch rode near the back of the caravan. His mother rode beside him. Rides the Buffalo shared a horse with Alisha.

Fights the Wind had told him it was only a short distance to the Jicarilla encampment. They would be there by late afternoon.

Mitch glanced at his mother, wondering if it was a mistake to move her. She looked haggard and worn out. Frail. He knew she was grieving for Elk Chaser, but her silence bothered him. She was too quiet, too withdrawn. It was as if she had lost the will to live. He had to make her realize that her life wasn't over, that Rides the Buffalo still needed her, that being the boy's grandmother was as important as being his mother.

"Mitch?"

He glanced over at Alisha. "Something wrong?"

"Where's Red? I just realized I haven't seen him since we got back."

"He went to be with his family. I reckon we'll see him soon enough."

Alisha nodded. She had grown quite fond of the man.

They reached the Jicarilla stronghold just before dusk. It was a larger village than the one in Apache Pass. An air of anticipation hung over the camp. She felt it as soon as they entered the encampment. Everywhere she looked, she saw preparations for war. The men all seemed to be working on their weapons—cleaning and repairing old ones, or fashioning new ones. Old men sat in the sun, telling tales of battles past to wide-eyed youngsters. Boys not yet old enough to fight stood in small groups, bragging about their fathers and brothers, talking excitedly of the battle to come, of the time when they would be given the chance to fight the Blue Coats. Women were preparing food and clothing. The shaman moved among the people, distributing hoddentin to the warriors.

Alisha saw Red Clements sitting in front of a lodge, cleaning a rifle. He looked up just then. Seeing her, he rose to his feet and walked briskly toward them.

"Well, hell," he drawled. "I never expected to see you here."

"I never expected to be here," Alisha replied with a smile.

Clements looked at Mitch and shook his head. "You crazy, bringing her here? We're going to war."

Swinging a leg over his horse's neck, Mitch dismounted. "It was her idea."

Clements looked at Alisha, his eyes thoughtful. "Is that so?"

Mitch slapped Clements on the shoulder. "She had

some idea that I'd regret it if I ran out on . . . on my people."

Red nodded slowly. "As wise as she is pretty," he said.

Reaching up, Mitch brought Alisha to the ground.

"I see you found the boy," Clements remarked. "How ya doin', son?"

Rides the Buffalo grinned. "I am well."

Clements glanced at White Robe, then looked over at Mitch. "How's yer ma doin'?" he asked quietly. "She don't look so good."

Mitch blew out a sigh. "She's grieving for her husband. This business with Rides the Buffalo has got her down, too."

"I reckon I kin understand that," Clements replied. "But, hell, it ain't like she's gonna lose the kid. She's his grandma, after all."

"I know. She'll come around," Mitch said. And hoped it was true.

"The boy and yer women can stay in my lodge," Red offered. "Course, you and me'll have to bed down outside."

"Thanks, Red."

Reaching out, Mitch drew Alisha to his side. He held her close a moment, then lifted Rides the Buffalo to the ground. He smiled at his son, then turned to help his mother dismount.

"*Ashoge, ciye*," White Robe murmured.

With a sigh, Mitch folded his mother into his arms and held her close. "It'll be all right, *shi ma*."

Looking around, watching the warriors prepare for battle, Alisha wondered if anything would ever be all right again.

*   *   *

The battle, when it came, came quickly. Scouts rode into the village the following afternoon, advising that the army was less than an hour away. The news spread rapidly through the village. The women hastily gathered their children to them. The men collected their weapons, then ran for their horses.

Alisha stood outside Red Clements's lodge, along with White Robe and Rides the Buffalo, watching as Mitch and Red got ready. Red Clements's wife, Mountain Sage, sat nearby. She was a lovely woman, much younger than Alisha had imagined, with a round face and huge dark eyes. Her three children, a girl of about six and two boys which she guessed were about two and four, sat beside her. Mountain Sage's expression was solemn as she handed Red a small pot of paint. He smiled at her, then dipped his finger in and began to apply it to his face.

Alisha watched with a sense of trepidation as Mitch spread a thin layer of black paint over the lower half of his face. It reminded her of a night when she had gone down to the river to meet him. She had been nine or ten at the time.

He hadn't been there when she arrived. She walked along the riverbank, noticing the way the moonlight danced on the water, listening to the sounds around her. Mitchy had taught her to be aware of the creatures that lurked in the shadows, those who only came out in the dark.

She paused near their rock, gazing down at the river. It glistened like a twisting black ribbon as it snaked its way along. She held her breath as a deer picked its way down to the edge of the water on the opposite side of the bank. The animal tested the wind a moment, then lowered its head to drink. She stood, frozen, until the deer bounded away.

Deciding that Mitch wasn't coming, she turned and started up the narrow path that led home.

She was about halfway up the hill when the most horrible creature she had ever seen jumped out at her from behind a tree. She had taken one look at its face, screamed, and ran for home.

"Alisha, wait! It's me."

She ran a few more steps; then, recognizing his voice, she turned. "Mitch? You scared me half to death." Hand pressed to her heart, she had stared at him, at the bold black slashes that covered his face. "What are you supposed to be?"

"A warrior!" he said proudly.

"What's that stuff on your face supposed to do? Scare your enemy to death?"

It had scared her then, she thought. It scared her even more now. He hadn't been in any danger when he'd been a boy; now he could be killed. Why hadn't she insisted on going home? She could live with his guilt and resentment better than his death.

All too soon, the warriors were ready. They were going to ride out and engage the cavalry on the prairie rather than let the cavalry bring the battle to the camp.

There was a last flurry of activity as the women bid their men farewell.

Alisha blinked back her tears, stifled the urge to beg Mitch to stay with her, when he came to tell her good-bye.

"Don't worry," he said as he pulled her into his arms.

She nodded, knowing she would burst into tears if she tried to speak.

She clung to him tightly, then stepped aside as he hugged Rides the Buffalo and his mother. He kissed her one last time, and then he was riding away with the other warriors, leaving her feeling cold and empty and wondering if she would ever see him alive again.

Mitch rode between Red Clements and Spirit Walking, his heart pounding with excitement and trepidation. There hadn't been time to be afraid back at Apache Pass, no time to think, no time to worry. The soldiers had attacked, and he had responded.

But now . . . thoughts of Alisha, of his mother, his son, crowded his mind. Never had he had more to live for, more to lose.

He rubbed his shoulder, which was still sore. He thought of Elk Chaser and the other Apaches who had been killed by the soldiers. He thought of his mother, who might have been killed, of the women who had been shot trying to protect their young, of the little boy he had seen clubbed to death, of the old woman who had been trampled beneath a cavalryman's horse, of the old man who had been bayoneted while trying to protect his aged wife.

The need to avenge their deaths rose up within him. He looked at the warriors riding ahead of him, and he knew their anger, their pain, their need for vengeance. The spirits of all the Apaches who had been killed, who had died protecting their families, who had watered the earth with their blood, seemed to call to him, demanding they be avenged. He heard the voices of Elk Chaser, of Cheis, of Diyehii, felt his own spirit swell within him. The blood of warriors flowed in his veins.

It tied him to the People, to the land. Though he hadn't been raised as a warrior, he was one of them, accepted as such. He was suddenly ashamed of the white blood that flowed in his veins.

Alisha wandered through the camp, too nervous to sit still, too upset to eat, to think of anything but Mitch. Had the battle started? What would she do if he were killed? How could she live without him?

She studied the other women, noting that they, too, seemed to be filled with nervous energy, but contained it better than she did. No doubt they were wondering and worrying, too. Some of them were tanning hides, others were drying meat, others were sewing, or sitting outside, nursing their babies. She wished she had something to occupy her hands, her time, something to take her mind off the fearful present, the uncertain future.

Finally, needing someone to talk to, she sought out White Robe. She found Mitch's mother sitting in the sun, staring off into the distance. Rides the Buffalo lay beside her, his head in her lap, asleep.

"May I sit with you?" Alisha asked.

For a moment, White Robe didn't acknowledge her and then, with a wave of her hand, she gestured for Alisha to sit down.

"Tell me about Mitch," Alisha said as she sat down.

"I would think you would know him as well as anyone," White Robe replied.

Alisha shrugged. "What was he like when he was Rides the Buffalo's age?" She hadn't known him then.

"Much like this one," White Robe said, stroking Rides the Buffalo's cheek. "Curious, always wanting to know why."

"He's still yours, you know," Alisha said quietly. "All that's changed is that you've taken your rightful place in his life. He still needs you. He still loves you. I only hope that someday he'll love me as much."

"Alisha." White Robe studied her face a moment. "I remember you."

"We never met."

"No, we never did. But I knew who you were. Otter spoke of you often. I remember seeing you one day."

"You do? When? I don't remember."

White Robe smiled faintly. "Of course you don't. You were asleep."

"Asleep! Where? When?"

"It was by the river. I went looking for Otter and found the two of you. He was sitting with his back against a rock. You were asleep beside him." She glanced down at Rides the Buffalo and smiled. "You had your head in his lap. I don't remember now why I had gone looking for my son. I only remember that he told me he couldn't come with me because he didn't want to wake you. You were the only friend he had."

"I'm sorry you and I never met before," Alisha said quietly. "It might have made all this so much easier. For everyone."

"I have behaved badly. Selfishly. Please forgive me."

"There's nothing to forgive."

White Robe placed her hand on Rides the Buffalo's shoulder, a world of love and tenderness in that simple gesture.

"You've done a wonderful job raising him," Alisha said. "No one . . . no one could have done better."

"*Ashoge*, my daughter."

Alisha drew a deep breath as she glanced into the distance, wondering where Mitch was, if the battle had started. She turned as she felt White Robe's hand on her arm.

"The waiting is never easy," White Robe said.

Alisha nodded, thinking how awful it must be for Mitch's mother, not knowing for certain what had happened to Elk Chaser. She didn't think she could bear it if Mitch didn't come back, if she never knew how he was killed, or where his body lay.

"Mitch . . . oh, Mitchy," she whispered. "Please be careful."

The noise. It pummeled him from all sides. The sound of gunfire. The shouts. The high-pitched scream of a dying horse. The gasps of the wounded. The sound of flesh striking flesh. The thunderous beat of his own heart.

Dust filled the air, so he saw everything through a dun-colored haze. Gun smoke stung his eyes, filled his nostrils, along with the cloying scent of blood.

His own blood, oozing from a bullet hole in his side.

He ducked, reining his horse in a sharp turn, barely avoiding a bayonet thrust. Turning in the saddle, he fired point-blank at the trooper. The force of the gunshot sent the man toppling from the saddle.

It seemed the fighting had been going on forever. He had no idea who was winning. Did anyone ever really win?

The numbness was wearing off the wound in his side, replaced by a throbbing, burning pain. Blood soaked his shirt, his leggings.

He fired at another trooper, missed, and fired again. He was lining his sights on another soldier when everything went black.

Chapter 34

"They come!"

The words were shouted through the village. Women, children, and men too old to fight hurried from their lodges, their faces anxious as they searched for their husbands, sons, and fathers among the returning war party.

Alisha stood beside White Robe, hardly daring to breathe as she searched for Mitch. Oh, Lord, where was he?

A high-pitched keening wail filled the air. It sent shivers down Alisha's spine. Mitch, Mitch . . .

She glanced at White Robe. "Do you see him?"

White Robe shook her head. "No . . . "

So many wounded.

So many dead. Alisha stared in horror at the blanket-wrapped bodies. Was he one of them?

She looked down as Rides the Buffalo slipped his hand into hers and gave it a squeeze. "There," he said, pointing.

She looked at the travois behind Fights the Wind's horse. Red Clements rode beside Fights the Wind. Mitch must be alive, she thought. They wouldn't haul him on a travois if he wasn't. With a cry, she ran across the sun-bleached ground.

"Mitch. Oh, Mitch." His eyes were closed. His face was pale. A bloody cloth was wrapped around his middle.

Fights the Wind reined his horse to a halt before Red's lodge. Mountain Sage embraced Red when he dismounted, then stood aside so he could hug his children.

White Robe and Rides the Buffalo had followed Alisha and now they stood on the opposite side of the travois.

"Rides the Buffalo, go for the shaman," Red said. He looked up at Fights the Wind. "Help me carry him inside, will ya?"

With a nod, Fights the Wind dismounted and the two men carried Mitch inside and laid him on a pile of furs.

Alisha followed close behind. It frightened her, how pale Mitch was, how still. His breathing was shallow, labored.

Red and Fights the Wind spoke a few moments, then Fights the Wind turned to leave the lodge.

Alisha laid her hand on the warrior's arm. "Fights the Wind, thank you."

Fights the Wind shrugged. "I owed him a life."

Alisha nodded, remembering that Mitch had saved the life of Fights the Wind when they fought the Comanche.

Alisha knelt beside Mitch and took his hand in hers. "Mitch? Mitchy, can you hear me? Mitch!"

Red placed a hand on her shoulder. "He'll be all right."

She nodded, wanting to believe him. But how could

she, when he looked so pale? When he lay so still? A fine sheen of sweat covered his brow.

It seemed like hours before Red Shield entered the lodge. Clements and his wife took Rides the Buffalo and their three children outside, but Alisha refused to budge from Mitch's side. She sat there, clinging to his hand, while the shaman examined the ugly wound in Mitch's side. White Robe sat near the fire pit, her hands tightly clasped in her lap.

Alisha turned aside, fighting the urge to vomit, as Red Shield dug the bullet from Mitch's side, cleansed the wound, sprinkled it with healing herbs. then bound it in a length of clean cloth.

When the medicine man had done all he could, he left Alisha some yarrow root for the pain, spoke briefly to White Robe, then left the lodge.

Alisha stayed at Mitch's side all that day, only vaguely aware of Mountain Sage moving about the lodge as she cared for her children.

White Robe lingered close by, as did Rides the Buffalo, all of them waiting. Waiting.

He writhed in pain. Hot, burning pain that throbbed through his right side, burning like all the fires of an unforgiving hell. He could see the flames all around him, shimmering fingers of fire that rose higher and higher, hotter and hotter, threatening to consume him.

He cried out, begging for water. One drink of cool water to put out the fire.

And an angel appeared beside him. An angel with a halo of honey-gold hair and brown eyes filled with worry and compassion. And love. So much love.

"Alisha . . . "

"I'm here."

She offered him a cup of water and he drank and drank, then fell back on the robes, exhausted.

When next he woke, it was to quiet darkness. Alisha slept beside him, her head resting near his shoulder.

Turning his head, he brushed a kiss across her brow.

She woke instantly. "Mitch?"

"Shhh."

"Are you all right?"

"Yeah. Fine."

The wry tone of his voice made her smile. "I've been so worried."

He glanced around the lodge. "How did I get here?"

"Fights the Wind brought you."

Mitch grunted softly. The last thing he remembered was someone hitting him across the back.

"Fights the Wind said they're leaving tomorrow."

"Leaving? For where?"

"They're going across the border to Mexico."

Mitch grunted softly. His mother had told him the Apache often sought refuge in the Sierra Madre Mountains of Mexico. It was a favorite hideout for Geronimo and his band.

Alisha took a deep breath. "Are we going with them?"

"Is that what you want?"

"I just want to be with you." She brushed a lock of hair from his forehead, worried by the fever still burning through him. "You should get some sleep."

"We need to talk."

"Later. You need to rest now."

"Could you get me a drink?"

"Sure." She filled a cup and held it for him. He

drank greedily, emptied the cup, and asked for more. Nothing had ever tasted better.

"Rest now," she said. "I'll be here if you need me."

He felt a little better when he woke again. His fever had gone down. The pain in his side had lessened, though not much. He started to sit up, but the movement sent pain splintering through his side and he fell back, cussing. From outside, he could hear the sounds of the camp being dismantled as the Apache prepared to move.

Damn! He had to get up, had to find Alisha and decide if they were going to the Sierra Madre with the Apaches.

Taking a deep breath, he pulled himself into a sitting position as Alisha entered the lodge.

"Here, now!" she scolded. "What do you think you're doing?"

"Getting up."

Hurrying toward him, she put her hands on his shoulders and pushed him back down. "Oh, no, you're not. You're not getting up for at least a week."

"A week! I can't lie here for a week."

"Oh, yes, you can." She placed a hand on his brow. "You've still got a fever."

"Dammit, Lisha, if we're leaving, I've got to get ready."

"We're not leaving."

"No?"

She shook her head. "You're in no condition to be riding a horse, or go bumping around on a travois. Besides, I don't think I want to go to Mexico. Do you mind?"

"No. But I'm not sure it's safe for us to stay here alone, either."

"We won't be alone. Red is staying, too."

"Is that right?"

"He said he needs to go see his wife in St. Louis, so he's sending Mountain Sage and their children to Mexico with Fights the Wind, and he'll meet them there in the spring. Are you hungry?"

"No."

"You need to eat. Mountain Sage made some rabbit stew."

Mitch shook his head. "Just get me something to drink, will you?"

He drained the cup she brought him, then grimaced.

"What is it?"

"I need to go outside."

"What? Oh." She glanced around the sparsely furnished lodge. "You need a bedpan."

Mitch snorted softly. "Well, you're not likely to find one here."

"No, I guess not."

"Go get Clements."

"I don't think you should get up so soon. Maybe I can find something for you to . . . "

"Lisha, just get Clements."

"All right."

Red came at Alisha's call, a broad grin on his face. "I told ya he'd be all right, didn't I, missy? Now, what can I do fer ya?"

"Mitch needs to . . . uh . . . go outside."

"Ahh. Well, come along then." Red helped Mitch to his feet. "You gonna make it?"

Mitch swayed a little, cursing the dizziness that swept through him. "Yeah."

"Here we go, then."

Step by slow step, they made their way outside and into the trees beyond.

"I hear you're staying behind," Mitch said.

"You heard right. I need to be getting to St. Louie 'fore winter sets in."

Mitch nodded, too out of breath to reply. "If I don't make it—"

"Here, brace yourself agin this here tree," Red said. "I don't wanna hear any talk about yer not makin' it. You got people what need you. Give me a holler when you're ready to go back."

By late afternoon, the Apaches were gone. Alisha stood outside Red Clements's lodge, staring at the emptiness that surrounded her. Nothing remained but patches of blackened ground where lodge fires had burned. It was quiet, so quiet. Red had gone hunting. White Robe had gone looking for wild vegetables. Mitch was sleeping.

She glanced at Rides the Buffalo, who was sitting in the shade. Thinking this might be a good time to get to know her son better, she went to sit beside him.

"How are you feeling?" she asked.

Rides the Buffalo shrugged. "I am all right. Why did we not go to Mexico with Fights the Wind and the others?"

"Because your father is badly hurt."

"Will we go with them when he is better?"

"No."

"Will we stay here?"

"No." She took a deep breath. "We're going home. To my home," she added quickly. "In Canyon City."

Rides the Buffalo frowned. "Where is this place, Canyon City?"

"Not too far."

"What tribe lives there?"

"No tribe," Alisha said, smiling.

"There are no Apache there?"

"No."

"It is the village of the white eyes then?"

Alisha nodded.

"They will not want me there."

"Maybe not at first. But only because they don't know you. Your grandmother White Robe used to live there, long ago, when she was married to Mitch's father." She saw no reason to tell the boy White Robe and Garrett had never married.

"She ran away."

"Yes," Alisha said. "But she didn't run away from the town. She ran away from her husband."

"Do we have to stay there?"

"I don't know. As soon as your father can travel, we'll go home. And then we'll see." Alisha smiled cheerfully. "You might like it, you know. I'll teach you how to read and write."

"What is read and write?"

Alisha picked up a stick. She wrote Rides the Buffalo's name in the dirt, and then pointed at it. "That's your name." She pointed to each letter and told him what it was. "Where I come from, people can read those letters, those words, and know what it says. We have books which are filled with words. Some of the books tell stories, called fairy tales. They're like the stories White Robe tells you about Coyote."

"Write something else," Rides the Buffalo urged. "Write my father's name."

With a smile, Alisha printed Mitch's name, and then drew a heart around it.

Rides the Buffalo looked at her strangely. "What is that?"

"It's a heart," Alisha said, giggling. "When you draw a heart around someone's name, it means you love them." She looked at her son, and then drew a heart around his name, as well.

Rides the Buffalo smiled at her. "I think I would like to know how to read and write." He took the stick from her hand and drew the letter *R* in the dirt. The lines were rough and wiggly, but it was definitely an *R*. He looked up at her, obviously waiting for her approval.

"That's very good," she exclaimed softly, and praised him lavishly as he spent the next half hour writing his name.

"What is this?"

Alisha and Rides the Buffalo looked up at White Robe's approach.

"I am learning how to read and write," Rides the Buffalo said proudly. He pointed at his name. "I wrote that."

"I see." White Robe looked at Alisha. "Perhaps you will teach me, too."

Alisha smiled, pleased by the warmth and acceptance in White Robe's voice. "Of course. I think there is much we can teach each other."

Six days passed before Mitch felt strong enough to travel, but Alisha insisted they wait another week. She said it was to give Rides the Buffalo's injuries more time to heal, but Mitch knew it was on his account.

On the day they were to leave, Mitch and Rides the

Buffalo sat in the shade while Alisha and Red packed their belongings, and White Robe dismantled the lodge.

Mitch looked at his son and grinned. "There are advantages to being laid up," he remarked, though it galled him to have to sit there.

"Laid up?" Rides the Buffalo asked curiously.

Mitch pointed at his son's broken arm. "Injured."

Rides the Buffalo nodded.

"Alisha tells me she's teaching you to read and write."

"Yes," he said proudly. "I can write my name."

"Your name," Mitch remarked. "What would you think about having a white name, too?"

"White name?" Rides the Buffalo shook his head. "Why?"

"Well, you do have white blood in you, you know. When we get back to town, you might be more comfortable if you had a white name. And you'll be going to school soon. It might be easier if you had a name that sounded like everyone else's."

"What name would I have?"

"I don't know. We'd have to talk it over with your mother and your grandmother."

"Is Mitch your white name?"

"Yes, Mitch Garrett."

"Mitch Garrett," Rides the Buffalo spoke the words slowly. "What does it mean? How did you earn it?"

"Well, Mitch was my grandfather's name. And Garrett was my father's name."

Rides the Buffalo thought about it a moment, and then nodded. "Will my name be Garrett?"

"Well, your last name will be Garrett."

"Last name?"

"White people have two names, a first name and a last name. Mitch is my first name."

Rides the Buffalo looked confused. "Can I wear your name?"

"If you like."

"We would have the same name, then?"

Mitch nodded. "Think about it. We don't have to decide now."

"Is White Robe going with us to the white man's city?"

"Yes." When Mitch had first mentioned it to his mother, she had said she would never go back to Canyon Creek, but she had quickly relented. Mitch and Rides the Buffalo were the only family she had left, and her bad experiences there were only because of her first husband.

"We're jest about done here," Red said. "You two ready?"

Mitch looked at his son. "I'm ready. How about you?"

"I am ready."

"Then let's do it."

The journey, which should have only taken four days at most, took seven. Red had suggested a travois for Mitch, but Mitch had refused. He was tired of being treated like an invalid, tired of the weakness that plagued him, the ache in his side.

They made quite a little caravan, with Clements riding at the head, followed by White Robe and Rides the Buffalo, with Mitch and Alisha bringing up the rear.

They stopped frequently so Mitch and Rides the Buffalo could rest. Alisha hovered over Mitch, her expression perpetually worried.

Rides the Buffalo was excited by the journey. Mitch had expected him to be reluctant, maybe even frightened, but his son seemed to be looking forward to seeing the white man's world. He was eager to learn to read and write.

As they rode, Alisha taught him the alphabet song and every evening after dinner, he asked Alisha to teach him how to read and write a new word. At the end of the fifth day, he could read and write all their names.

They rode into Canyon Creek at midmorning. Mitch took a back trail to the house, avoiding a trip through the center of town.

Rides the Buffalo slid from the back of his horse, his eyes wide as he looked at Mitch. "Is this your lodge?"

Mitch nodded.

"It is very big."

"Yeah, it is that." Lifting his leg over his horse's neck, Mitch slid to the ground. He smiled at Alisha. "I'd like to carry you over the threshold, but I'm afraid I can't quite manage it."

She laughed softly. "That's okay. We aren't legally married, you know."

Mitch grunted softly. "I guess you're right. We'll have to do something about that."

"We gonna stand here jawin' all day," Clements muttered, "or go inside?"

"We're going in, old man."

"Old! Who you callin' old?"

Mitch looked at his mother. "You coming, Ma?"

White Robe nodded slowly. She stared at the house for several moments before dismounting. Her steps were heavy as she climbed the stairs, her eyes sad, making him wonder if it had been a mistake for him to bring her back here.

As soon as they were inside, Alisha drew back the drapes and opened all the windows, then she stood in the middle of the parlor and looked around.

"Well," Mitch said, "what do you think?"

"I think it needs a coat of white paint to brighten it up."

"Yeah." Mitch grinned. "That's what my mother always said, right, Ma?"

White Robe nodded. "Living in this house was like living in a cave. Always dark."

"Well," Alisha said briskly, "if you and Mitch have no objections, I think we'll have to do some serious redecorating."

"Feel free to make any changes you want," Mitch said, glancing from Alisha to his mother. "I want the two of you to be happy here."

Alisha winked at White Robe. "It might cost a lot of money."

"That's okay," Mitch said. "We've got a lot of money." He sank down on the sofa. "Ma, why don't you show Rides the Buffalo around. Let him pick out a room for himself. Red, you're welcome to stay as long as you've a mind to."

"Obliged," Clements said. He sat down in the big leather chair that had been Con Garrett's favorite. "I reckon I'll be movin' on in the mornin'. I'm kinda anxious to get back east."

"I don't suppose there's any food in the house," Alisha remarked. "I think I'll go into town and stock up."

Mitch nodded. "Good idea."

"I think I'll go along with ya," Red said. "Send Dorothy a wire to let her know I'm on my way."

Alisha glanced down at her tunic. "I can't go into town like this."

Mitch grunted softly. "There's a trunk full of my ma's clothes up in the attic. My old man wouldn't let her take anything with her when she left." He looked over at Red. "There's a buggy out back."

"I'll be ready in a few minutes," Alisha told Red.

With a nod, Clements went outside to hitch his horse to the buggy.

Eager to get out of her worn and stained tunic, Alisha ran up the stairs. The attic was dark and musty. The trunk was near the door. She blew the dust off the top, then opened the lid.

She pulled out several dresses, none of which suited her. She settled on a white shirtwaist with a froth of lace at the throat, and a dark blue skirt. She found some undergarments near the bottom, along with a comb and a brush and a package of pins. She also found some stockings and several pairs of shoes and boots. Gathering everything together, she went downstairs.

There were several bedrooms on the second floor. She went into one, shut the door, and changed her clothes. The shoes were a little too big, but they would do.

Taking up the brush, she ran it through her hair until all the tangles were gone, then she pinned it in a neat coil at her nape.

She stared at herself in the mirror. She looked much the same as always, she thought, except for her sun-tanned skin.

She met White Robe and Rides the Buffalo in the hallway when she left the bedroom.

Alisha smiled at her son. "So, how do you like the house?"

"It is very big. My . . . " He frowned, searching for the right word. "Bedroom is bigger than our wickiup. It has a bed that is softer than a buffalo robe. And a huge kettle to wash in."

Alisha laughed as she moved down the hallway toward the stairs. "That's a bathtub." She glanced over her shoulder at White Robe. "I'm going into town. Can I get you anything?"

White Robe shook her head. "No."

"I hope you don't mind my wearing your clothes."

"No. You are welcome to them."

Alisha paused at the head of the stairs. "Are you coming down?"

"No. I think I will go up and see if I can find a change of clothes." White Robe looked at Rides the Buffalo. "And I think it is time this one had a bath."

"I think so, too," Alisha said. She grinned at her son. "I'll see you both later."

Turning, she went down the stairs.

Red was waiting for her. "You ready?"

"Yes. Do you want anything from town, Mitch?"

He shook his head. "I don't think so."

"All right." Crossing the floor, she bent down and kissed his cheek. "I'll be back as soon as I can. Get some rest, all right?"

"I'm fine."

She kissed him again, then followed Red out the door.

She knew it was only her imagination, but Canyon Creek seemed bigger than when she left. She nodded at Mrs. Moss and Mrs. Hazelwood as they drove down the street, conscious of their curious stares. She hadn't told anyone but Chloe that she was leaving town, and even then, she hadn't told her why.

Alisha laid her hand on Red's arm when they approached the office of the *Canyon Creek Gazette*. "Pull up here, will you, Red?"

With a nod, he reined his horse to a halt. Leaping lightly to the ground, he rounded the buggy and helped Alisha down.

"I won't be long. Why don't you go over to the telegraph office and send your message, and I'll meet you at the mercantile?"

"All right, missy." Climbing up on the seat, he lifted the reins and clucked to the horse.

Lifting her skirts, Alisha went up the stairs, thinking how strange it felt to wear petticoats and drawers and stockings again. Opening the door, she stepped into the newspaper office.

"Hello, Mr. Quimby. Is Chloe here?"

"Miss Faraday! Where in tarnation have you been? Chloe's been worried sick about you. Chloe! Come on out here."

"What's wrong, Sylvester? You don't have to shout. I'm not . . . Alisha!" Wiping her hands on the big white apron that covered her dress, Chloe hurried across the room and embraced the younger woman. "Where have you been? I've been worried to death."

"I took a rather long trip."

Chloe held Alisha at arm's length and looked her up and down. "Well, you don't look any the worse for the journey. Where on earth did you go?"

"It's a long story, Chloe." Alisha glanced at Sylvester. "I'll tell you all about it some other time, all right?"

Chloe nodded, but her expression was doubtful.

"I need to pick up my things. Are they still here?"

"No, they're up at the house. Where are you staying? I'll have Sylvester drop them off after work."

"I don't want to put him to any trouble."

"Oh, pish posh, it's no trouble at all. Just tell us where you want them."

Alisha took a deep breath. "I'm staying up at the Garrett place."

Chloe blinked several times, slowly. "The Garrett place?"

"Yes."

"The Garrett place," Chloe repeated. "Why would you be staying there?"

"Well." Alisha glanced from Chloe to Sylvester and back again. "That's where my husband lives."

"Husband!" Chloe exclaimed.

"Husband!" Sylvester blurted.

Chloe dropped into the chair beside her husband's desk. "When did this happen?"

"Recently . . . I really need to go," Alisha said.

"Oh, no, you don't!" Chloe jumped out of the chair and grabbed Alisha by the arm. "You're not leaving here until you tell me everything."

Red Clements was sitting in a rocker outside the general store when Alisha arrived.

"Wal, I about gave up on ya," he said.

"I'm sorry. I got detained."

Red grunted. "I been waitin' here near an hour."

"I know. I'm sorry. I won't be long."

With an apologetic smile, Alisha opened the door and stepped inside. She nodded at Mr. Halstead, picked up a basket from beside the front counter, and made her way down the first aisle.

It was Saturday afternoon, and the store was crowded. She was aware of the whispers that followed her, people wondering where she had been, what she was going to do now that her father was gone and the school board had hired a new teacher.

Alisha felt a twinge of regret when she heard about the new teacher. She had loved teaching and hoped she might be able to go back to it, but it was her own fault they had replaced her. She should have notified the school board before she left town, but she simply hadn't thought of it in the rush to find her son.

She walked up and down the aisles, automatically filling her basket with foodstuffs. But food was the furthest thing from her mind. She was a mother now, with a son to think of, yet they were still strangers to each other. Her mother-in-law was living with her, and she wondered what problems that was going to cause. White Robe had been Rides the Buffalo's mother for the last four years. She was accustomed to raising him, disciplining him. It wouldn't be easy for her to relinquish that position. And Mitch . . . they were married, and yet that marriage, performed by an Apache medicine man, would not be recognized here in town.

She moved to the back of the store where the clothing was kept. Rides the Buffalo needed clothing. She picked out a couple of shirts that looked to be the right size, two pairs of corduroy trousers, a suit of underwear, several pairs of socks, a pair of boots. She wondered how he would feel about his new clothes, if he would object to giving up buckskin in favor of wool and cotton.

She paid for her purchases at the counter, waited while Mr. Halstead wrapped them for her.

Red stood up when she exited the store. Coming forward, he took a couple of her packages. "Got everything you need?"

"Yes, I think so."

They stowed her purchases under the seat, then Red helped her into the buggy, and they were on their way.

"Somethin' troubling you, missy?" he asked as he put the horse into a trot.

"No. Yes. I don't know."

Red grunted. "Well, which is it?"

"Oh, Red, I'm so confused. I was so eager to find my son, I never thought past that. Now he's here, and I'm not sure what to do. I'm his mother, but I'm not, really. White Robe is. She raised him. She's the one who's taken care of him his whole life." She sniffed back her tears, torn by the question that had plagued her from the beginning. "What if he never thinks of me as his mother?"

"Here, now," Red chided. Reining the horse to a halt, he patted her shoulder. "Give the boy some time. Lotta changes in his life, kind of sudden like, you know."

"I know." She sniffed.

"Lotta changes in your life, too, I reckon."

Alisha nodded. A broken engagement. Her father's death. A child. A husband. A mother-in-law. The loss of her teaching position. "You could say that."

"Change is never easy, but it's necessary sometimes, ya know?"

"I know." She blew out a sigh. "Thanks, Red."

"Nothin' to thank me for." He patted her arm again, then picked up the reins and clucked to the horse.

"I wish you didn't have to leave," Alisha said, meaning it. He had become a good friend in a short time.

"Wal, I'd like to stay, but . . . " He shrugged. "You know how it is?"

"I'm sure they're anxious to see you, too."

Red grinned. "Yeah, I reckon. Don't you worry now. Everything's gonna be jest fine."

Alisha stared up at the ceiling. It seemed strange to be sleeping under a roof, in a real bed again. Stranger still to be sleeping in the bed that Mitch's parents had shared. Mitch had objected at first, but it was the only double bed in the house.

She had aired out the room and the mattress and pillows, put clean sheets and blankets on the bed, re-arranged the furniture in an effort to make it *their* room instead of his father's.

In spite of Mitch's misgivings, he had quickly fallen asleep. Even though he insisted he was all right, she knew his injury still pained him, that the long journey had tired him more than he would admit. She snuggled closer, her shoulder pillowed on his arm.

Red had insisted on sleeping outside, saying he'd have plenty of indoor living when he got to St. Louis.

White Robe and Rides the Buffalo were asleep in their own rooms. White Robe had gone to bed early, saying she was tired, but Alisha had the feeling that her mother-in-law was giving her and Mitch an op-portunity to spend some time alone with Rides the Buffalo so they could get to know each other better.

They had spent a pleasant evening, just the three of them. Mitch had promised to get Rides the Buffalo a pony, then told him a Coyote story. Later, Alisha had tucked Rides the Buffalo into bed and, after a brief hesitation, she had kissed him good night. He hadn't seemed to mind.

With a sigh, she closed her eyes, completely at peace.

"Alisha! Alisha! Wake up!"

She bolted upright, overcome by a sense of panic. "Mitch?"

"I'm here. Shh, it's all right. You were having a nightmare."

"Oh." She fell into his arms, remembering. "It was awful."

He drew her up against him. "It was just a dream, darlin'."

"I know, but it was so real." She took a deep breath. "So real."

"What was it about?"

"We were in town. We . . . we were walking . . . down the street. It was night. You were the sheriff again, and . . . " She shivered. "Someone shot you."

Mitch lay down again. Tucking Alisha against his side, he stroked her hair. "Try not to think about it any more. It was just a bad dream. Nothing more. Besides, I've already been shot—twice—and I'm all right." He grinned and she smiled, reassured.

Red left for St. Louis the next morning. Alisha hated to see him go. He promised to stop for a visit in the spring on his way to see Mountain Sage.

She thought about what he had said often during the next few days. *Everything's gonna be just fine.* She repeated those words in her mind when she was caring for Mitch, when she was getting acquainted with her son, when she was learning to adjust to having a husband and a son and a mother-in-law.

Sylvester Quimby had dropped off her things, and she felt more like herself in her own clothes. It gave her a sense of being home to see her few knickknacks scattered around the house, to see her father's Bible on the table beside the sofa.

Mitch said he would paint the inside of the house when he was back on his feet, and she spent a day at the general store picking out fabric for new curtains: a bright blue for Rides the Buffalo's bedroom, a yellow check for the kitchen, a light green for the parlor, white for their bedroom. White Robe picked a soft blue print for her room.

She rearranged the furniture in the parlor, ordered wallpaper for their bedroom.

Mitch told her to buy whatever she wanted. It was a strange feeling, knowing she could spend as much as she pleased. Growing up, Mitch had always thought of her as being rich because she had nice clothes and lived in a big house. But the house had belonged to the church. True, they'd had plenty to eat, and she'd always had nice clothes, but money for extras, for frills and doo-dads, had always been scarce.

She bought a crystal swan just because it was pretty. She bought Mitch a blue shirt because it was the same color as his eyes. She bought Rides the Buffalo a set of toy soldiers, a new dress for White Robe, and one for herself.

After her initial shopping spree, she stayed close to home, busying herself with housework. While Mitch and Rides the Buffalo sat out on the porch, getting to know each other while their injuries healed, she scrubbed the floors and shook out the rugs and waxed the furniture. She went through drawers and cupboards and closets.

At first, Alisha had felt ill at ease. The house had been White Robe's home, and Alisha couldn't help feeling like an intruder at worst, a visitor at best, but White Robe had quickly assured her that this house had never been home, and that it held only bad memories for her.

"We'll have to change that," Alisha had told her, determined to make it so.

They worked comfortably together after that. Sometimes, while they were busy with a task, White Robe reminisced about days gone by, telling Alisha stories about Mitch, about how he had always loved the water, about the time he found a wounded fawn and nursed it back to health.

As the days went by, Alisha began to feel that Red had been right and that everything would, indeed, work out for the best.

Chapter 35

They had been in town almost three weeks when Alisha bumped into Roger. Mitch had dropped her off at the general store, then went on to the blacksmith shop, saying he'd be back for her in a half hour or so.

She paused to look in the window of the store, but her mind wasn't on the display, or on the thread she had come to buy, or the curtains she was making for the bedroom. She had missed her monthly flow, and she was contemplating the fact that she might be pregnant when she opened the door to the mercantile and came face-to-face with Roger.

"Alisha!" he exclaimed. A smile lit his face, and then his expression turned sour. "I heard you were back in town."

"Hello, Roger."

"Folks tell me you're staying with Mitch Garrett."

"Yes." She lifted her chin. She knew what people were saying, that she was living in sin with a half-breed. But she didn't care. She wasn't living in sin. Mitch was her husband in every way that mattered, and soon they would be married in a church. She hadn't said anything to Mitch about the whispers and gossip she overheard, nor had she brought Rides the Buffalo into town with her. The old cats had enough fat to chew. Hopefully, all that would change once she and Mitch were married.

She was going to make the arrangements with the new preacher when she finished her shopping.

"Can we go someplace and talk?" Roger asked.

"There's nothing to say."

"I think there is." He looked around. It was Saturday, and the street was crowded. Women hurried along the boardwalk, or clustered in small groups, chatting. Men sat in the rockers outside the mercantile, talking and whittling while their wives shopped. Kids played near the horse trough. A group of men stood near the blacksmith shop, arguing politics. "We can't talk here."

"Roger . . . "

"I think you owe me that much, don't you?"

"Yes," she agreed with a sigh. "I suppose so."

"Come on," he said, taking her by the arm.

"Where are we going?"

"To the hotel. We can talk over a cup of coffee."

Something told her it was a mistake, but it was too late to back out now. And she did owe it to him, she thought as they crossed the street. He was right about that.

There were only a few people in the hotel dining room. Roger held her chair for her, they ordered pie and coffee. Alisha glanced around, trying to think of something to say.

Roger took a deep breath, and then got right to the point. "I was wrong, to behave the way I did. I should have been more understanding of what you were going through." He paused. "Did you find your . . . your son?"

"Yes."

"I'm . . . I'm glad. Is he . . . where is he?"

"Up at the ranch."

A shadow passed through Roger's eyes, and was gone.

"I still love you, Alisha. I want you to marry me, the way we planned. The house is finished, just the way you wanted it."

"Roger, please, don't."

"We were good together, Alisha. It can be that way again."

"No, Roger, it can't. Nothing's the same as it was."

"Alisha . . . "

"Listen to me! I'm in love with Mitch. I always have been, and I always will be."

Roger shook his head. "No, that's not true," he said, his voice rising. "You loved me."

Alisha looked around. "Roger, please, don't make a scene."

"You loved me! I know you did."

"Yes, I did, but not in the way you deserve. Not the way a woman should love the man she marries. I'm sorry, but that's the end of it. Mitch and I are going to be married soon."

Roger shook his head in denial.

"It's true, so please try to accept it."

Roger raked his hand through his hair. She could see by the expression on his face that he wanted to argue with her, but something, his pride perhaps, or the fact that he still cared for her, kept him from speaking.

"I'm sorry, Roger, truly I am. I never meant to hurt you."

He nodded. "I hope you'll be happy with him," he said, and though there was a lack of warmth behind the words, she counted it as a step in the right direction.

"Thank you." She glanced out the window at the clock across the way. "I've got to go," she said, rising. "Good-bye, Roger."

He stood up. "Good-bye, Alisha."

Mitch was waiting for her in front of the general store when she left the hotel. She crossed the street, wondering if she should tell him about Roger.

Mitch frowned as he lifted her into the buggy. "Where were you?"

"Over at the hotel."

"Oh?" He looked up at her for a long moment.

"I ran into Roger."

He hesitated a moment. "I see."

"No, you don't," Alisha said. She stared at him a moment, felt her cheeks grow hot. "Mitch, you don't think . . ."

"Of course not." He vaulted up onto the seat beside her. "What did he want?"

She settled her skirts around her as he picked up the reins. "He said he still loved me, that he wanted to marry me."

She felt his body tense. "Go on."

"I told him I loved you, that we were going to be married. He said he hoped we'd be happy."

"I'll bet. Are you still in love with him?"

She stared at him in exasperation. How could he even think she loved another man? After all they had been through, didn't he know by now that she loved him, only him? Always and forever him? He was her heart, her soul, her reason for being.

"Mitch."

He grunted softly.

"I love you."

Three simple words, fervently spoken. She watched the anger, the tension, drain out of him. His shoulders relaxed, his jaw unclenched, he loosened his tight grip on the reins.

And then he pulled off the road, following a narrow, winding path that ended at the river.

He climbed out of the buggy, lifted her to the ground. Taking her by the hand, he led her into a secluded thicket. Wordlessly, he drew her into his arms and kissed her. She had the feeling it wasn't so much a kiss as a brand, a reminder that she belonged to him.

She slid her hands up under his shirt and caressed his back, reveling in the warm skin beneath her fingertips, the power of the arms wrapped so tightly around her. She felt his need pressing against her belly, felt an answering need uncoil in the innermost part of her body, yearning toward him, aching for the pleasure only he could give, and she leaned into him, her hips thrusting forward, provocative, inviting.

Still entwined in each other's arms, they sank down on the soft grass. He kissed away her clothing, his mouth trailing fire as he rained butterfly kisses over every inch of exposed flesh. Her hands were equally busy, removing his shirt, tugging off his trousers, giggling when she realized she should have removed his boots first.

He laughed with her, a deep, sexy sound that made her heart beat even faster, made her hands clumsy as she pulled off his pants. He wasn't wearing anything underneath.

The grass was cool beneath her back, but the heat radiating from Mitch's body soon made her forget everything else. She wrapped her arms around him.

"Tell me," he said. "Tell me that you love me. Just me."

"I love you," she gasped, her nails raking his back. "Only you."

Thrusting deeper, he covered her face and neck with kisses, his hands working their familiar magic, until she thought she might shatter into a million pieces of pleasure, until she did shatter, as wave upon wave of ecstasy exploded within her, then slowly, slowly coalesced into a feeling of sweet satisfaction.

With a sigh, she held Mitch close, basking in the warm afterglow of passion, in the welcome weight of his body on hers, the touch of his heated skin, the feel of his hair brushing against her breasts.

"Mitch?"

He feathered kisses over her cheeks. "What is it, darlin'?"

"I think I'm pregnant."

He pushed himself up on his elbows and gazed down at her. "What?"

"Pregnant? With child? In the family way?"

He stared at her, a slow smile spreading over his face. "Are you sure?"

"Pretty sure. Do you mind?"

"Mind? No, I think it's great." He rolled onto his side, carrying her with him, then slid his hand between their bodies and rested it on her belly. "Damn. How do you feel? Dammit, Lisha, why didn't you tell me? What if I hurt you? Maybe we shouldn't have . . ."

She put her hand over his mouth, stifling his outburst. "Hey, it's all right. You didn't hurt me." She laughed. "We have months and months until I might be too big and clumsy to do this."

His gaze softened, grew tender as he kissed her gently. "I'll be here for you this time, Lisha. I promise." He kissed her again, joy thrumming through him. "Come on, let's go tell Rides the Buffalo he's going to have a little brother."

Alisha made a face at him as he helped her to her feet. "Or a sister."

"A girl?"

"Yes, you know, a girl."

"Oh, right." He picked up her chemise and tossed it at her. "A girl."

"You wouldn't mind if it was a girl, would you?"

"Of course not." Grinning, he pulled her into his arms and kissed her soundly. "In case you haven't noticed, I like girls."

They told White Robe and Rides the Buffalo about the baby as soon as they got home. White Robe looked pleased. Rides the Buffalo stared at Alisha's stomach.

"How did the baby get in there?" he asked.

Alisha looked at Mitch, who looked at White Robe, who laughed.

"I think his mother should tell him," Mitch said.

"I think his father should tell him," Alisha said.

"I think his grandmother should tell him," White Robe decided, and taking Rides the Buffalo by the hand, she led him out of the room.

"Well," Alisha said, her lips twitching. "We handled that really well, didn't we?"

Mitch laughed. "Well, at least we've got plenty of time to think of a good answer for the next one." He pulled Alisha into his arms and patted her stomach. "Maybe we'd better think about getting married before he . . . " He grinned at her. "Or *she* gets here."

"Are you proposing to me, Mr. Garrett?"

"I am indeed, Miss Faraday. For the second time."
He quirked an eyebrow at her. "Well?"

She batted her eyelashes at him. "I'm thinking it over."

"Is that right?"

She shook her head, then laughed softly. "Silly. The answer is yes, of course."

Mitch grunted. "Name the day."

"Is tomorrow too soon?"

"I don't know. *I* may have to think it over."

Alisha punched him on the arm. "Very funny, mister."

He kissed the top of her head. "Did you mean it, about getting married tomorrow?"

"No. I'll need a week or so to find a pattern and make a dress. How about a week from Sunday, if the preacher is available?"

Mitch nodded. "Guess that means new duds for the men in the family, too."

Alisha smiled. In all the years she had known Mitch, she had never seen him in a suit and tie. It was a pleasant prospect. "You'll need someone to stand up with you."

He grunted softly. "I don't have any friends in town, you know that."

"Well, I'm going to ask Chloe to be my bridesmaid. I can ask Sylvester to be your best man, if you don't mind."

"I don't mind. I don't care who else is there, as long as you show up."

"I'll be there." She poked her finger into the center of his chest. "Just be sure *you're* there!"

They broke the news at dinner that night.

"Are you not already married?" Rides the Buffalo

asked. He looked at White Robe. "Red Shield married them."

"That is true," White Robe replied. "But they are going to be married again, according to the white man's custom."

Rides the Buffalo nodded, his expression thoughtful. "My father said I should think of taking a white man's name. Do you think I should take a new name?"

"You come from two worlds," White Robe said. "When you are with the People, you are Rides the Buffalo. I think it would be wise for you to have another name, one that reflects your white heritage, as well."

Rides the Buffalo looked at Mitch. "I have told my father I would like to have his name."

"Oh?" Alisha glanced at Mitch, a question in her eyes.

He shrugged. "We talked about it a while back."

"I have no objections," Alisha said, smiling. "Mitch Garrett, Junior, is the name I would have given you."

"Junior?" Rides the Buffalo asked. "What is junior?"

"Your father is senior, older, and you are junior, younger."

Rides the Buffalo looked at his grandmother. "Do you like my new name?"

"Yes, very much."

Rides the Buffalo glanced around the table. "I will be Mitch Garrett, Junior," he declared proudly.

Epilogue

Alisha sat on the sofa, nursing her seven-week-old daughter, Catherine Amanda. True to his word, Mitch had been there when their daughter entered the world. He had held Alisha's hand, offering her encouragement, wiping the perspiration from her brow, kissing her between contractions.

Alisha smiled at her daughter. She was so beautiful, so perfect with her tawny skin and deep blue eyes. Her hair was black, like her father's. So tiny, to hold such a big place in her mother's heart.

Young Mitch adored his little sister. He spent hours holding her, telling her stories. Of course, in true grandmotherly fashion, White Robe also did her part to spoil the baby, but Alisha didn't mind.

The ranch was home now. They had painted it inside and out, bought new furniture and carpets, filled the rooms with love and laughter that had chased all the old ghosts away.

Alisha sighed as she patted the baby's back. She had never been as happy as she had been in this past year. Mitch had agreed to act as the sheriff until the town could find a new one, and he had collected a sizable reward for catching a notorious bank robber. They had used the money to stock the ranch with cattle. At White Robe's request, Mitch had built his mother a small house of her own. Two months ago, to her relief, the town had finally found a new sheriff.

In the summer, Red and his family were coming from St. Louis for a visit. Alisha couldn't wait to meet Dorothy Clements. Right or wrong, she couldn't help being curious about Red's other wife.

Rising, Alisha walked to the back door and stepped out onto the porch. Mitch had bought their son a new horse, and she smiled as she watched young Mitch put the animal through its paces. Only five years old, yet her son seemed so grown up. Every day, he looked more like his father.

White Robe sat in the shade, making a pair of moccasins for the baby. She looked up and smiled, then went back to her sewing.

Alisha looked at Mitch, her heart overflowing with love. He was everything she had ever hoped for, every dream come true.

He waved when he looked up and saw her watching him. And then he was walking toward her, his dark eyes alight with love and desire. As always, her heart beat a little faster when he was near, when she saw that look in his eyes. Warmth uncurled deep inside her.

Drawing close, Mitch slipped one arm around Alisha's shoulders, then bent down to kiss the top of his daughter's head. "How's our angel doing?"

"She's fine. Full and happy and ready for a nap, I think."

"A nap, eh?" Mitch faked a yawn. "I'm feeling a little tired myself." His gaze moved over her, hotter than the sun shining overhead. "How'd you like to put me to bed?"

Happiness welled up inside Alisha and spilled out in soft, joyous laughter as she took her husband by the hand. "My pleasure, as always," she said.

And it was.

Dear Reader,

I hope you've enjoyed Mitch and Alisha's story. I want to take this opportunity to thank Mitch Dearmond for the lovely poem in the front of the book. I also want to thank Spirit Walker for his help and advice.

A heartfelt thank you to all of you who have taken the time to write. I love hearing from you, and appreciate your support.

If you have access to the Web, I hope you'll check out my Web page at

<u>http://www.angelfire.com/ga/apachefire/</u> <u>index.html</u>

Happy reading!
Madeline